D0915020

NOW & WHEN

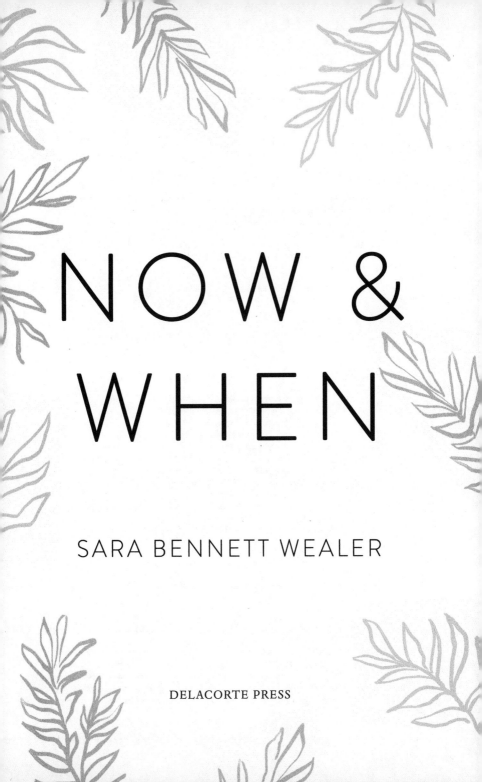

NOW & WHEN

SARA BENNETT WEALER

DELACORTE PRESS

Text copyright © 2020 by Sara Bennett Wealer
Jacket art copyright © 2020 by Ewelina Dymek

GetUnderlined.com

Educators and librarians, for a variety of teaching tools, visit us at RHTeachersLibrarians.com

Library of Congress Cataloging-in-Publication Data
Names: Bennett Wealer, Sara, author.
Title: Now & when / Sara Bennett Wealer.
Other titles: Now and when
Description: First edition. | New York : Delacorte Press, [2020] | Summary: To the shock of high school student Skyler Finch, her romantic future, as revealed by a mysterious website, lies with the arrogant and annoying Truman Alexander.
Identifiers: LCCN 2019022446 | ISBN 978-1-9848-9624-7 (hardcover) | ISBN 978-1-9848-9626-1 (ebook)
Subjects: CYAC: Dating (Social customs)—Fiction. | Love—Fiction. | Friendship—Fiction. | High schools—Fiction. | Schools—Fiction.
Classificaton: LCC PZ7.B447111 No 2020 | DDC [Fic]—dc23

The text of this book is set in 11-point Dante.
Interior design by Trish Parcell

Printed in the United States of America
10 9 8 7 6 5 4 3 2 1
First Edition

Mom and Dad, I love you.

CHAPTER ONE

There's nothing I hate, and nothing Truman Alexander loves, more than the sound of Truman Alexander's voice.

"I found the ending solipsistic, manipulative, and metaphorically facile."

That's Truman now, treating sixth period to his opinion of *The House of Mirth*. And yes, vocab bombs like *solipsistic* are part of Truman Alexander's everyday speech.

"I can understand why some people would be moved by it," he says, lacing his fingers on top of his desk. He shoots a glance in my direction. "But they're just playing into the author's hands. At the end of the day, it's not very sophisticated."

I note the emphasis on that last word at the same time Truman's eyes dart away, as if to leave just the trace of a doubt in my mind whom he was referring to. He's both courting and dodging one of our legendary arguments. Because the last time we clashed, I wiped the institutional tile floor of the AP English classroom with him.

Metaphorically, of course.

"Lily Bart's ridiculous pride is what killed her," Truman continues, his tone growing even more self-important. He's forgotten yet again that he is in a classroom, and not one of his precious debate tournaments. "She had plenty of opportunities to improve her situation, but she insisted on maintaining a façade of misplaced honor that was, frankly, tiresome."

I have to roll my eyes at that one. Because Truman Alexander is the very definition of tiresome. He sits across the aisle in a button-down shirt, freshly pressed shorts, and loafers—a formal island in a sea of sweatshirts and slides—pontificating as he stares with that unblinking gaze that lets everybody know Genius Truman is in the house. We've all been listening to Truman since he was a seventh-grade brainiac with a compulsive need to tell everyone exactly what was on his mind.

High school Truman isn't much of an improvement. You'd think being Alton High's master debater would give him all the outlet he needs for listening to himself talk. Instead, it's rendered him even more in love with the sound of his own voice—a voice that makes my skin crawl. Especially when Truman seems to have completely and, I suspect, willfully missed the point of a book I absolutely loved.

Rather than give him the satisfaction of knowing I noticed his passive-aggressive digs, I sneak a text under my desk. Jordan and her prom committee cochairs are out scouting locations right now.

> Where you at?

Jordan responds with a photo. It's the courtyard garden from the Blessing mansion where Harper, the third in our trio of best-friends-since-toddlerhood, volunteers every weekend. Harper calls it her "happy place," and who could argue with that? Sculptures

2

peek from behind shrubberies, and trellises of budding flowers frame an open space that manages to be sprawling and intimate all at once. In the background, an old brick wall supports masses of ivy and the skeletons of what look like climbing roses.

This is THE place. Search over. It's perfect.

Ten other pics follow, and it's clear Jordan has embarked on one of her epic party-planning crusades—more than embarked; the boat has left the harbor and is sailing away to Prom Paradise. Looking at that garden, I envy her. Today is the first truly pretty day of spring: crystal-blue sky, warm enough to go without a jacket but chilly in the shade. The world outside the window behind Ms. Laramie's desk sparkles. Jordan is out there while I am stuck in here, listening to Truman freaking Alexander's freaking infuriating voice.

"Furthermore," he adds, "if Lily hadn't been so spineless and indecisive, she wouldn't have made such a mess for herself in the first place."

"Okay, that's just wrong," I blurt out. I told myself I wouldn't engage Truman today, but he's managed to pull me in as only Truman can. "First of all, Lily Bart's mistakes are part of what make her an interesting and *realistic* character. Second, Lily might be the only truly honest person in the circles within which she has no choice but to sink or swim. Which leads me to my third point, which is that Lily is backed into a corner. She has no other options."

"Lily has options left and right," Truman counters. "She either doesn't choose, or she chooses the wrong ones."

This is rich coming from Truman. His family is one of the

wealthiest in Alton. There's no way he could identify with a well-born but penniless girl who falls prey to the schemes of those whose acceptance she needs to survive.

"Every option is one that forces her to subvert her true self," I inform him.

"Everyone in the book is subverting themselves in one way or another. Do *they* overdose on chloral hydrate?"

"Have you ever been a woman without choices?"

"Have *you*?"

I feel my cheeks redden, feel my grip on the discussion start to slide. "I don't think you're exactly qualified to talk about this book."

"That's an ad hominem argument. So I win."

He sits back smugly, while the heat in my face dissolves into the sensation of a million tiny worms wriggling down my neck and arms. I can't be the only person who's repulsed by Truman right now. I look around for confirmation of this, only to see that everyone else in the room is half-asleep. Even Ms. Laramie looks like she's nodding off on her perch at the edge of her desk.

The bell rings, jolting them all awake. I snatch up my bag, ready to bolt. But Truman isn't done arguing. Of course. He decided years ago that I was his extra-superfun intellectual punching bag—the one person who can never be allowed to express an opinion without challenge. It's probably because *I'm* the one person who ever challenges *him*. Everybody else is smarter than me; they let Truman talk in class so they don't have to deal with him after.

I put my bag back down on my desk. I rummage around for some lip balm. I take my time unwrapping a piece of gum and putting it into my mouth. I pray Truman will get tired of waiting and leave.

He remains at his desk. And I can't hang out here forever. I have to walk by him in order to get out of the room. I gather my things and make a beeline for the door.

"Skyler."

"Truman."

I avoid eye contact, leaving no opening for further conversation. The last time we sparred in class he followed me afterward, trying to argue that Jay Gatsby was a tragic figure and not a social-climbing thug. He used words like *archetype*. He recommended websites I might like to check out for additional reading. He made me want to punch him in the throat.

I can't do that today—deal with Truman in general *or* punch him in the throat specifically. I have to let it go, if for no other reason than that boring to sleep an entire roomful of our classmates is bad karma. I'm not boring. Nor am I anywhere near as hateful as hating Truman makes me seem. If you asked any random person who knows me, they'd say, "Oh, Skyler Finch? She's cool. Fun. Just your average cool, fun girl."

Truman Alexander brings out the worst in me. Of all the reasons to hate him, that is probably the biggest.

Second biggest? His refusal to take a hint and *back off.*

"When you're navigating the high-stakes world Lily Bart was, you have to be calculating and logical," he says.

"Lily followed her heart," I respond against my better judgment. "It wasn't in her nature to be calculating."

"So she faced the consequences."

Now that I've had a chance to collect my thoughts, what I should have said earlier comes to me. I take off my glasses and rub my eyes, trying to massage away an oncoming headache.

"You know, Truman, the whole purpose of that book was to make you feel a little something about those consequences. Maybe question whether we want to live in a society where people who aren't equipped to play the game—or who choose not to—get crushed like Lily Bart did."

This shuts him up, momentarily at least. I might not have wiped the floor with him, but we're even now.

He shakes dark hair out of his eyes, and I'm forced to admit that, objectively speaking, Truman has more than a few things going for him in the appearance department. His face may be moon-shaped, but his eyes are bottle-green, and he wears those crisply ironed shirts and shorts quite well. He could be more popular if he weren't so Future CEOs of America. He could even be considered hot if you find bulging backpacks and brows furrowed deep in thought attractive.

I don't. When I'm not in class with Truman, I try to think about him as little as possible.

"I need to get going," I tell him. "Was there something you needed?"

"Yes. I had an idea just now."

He pauses, leaving me unsure whether this is a dramatic interval, or whether I'm supposed to dig for more. I hold up my hands, begging him to get on with it.

"I was thinking we could use you in debate. Have you ever considered joining?"

"No. I'm busy enough."

It's the truth. Show choir, clarinet in orchestra, yearbook . . . I'm involved in pretty much everything but sports, and that's only because I don't have an athletic bone in my body.

"What are you focused on, though?"

I squint, trying to figure out how we went from *The House of Mirth* to what Truman seems to be implying is my unimpressive lineup of interests and activities. "Are my extracurriculars a problem?"

"It's not my place to say. . . ."

"Apparently you're making it your place."

"Well . . ." He casts his gaze toward the ceiling. When he looks at me again, it's down the nose. "There's no disputing you do a lot. But is there anything you excel at?"

A surge of righteous rage steals my voice. I bite my tongue until I can shake the words loose. "I excel at *life*. You know, living in the now? You're always either in some debate tournament or acting like you're practicing for one."

"There's nothing wrong with being the best at what you do. Striving for success isn't a bad thing."

It is if it makes you an arrogant pain in the butt. The only thing that keeps me from saying this out loud is Ms. Laramie shooing us both out into the hallway. I'm not sure, but I think I hear her door lock behind us.

"So I lack focus. Then why would you want me on your debate team?"

"Trishna is moving and there are still qualifying tournaments coming up."

I look past him to where his debate friends are gathering for practice outside the speech and forensics room. Every one of his teammates looks like a puffed-up Truman wannabe.

"If you stick with it into next year, it'll look good on your college applications," he says.

"Not a concern. I already know where I'm going."

"How can you know that as a junior?"

"I mean I'm only applying at State." He makes a face. "What? All my friends are planning to go there."

"I just thought you'd want to be better than all your friends. Never mind."

"No, wait. Don't say *never mind*. What does *never mind* mean, anyway?"

"Just that you've clearly got your life set up the way you like it. Far be it from me to suggest any improvements."

"Oh . . . kay . . ." If anyone needs a life improvement, it's Truman, with his uptight pseudo-intellectualism and his tiny squad of debate nerds who treat him like their savior. He's got his nose so far in the air—and they've got their heads so far up his butt—that it's a wonder he can even find his way around school. "First, implying that I lack the drive to succeed is presumptuous. And second, how do you know my life is so perfect?"

He deflates slightly. "I brought up debate because I thought it was something you'd enjoy and benefit from. It's not like I asked you to rob banks or clean toilets."

Now he looks hurt, and I feel bad—but also mad that Truman has put me in a position to feel bad and mad. I hoist my backpack onto my shoulder, forcing myself to take a friendlier tone.

"Well, thank you. But I'm good. And now I really do have to go. So . . . bye?"

He waits a beat before dismissing me with a nod. "Have a nice afternoon."

I turn and start walking away, feeling pretty good about how that ended. I made my point. We said a civil farewell. And here's the real win as far as I'm concerned: nobody had to have the last word.

"I still think you should try it!" Truman shouts after me. "You could start tomorrow and be ready for the Westwood tournament next week!"

8

Luckily for my sanity, Eli the anti-Truman is waiting for me at our bench in the commons. He bolts to his feet when I walk up.

"Hey, Skyler. How was English?"

I pull in a cleansing breath and try to relax. Eli is sweet and laid-back. He navigates the social waters of our school like the captain of some amazing cruise ship. In the seven months that we've been dating, I've become convinced I am probably the luckiest girl alive.

"English sort of sucked, but it's fine now," I tell him. "Why do you look so weird?"

"No reason." He flashes a shy smile, which widens to a full-on grin. "Well, maybe there is *one*."

He turns me around to face the end-of-day crowd; then he reaches into the pocket of his shorts and pulls out a pitch pipe.

"I have something to ask you."

Out of the traffic steps Mitch, Eli's best show choir friend. Eli blows a long E, and Mitch starts to sing.

"Well, a certain dance is coming in the month of May. . . ."

Next to Mitch appears Ravi, second tenor in the Glee Club barbershop quartet.

"A special night of romance, so that's why we're here to say . . ."

The last two guys in the quartet pop out. *"Eli would be honored if you'd make his dream come true. . . . Please, oh, please let Eli go to prom with you!"*

At the last line, seven of our closest friends pop out of the crowd holding hand-painted signs, each bearing a single word.

WILL

YOU

GO

TO

PROM

WITH

ME?

The last sign is held by none other than Harper. She steps out of the group and starts working the crowd, getting the rest of the commons cheering. And now Jordan's at my side with her phone, capturing for posterity the fact that I have no words. Literally, I can't say anything except for "Oh my God" and "This is amazing" and "I can't believe it," which, okay, is actually a few words. But if I were to try and say something eloquent like, "Eli, this is such a sweet surprise and I'm honored and humbled by the whole thing," I would be unable.

Because amazing. Oh my God. I can't believe it.

"So will you?" Eli asks.

"Of course!" I squeal. Like there was ever any doubt. He could have leaned over in the middle of a movie and grunted "Prom?" and I would have said yes. Prom was a foregone conclusion as far as I was concerned, but Eli made it special.

And the surprise isn't over. Out of his backpack he pulls a teddy bear clutching a rose and the menu to my favorite restaurant in its furry little paws.

"It's perfect." I take his face in my hands, standing on tiptoe to kiss his sweet, show choir–loving lips. "Thank you for this. I can't wait."

"I have to get to track, but I'll call you tonight, okay?" he says. "Start looking at dresses, or whatever it is you're supposed to do now!"

He backs down the staircase, waving all the way, while Harper

collects everybody's signs, and Jordan posts her video to ever̠
she manages. My phone vibrates in my bag as she tags me.

"Best promposal ever!" Jordan gushes. "I'm not allowed ι
vote for you since I'm running the contest, but that might be our
winner. Javier's just put in for the prizes—free burritos for a year,
baby!"

"I'm just glad it happened," says Harper. "We were starting to
wonder if you were ever going to show up."

"I got ambushed by Truman Alexander." I shudder at the memory. "Apparently he thinks my life would be much more worth-
while if I joined—get this—debate."

Jordan snorts. "You can't do debate. I need you for prom."

"Did you see where we're having it?" Harper says. "I told the
volunteers at Blessing they should start opening up the garden for
events again. They could make so much money."

"I'll pay them however much they want," Jordan says. "Even if
I have to force people to sell popcorn to cover it. As the first junior
ever to get voted committee chair, I refuse to have the first prom
I'm in charge of at some crappy hotel like they do every other year.
This is going to be the prom to end all proms."

"Then that's the place to have it," I agree. The Blessing place is
one of the few historic sites in town that hasn't been replaced by
a subdivision or strip mall. When Mr. Blessing was alive, he'd host
these amazing holiday parties in the garden. There were twinkle
lights in the trees, carolers in Victorian garb, and hot chocolate in
the gazebo, and everybody went, whether they celebrated Christmas or not. It was a chance to meet up with people you didn't see
much at other times and soak up the general magic of the season.
I have a photo by my bed of the three of us at the last party, four

years ago, before Mr. Blessing died: Jordan, sleek, dark, and stylish; Harper, whose pale complexion and auburn hair give her the look of a fairy princess; and me, bespectacled and blondish, with hair that manages to look bushy on one side and stringy on the other no matter what I do to it. If Jordan's first prom is half as great as those parties were, then she'll be a legend at our school.

Harper ducks into the choir room to stash Eli's posters. I pull out my phone to check the promposal video.

"Did you get it?" Jordan looks over my shoulder.

I try Instagram, but all I get is my phone's home screen with the apps grayed out and little spinning circles under each one.

"My phone is being a butt." I swipe left. I swipe right. Somehow my screen decides to swipe up.

"God, Sky, that really is tragic."

I make a sobbing noise in agreement because I am the owner of the most craptastic phone that anyone my age has ever been forced to carry. I wish I could blame it on being broke since my dad got laid off, but my crappy phone situation has more to do with building character—at least according to my parents. They don't believe in giving kids expensive gadgets; if I want something better than the free bargain-basement smartphone offered by their service provider's plan, then I have to pay for it myself. And since I don't have a few hundred dollars just lying around, nor have I built up something like a babysitting business to earn a few hundred dollars, I'm stuck with a phone that takes forever to load stuff, has been known to drop entire text conversations, and sometimes randomly spits out junk from my email's spam filter so that I get pinged with male enhancement notifications while I'm attempting to Snapchat.

Jordan shows me the video on her phone instead. I watch Eli

and myself as the whole promposal unfolds again—the way people stop to look, all the friends he got to participate. We look popular and fun. It's nice.

When Harper returns, we continue our trek to the parking lot.

"Hey, Mr. Ortiz," she calls as we pass our Spanish teacher in the quad. "Did you hear about the nosy pepper?"

"What about the nosy pepper?" he says, slowing down.

"He was jalapeño bizniz."

Mr. Ortiz cracks up, and Harper grins. This is classic Harper, going out of her way to make someone else smile. These days, though, it's *her* smile I crave. There's a certain spark to Harper— this totally in-the-moment energy that sweeps you up and makes you willing to go along with whatever cosmic social justice thing she happens to be into at the moment.

It's easy to make excuses for why none of us noticed when that spark started to flicker. I was busy with show choir and the winter musical. Then there were the holidays. Right around then her dad got laid off, like mine did when Eagle Mills closed its plant and re-located. A week later, her brother got kicked out of college after gambling his student loan money away online. Her mom went back to work, piling on extra hours to keep everything together. And none of us had any idea that Harper had started cutting herself.

Truman thinks my life is perfect; up until a few months ago, it was probably as perfect as anyone could possibly expect. No matter what happened at home, I had the constant and comfort of my two best friends. But when one leg of a tripod gets weakened, the whole thing goes wobbly. Harper's come home from the hospital and her spark seems to be returning, but I never considered the possibility of a world without that spark. Knowing it could go out has definitely made my life less perfect than it was before.

13

Her laughter carries us into the school parking lot, where we say goodbye to Jordan and get into my car. For the ten minutes it takes to drive to her house, she's the Harper I've always known—fighting over the music, keeping my head from getting too big over Eli's promposal by reminding me how cheesy barbershop quartet is, complaining about how much schoolwork she still has to make up. But when we get closer to her house, she grows quiet.

"You okay?" I ask as we pull into her driveway.

"Yeah," she answers. "Just tired. I have therapy in an hour."

"Oh . . ." I'm glad she's getting professional help, and from what I can see it's been a good thing. But I'll be the first person to admit I don't know anything about it. So I ask her, "What's that like?"

"Good, I guess. I'm supposed to be doing this worksheet, basically mapping out my emotions and how I deal with them. It's sort of like a personality test, only I don't get to find out what Disney princess I am at the end."

"You gotta love having even more homework to do."

"Well, my therapist calls it an action plan, but yeah . . . it's pretty much homework." She smiles as she opens the car door. "Thanks for the ride. And congrats on prom. You and Eli are super cute together."

I watch her go up the sidewalk and wait until her front door closes before driving to my own house. When I walk in, the soul-healing aroma of tomato sauce and melted cheese greets me. I burst into the kitchen, eager to tell Mom about Eli's promposal, only to find the room empty. The slow cooker sits on the counter with something resembling a lasagna inside, its red light reminding me that, oh yeah, my mother works now too. Dad followed his bliss and went to work for Legal Aid when Eagle Mills cut back their team of corporate attorneys. Mom took a job at Planned Parenthood, because we can use the money, and because she believes "all women have a right to health care." Also because she enjoys "pissing off the patriarchy."

They haven't been happier in years. Good for them.

That thing in the slow cooker, though, looks like a big fat nope.

My phone buzzes. It's my sister, Piper, wanting to chat. She's in her first year of law school up at Baldwin, and it's officially a Big Deal. I consider declining her call. She and I had a fight over Christmas, and things have been strained ever since. But I don't want to be an ass if she's making an effort, so I accept. All I can see when I try to connect, though, is myself in the camera window, shouting "Hello? Piper?" The buzzing stops.

I try calling back. Now it's her turn to shout while I fiddle with my volume, trying to figure out why I can hear her, but she can't hear me.

"Skyler, I'm going to hang up," she says. "I just wanted to say hi and check in."

I text her a Hi, things are good here. Sorry my phone's busted.

She texts back a thumbs-up, and I cross *communicate with Piper* off my mental to-do list. She made an effort; I made an effort. We didn't make up or talk it out or come to anything resembling a resolution, but we both did the Good Sister thing. So I guess that means it's all good. For now.

I've got a quiz in trigonometry this Friday, plus a test next week. So I drag myself to my room, force myself to open my notes, and then read the first page three times. Without understanding any of it.

I push my math to the floor and pick up the next book in Ms. Laramie's semester-long unit on female authors whose works were commentaries on their societies. This is much better. Except it's Austen, which Truman will no doubt willfully mangle and misinterpret.

Ugh, Truman.

My phone's buzzing again. I pick it up to find a new post notification. Finally, I'll be able to watch the promposal video on my own phone!

When I open Instagram, however, it looks weird. Instead of my photos, I see pics of sunsets and mountains and food. There are also a few featuring a smiley mutt of a dog.

I open my DMs and find a new one from Jordan.

Thanks for helping make the reunion so wonderful. Here's a link to the album. I'm still adding features but wanted you to be the first to see.

"Wait . . . what?" I tap the link and . . .

The website that comes up looks like it's for an event that's already happened. It's packed with photos of people dancing, hugging, celebrating. At first, I wonder whether someone else got the domain first. Then I spot a name I recognize under one of the photos: Ryan Oard. Only it's *not* Ryan Oard—at least, not as I know him. The guy in this picture is stockier, and his face has the weathered look of someone who's spent several years in the sun. Ryan *is* way into golf so he's outside a lot, but this guy looks like he's in his late twenties, maybe even older thanks to the sun damage.

I scroll, taking a closer look. The captions contain names of people from our class. But it's as if someone put makeup on everyone to age them several years. Most are easy to recognize; a thinner face here, a different hair color there—but I can still tell who's who.

Then there are some that make me do a double take. Samantha Voltaire has lost a ton of weight. Karter Listermann, on the other hand, has put on an alarming amount, in addition to losing most of his hair. If I look closely, I can see teenaged Karter underneath it all, but I have to use my imagination.

If this is a joke, then Jordan must have some secret stash of spare time that I'm not aware of. When did she put the site together? Where did she find all these people willing to masquerade as older versions of our classmates?

And where am I in all of it?

I find the search bar and enter my name.

My initial thought when the first photo pops up is that I look good. My normally drab hair has professional highlights, and it falls in loose waves to my shoulders. My makeup is sophisticated, my smile confident.

In the next photo, I'm posing with Jordan, who wears her hair in a daring buzzcut. In another, I'm hugging a boho Harper, who looks magnificent with waist-length hair and a flowing dress.

But it's the photo after that that makes me gasp.

I'm with Truman Alexander. Or, to be precise, an older version of Truman Alexander. Same green eyes, same dark hair, but he looks taller and his face isn't as round. He has an arm around my shoulder, but it's clear we aren't just posing as friends. I'm leaning in too intimately. His face is turned to mine as if he's getting ready to kiss my forehead.

And is that . . . ?

I zoom in, swearing under my breath. A diamond rests on my left hand, above a platinum band etched with a motif of gold leaves.

A matching band circles Truman's left ring finger.

CHAPTER TWO

"Ha-ha, very funny," I say as soon as Jordan's face appears on my laptop screen.

"What?" she asks. "What's funny?"

"You know what." I hold up my phone to the webcam. "This. Fake reunion site. Did you find an app that goes through the yearbook and adds ten years to everybody or something? Nice touch putting me with Truman."

She sighs. "Skyler, I have no idea what you're talking about. What reunion? What site?"

"The one you sent me a link to. It says you sent it an hour ago."

"I was with you an hour ago. If I was sending you something, I would have told you about it."

"You definitely sent it. I'm sending it back to you. Here."

I wait while she watches her own phone screen.

"Has it come through yet?"

"No. Not to sound like I don't care, Sky, but I've got a chemistry test tomorrow. I don't have time for this right now."

"And yet you found time to prank me?"

"Fine, whatever. You can believe what you want." She pulls her cat, Bea, into her lap and moves the kitten's paw in a mini mock wave. "I'll see you in the morning, okay?"

She signs off, leaving me with the vaguely unsettled feeling I've been having for a while now. Jordan is the kind of person who always knows what she wants, and she has this uncanny ability to make whatever that is a reality. It could be a fabulous party or straight As or the perfect outfit—all she has to do is touch it and it comes out just the way she envisioned. Lately, I feel like there's something she wants me to be but can't make materialize. I'm not sure I could find the words to ask what was wrong if I ever really wanted to know, but I can sense it; I'm frustrating her.

Or maybe I'm losing my mind. How else to explain what I'm looking at right now? I prop myself up on some pillows and start searching again. First, I look up Eli. In every photo, he's with a bunch of other guys. No rings on his fingers.

Next, I search Truman, and the vast majority of images have me in them. We're laughing, dancing—even kissing, which creeps me out exactly as much as you'd think it would. The only other person Truman appears with more than once is an older woman with red hair. The caption says her name is Margaret Olmstead, and apparently she's some sort of guest of honor. In one photo, Truman, Jordan, Harper, and I stand on a stage with her. She's shaking Harper's hand.

I take a bathroom break; then I'm back to scrolling, trying to unravel what all of it means. As I scroll, an idea wiggles in—the most outrageous explanation possible.

Is there a possibility this could be real? Am I somehow looking into the future?

And if I am, does that mean I'm going to end up with Truman Alexander?

The room tilts. Invisible bugs scuttle down my back, across my arms, everywhere. Everything buzzes. It's impossible. There is no way I would so much as go on a single date with Truman, let alone marry him.

The creepy-crawlies bring a new, more plausible thought: Maybe Truman is behind all this. Maybe the website is some new manifestation of his fixation with me, in which case it's violating and gross. The fact that I even gave a second thought to the idea of marrying him means he's crept into my brain, turning what up until now has been a mostly academic rivalry into something far more insidious.

If this is his doing, then we've moved beyond passive-aggressive sparring in English class and into personal territory. All those years of hating Truman are nothing compared to how I feel now.

Now? I straight up loathe him.

"Can I ask you something crazy?"

"Sure." Harper takes off her cardigan and sits next to me on the choir room risers before first bell. Next to her backpack sits a bag of her famous vegan cookies, which I know are for Nick Kroger, whose brother was in a bad car accident two days ago. She smiles at me over her takeout tea, looking pretty with her hair in a loose side braid.

"Can I see your phone?"

She hands it over and I pull up my IG through her feed. Harper's phone shows my regular profile and pics—the "artsy" Christmas-tree photo I took over break, the photo of Jordan sticking her tongue out at lunch, the selfie I took two days ago when I got new glasses frames. My phone, on the other hand, is still showing the dog and the food and the mountains. I thumb the URL from my DMs into Harper's browser, trying to pull up the reunion site, but nothing happens.

"What the . . ." I refresh, getting the same result.

"Is something wrong?" she asks.

"Maybe?" I give her her phone back, trying to figure out how to explain what's going on so I can ask her opinion about it. "I don't know. It's this—"

"Whatcha looking at?" Eli plops down in the chair on the other side of me.

"Nothing." I shove my phone into my bag. Harper gives me the quickest look of concern before lighting up when Eli leans across to smack a kiss on her cheek.

"Did you see our video from yesterday?" he asks me. "The likes are through the roof!"

"There were two more promposals last night," Harper says. "They were weak compared to you guys."

"So I was thinking for actual prom, we could do a spa thing," Eli continues. "Skyler, you get your hair and makeup done. Me and Mitch get manicures or something like that. We get a limo, hire a videographer . . ."

I nod agreeably while my stomach clenches at the thought of trying to scrape up money for spa treatments. A year ago, I wouldn't have thought twice about it. And I envy the fact that Eli doesn't have to think twice about it now. My friends whose parents didn't work for Eagle Mills have continued on their wealthy way—people like Jordan, whose dad is an orthodontist, and Eli, whose mom is in advertising and whose dad is a lawyer too, but with his own practice. I miss the blissful ignorance that they still get to enjoy, not having to worry too much about money and not even realizing that they don't have to worry about it. I'm happy for them. Really.

But pedicures and videographers? Thank God show choir is starting. Eli's distracted, so he doesn't see me stressing out. He and Harper head down to the piano for warm-ups while I check my phone one more time.

The reunion site is still there, just like last night, with those same photos of Truman and me, matching rings on our hands. I look up at Eli with his track-toned body and his gorgeous brown eyes, everything about him radiating sunshine, and wonder how in the world anyone could ever imagine me with anybody else, much less a pompous windbag like Truman Alexander.

As if on cue, Truman sends me a text.

Last chance—Debate?

My fingers fly in response.

Not interested. Leave me alone.

"Skyler, are you joining us?" Mr. Easterday gestures toward the empty spot in the back row of the formation. I scurry down, take my place, and try to focus on matching choreography to four-part harmony.

Our first number is a mash-up of rock classics. It opens with a duet—Harper and Eli, singing "Don't Go Breaking My Heart."

They get all the solos, because Harper sings like nobody else, and Eli is irresistible in front of an audience. I, on the other hand, am content to be part of the chorus. There's less pressure when you're in the back—less chance of looking dumb, getting put on the spot, or being judged for making mistakes. I can be a part of it all, but not be the one everything relies on. I'm a supporting player, and I like it that way.

I watch as Eli thrusts a hand out to Harper. She takes it. He pulls her toward him, and they sing to each other—the guy I love and the girl I worry about. She belts out the music, eyes sparkling. Eli beams at me over his shoulder as we move into place for the next song. Right now, things are good. I like things now. Why do I even need to think about the future?

I don't. That reunion site is nothing more than joke, and I'm not going to let Truman get away with it. He and I have been in a simmering kind of war for years, but I'm not letting it escalate. Whatever he's up to, it stops now.

"Quit it."

Truman looks up from his desk. He glances around as if I might be talking to somebody else.

"Excuse me?"

"You heard me. Stop with the website stuff. It's not funny."

He squints in confusion, a look echoed on the faces of everyone around him, but I don't care. English is starting soon. I want to get this over with.

"Skyler," he says. "I have no idea what you're talking about."

"You seriously want me to believe that? Who else could have done it?"

"Did you check the coding club? If we're talking about a website—and that *is* what we're talking about, right?—then that would seem to be your best bet. Web design is not one of my many talents."

A smirk plays across his lips. I clench my fists, tempted to shake him by the lapels of his logo-breasted fleece.

"You don't have to be a coder to do what you did. It's harassment and I don't appreciate it. I want it taken down. Immediately."

"If you're a victim of cyberbullying, then there are resources available to help. In fact, isn't there a packet they send home to our parents every year? Maybe get a copy from the office."

"Skyler and Truman, could you wrap up your conversation so we can get started?" Ms. Laramie stands at the front of the room with her copy of *Pride and Prejudice,* looking wearier than usual.

"Take it down," I tell him before stalking back to my seat. "Or I'll report you."

Ms. Laramie lectures about wealth and social status in Regency England. I watch Truman. Halfway through the lecture, he takes out his phone. He thumbs the screen under his desk, then glances at me as he puts it away, and it's all I can do to wait until the end of class to make sure he definitely deleted the site. He exits right away when the bell rings. I stay at my seat, pull up Instagram and . . . it still looks weird.

I open the link in my DMs. The website is still up.

"Are you freaking kidding me?!?"

I march out of English and two doors down to the speech and forensics room. It's empty. I head for the yearbook office to find Jordan coming out, putting on her jacket.

"What's the matter?" she says. "Why do you look like you're going to murder somebody?"

"Can I show you this?" I hold up my phone. "It's that website I told you about last night. I want to know what you think about it."

"Can you show it to Harper? I have to drop off deposits right now."

"She's volunteering."

Jordan checks her own phone. "What if I come over later?"

"Fine. I'll see you then."

I don't want to wait, but I need her sensibleness. If Harper is the soul of our trio, then Jordan is the one who keeps everything grounded. Years ago, when we were kids living on the same street, she and I didn't like each other. I thought she was bossy. She thought I was hyper. It was Harper who brought us together, coming by every day to knock on my door, then Jordan's, creating a neutral space in her backyard where we could play, fight, talk, and learn to love each other. As the years went by, we started to feel like three aspects of the same person: Me, impulsive and headstrong; Harper, dreamy and thoughtful; Jordan, practical and ambitious. By the time we all moved to bigger houses and better streets, we were inseparable everywhere else.

Now I need a good dose of common sense as only Jordan can deliver it.

Walking through the commons on my way to my car, I get an email from Piper. *FW: 101 Quotes to Motivate and Inspire You.* Every other week she sends me these things—gems like *Michelle Obama Believes in You, So Don't Let Her Down* and *Disabled Dog Teaches Prison Inmates the Power of Perseverance.* My sister lives for this stuff.

I shut off my phone, get in the car, and turn on the radio. Then I drive around town, taking the long way home because home is too quiet these days. And that's not exactly bad; it's just . . . different. On days when the rest of my world is going the way it should, then different and I are cool. But when things are weird—when, for example, I am being harassed online by my archnemesis—then different and I are not friends.

In fact, I'm not a fan. Not even a little.

CHAPTER THREE

"What's on for tonight, Sky?" Dad hands me a slice of pizza, then starts serving up salad from the foil take-out container. I get up to grab pepper flakes and Parmesan cheese before joining him back at the table. Mom just got home and is getting washed up. I can hear her humming to herself in the bathroom.

"Tons of homework," I say as I doctor up my pizza. "Trig test tomorrow and quizzes coming up."

"Ah, I hated trigonometry." Mom comes into the kitchen wearing one of her sympathetic looks. "I remember when I was your age, I could not wait to be done with math."

"The struggle is real." Overall, my GPA is pretty good; the weighting from my AP English and History classes helps balance out the mediocre grades I bring home in math every year. "But honestly, this one might kick my butt."

"Can I help?" Dad offers.

"No, it's okay. I'll go to review night."

My dad hasn't tried to help me since seventh grade, or what Piper ever so graciously dubbed "The Year of Tears." Mom was out of town a lot helping my grandparents sell their house and move to a retirement community. I, meanwhile, had a math teacher with the personality of a drill sergeant, who expected that everyone in our class turn out to be mini Stephen Hawkings. Dad tried to see me through my homework each night, but his explanations made no sense. I ended up wading in a swamp of anxiety, numbers sliding around the page like one of those carnival games where you have to guess which cup a little red ball is hiding under. Dad, the *let's get 'er done* workaholic, tried to hide his frustration. He failed, which sent me into an even deeper tailspin.

Meanwhile, my sister breezed through her work, making my troubles look even more pathetic.

"Maybe Skyler wouldn't have such a hard time if she didn't turn everything into so much drama," she sniped one night. "She can't freak out like that when she gets to high school."

And that right there says a lot about my relationship with Piper. She floats through life while I get stuck knee-deep in it. She blazes trails that I can never hope to follow. Then, every once in a while, she drops in with some unsolicited advice.

Most recently, the day after Christmas, right before she left to go back to school. Mom and Dad had gone over to see the neighbors, and we were sitting in the den finishing off a leftover cheese ball, when she said, "How's school?"

"Fine," I replied, thinking she meant *school* as in friends, show choir, yearbook . . . the whole shebang.

"You should really try and buckle down this next semester. Bring up your grades."

A cracker got stuck in my throat. I coughed and said, "My grades are fine."

"They might not be if you want scholarships for college." She reached for the last Triscuit, sounding very worldly. "And maybe you should be applying for some. Mom and Dad can't really afford full tuition now."

"We have college savings."

"But you'd be surprised how expensive everything is. Mine didn't last long when I had to figure in books and food and the dorms and everything else."

"I'm applying to State. How expensive can that be?"

"Get online and look—it's a lot more than you think."

She went back to her cheese and crackers, while I had lost my appetite. Before Piper left for college, I constantly had to listen to people rave about her bright future. Now here she was lecturing me about mine. I couldn't let her have the last word.

"Where I go and how I pay for it is none of your business, Piper. Especially since you already got your expensive college at Duke. Now you've got law school, which I'm sure is not cheap either, so who are you to say anything about what I'm doing?"

"Geez, calm down," she said. "I'm just telling you the truth. You can't coast by anymore and assume things are going to be okay. You have to step up and take more initiative."

That sparked a shouting match, which led to a superawkward rest of the day and an even more awkward goodbye when she left for Lake Champion the next morning. And now things are awkward between us, and they'll be awkward between me and Dad, too, if he tries to help me with trigonometry. So I tell him "I think I can handle the test," and count it a win when he and Mom start talking about his casework at Legal Aid.

The doorbell rings. Jordan's voice carries down the hall as she makes her way toward the kitchen.

"Oh yeah, and Jordan's here." I get up, grabbing more pizza for me, plus a slice for her. "We're doing some prom-planning stuff."

"I saw the video of Eli asking you yesterday," Mom says. "That was sweet of him to go to so much trouble."

"I know. Isn't he perfect?"

Maybe sometimes too perfect. The thought pops into my head out of nowhere, making me frown. That reunion site is messing with my head, making me doubt things I was certain about less than twenty-four hours ago.

All the more reason to figure out what the hell it is.

"So look at this." I tap the link and wait while my phone decides whether or not it's going to work. When the site comes up, I scroll through, giving Jordan a mini tour. "You really didn't do this?"

She studies the screen. When I land on a thumbnail with her name below it, she commandeers my phone, pulling the photo up big.

"Wow, my hair looks awesome. Yours too, Sky. Everybody wonders what they're going to look like when they're pushing thirty but you and I don't need to worry. We are fiiine!"

She chuckles to herself. The sound jangles my nerves.

"Looks are the least of my concerns right now."

"I'm just saying. If we're going to have to start going to bed early and taking calcium and paying taxes, we should at least look fierce doing it."

I take back the phone, scrolling away from Jordan's photos. None of us should be surprised that she would strut into the future with impeccable style, but that's not what this is about right now.

"I don't even know if it's real. We could be looking at ourselves put through the world's best aging filter. Or Photoshop."

"If that's what it is, then it's extremely good Photoshop." She pokes around my bedroom, peeking behind my desk and under the bed. "Are there hidden cameras in here? Because if you're going to end up on some prank compilation you might want to wear something a little nicer than holey old sweatpants. I see London, I see France . . ."

"Nice." I shift to a position that doesn't allow any part of my London or France to be seen. "Way to make me paranoid."

"But here's the thing. If this whole site is a joke, how come you're only in, like, twenty percent of it? Someone would have had to doctor up hundreds of pics of everybody else, too. It seems like a lot of trouble for a prank on just one person."

"Maybe other people got the link too, not just me."

"No. If something like this was going around, people would be talking."

I click some more. "But what *is* it?"

She scrolls and scrolls. She goes back to my Instagram, then back to the reunion site. Her whole being radiates excitement as she opens picture after picture.

"I know this sounds unreal, Skyler, but maybe it's exactly what it looks like."

Her expression is full of awe now, and my stomach drops like I just went over a speed bump at full throttle. I expected her to have a plausible explanation; instead, my most practical friend looks like she's just seen the ghost of reunions yet to come.

"Oh my God, what if it really is real?" she says. "Wait a minute, can you see my future Instagram too?"

She taps the profile that sent me the reunion URL. Nothing happens. "Damn." She goes back to my Insta and looks at the dog, the coffee shops, the sunsets. "You need to make a note to your future self to have a more interesting feed, Sky. This is boring AF."

"That's not funny. . . ."

"You're right. There is absolutely nothing funny about this sad future feed."

"Stop it. This is horrifying!" I feel like I might throw up. "What if we really are looking at the future? And why is this only happening to me?"

She pulls up the DM again. "It says I sent it, but that's not my profile. At least not right now. Maybe, for some reason, Future Me thought you should see this?"

I take off my glasses to scrub my eyes with the palms of my hands. "My brain hurts. This is some serious *Doctor Who* shiz, Jordan."

"It's also seriously awesome." She jumps back onto my bed. "What else can we see?" More scrolling, more tapping. "Okay, note to Future *Me*: make sure the reunion site has a current events section or something. I can't even tell who's president. We also need some bios. I can't see who *I* end up with. I don't know what my career is . . . Future Jordan, do better!"

"Future Jordan probably had no idea High School Jordan would want that information," I say.

"At least we can see how everybody else turned out." She rubs her hands together. "Who should we look up first? How about Brynn Lischer?"

"Ugh, Brynn." Top of the Alton High School A-list and class-A bitch. I watch as Jordan types Brynn's name into the search bar.

"You know what they say. The most popular people in high school end up being losers as adults. They peak early and it's all downhill from there."

I point at the perfectly turned-out woman whose image pops

up. "If that's really Brynn, she doesn't look like a loser at all. She looks even more fabulous."

Jordan points out the other figure in the photo: Brynn's trusty sidekick today and, it looks like, as an adult too. "McKinley Peterson, on the other hand . . ."

". . . definitely looks like a train wreck. Though is anybody really surprised what smoking and obsessive tanning will do to a person?"

"Hold up," Jordan says. "Who's that?"

I tap the thumbnail. "Looks sort of like Kevin Kallaos in a dress and long hair."

"The caption says Kristin."

"Unless they have a sister we don't know about, it looks like there are some changes coming."

"Huh," Jordan says. "Good for Kristin."

Exploring further, I open an album titled *Recognition*. What I find there makes me do a double take. "Check this out: Ten-Year Achievement Award. It's Anna Larkin."

"Awkward Anna? The one Brynn and McKinley love to torment?"

"Apparently she's going to get the last laugh." I read the caption under the photo. "Started her own company, a multimillionaire by age twenty-five—"

"And what a makeover! I never would have recognized her."

I sit back against my headboard, feeling lost. "I guess it's nice that everybody turned out so great. Except . . ."

"Except for the part with you and Truman. Are you positive you don't have *any* feelings for him at all? I mean besides complete and utter loathing?"

"No! Gross! It's Truman Alexander."

"Yeah. He's weird."

"Even in a bizarro parallel universe, there's no way he'd be the love of my life."

"But maybe you're the love of his." She gasps. "Maybe this is part of the most epic promposal of all time!"

"But why? I already have a prom date."

"Do you really think that would stop him? You know how the guy loves to win. Even though I'm supposed to stay neutral, I can tell you that this beats Eli's barbershop thing hands down."

"Ughhhh . . . no." I bury my head in my arms. "Truman argues with me in class. Truman does not compete with me—or for me, or whatever—in private life. And most of all, Truman does *not* love me."

Jordan lets me moan and protest until she checks her own phone and finds it's later than either of us realized.

"I need to go." She nods to my screen. "What are you going to do?"

I look at the image of Truman and me smiling with our arms around each other. I turn my phone off.

"I don't know. But until I figure it out, don't tell anyone, okay? Especially not Eli. He doesn't need to know how ridiculous this Truman drama has gotten."

"Eli wouldn't care," Jordan says. "It's not like Truman is competition. Is he?"

"No!" I smack her leg as she slides off the bed. "Truman's probably doing this *because* he knows it'll freak me out, which is why from now on I'm keeping calm and keeping it to myself. Truman is screwing with my head, and it's not going to work. He's messing with the wrong girl."

Which is why, when I arrive for prom committee after school the next day, the sight of Truman there nearly makes me turn around and walk right back out again.

He's sitting on a bench slightly apart from the rest of the group, next to the arched door of the garden. When Harper and I walk in, he locks eyes with me. Harper goes to talk with some of the volunteers, while Jordan grabs my arm and drags me behind a bush.

"Before you say anything, I knew you wouldn't want him here," she says. "Which is why I didn't text you in advance. Truman asked if he could come."

And of course, who should pick this very moment to appear around the corner? Truman eyes Jordan and me.

"Everything okay?" he asks.

"I'm just trying to figure out why you're gracing us with your presence," I tell him. "Did you join prom committee? Or have you decided to torment me literally everywhere now?"

"Actually," says Jordan, "Truman has something we all need to hear."

She pulls us both back to the main courtyard as the other committee members put down their phones. She calls the meeting to order, making sure we take a moment to appreciate our surroundings.

"I decided to meet here instead of school because I'm really excited about this place. I think we all agree it would be amazing to have prom here, am I right?"

People are nodding, envisioning photos in front of the rose wall, hookups by the fountain, couples in tuxes and gowns swaying under the stars.

"But there's a problem. That's why Truman is here."

Jordan has just answered the question everyone's been thinking: Why is Truman, who no one would ever expect at a prom meeting, standing there next to her? They're an odd couple, but for the moment they appear to be a team.

Truman clears his throat.

"I'm sure you've all heard that the city is bringing Everest Outfitters to town."

Of course, we've heard. For the past six months, the Everest deal has been topic number one in the news. The company wants to open a massive distribution facility here. It's going to bring a ton of new jobs.

"Well, they've already bought the Eagle Mills plant," Truman continues. "But they're buying up smaller properties too. One of the places they're looking at is right where we're standing."

"Everest is buying the mansion?" I ask.

"This year's debate topic is property rights, specifically imminent domain, so I went to city hall for some case study materials, and I found a paper trail of plans in the zoning office that nobody outside of city council has paid any attention to—at least not that I know of so far."

He pauses, expecting the rest of us to be as fascinated as he is by the details of his tournament prep. I raise an eyebrow and roll my finger, signaling him to get on with it.

"According to what's on file with the city, the mansion would house some of the Everest offices," he continues. "This garden would be a parking lot."

Gasps ricochet through the group. I look around for Harper, but she's off helping in the shed. I can hear her laughing while the volunteers haul bags of potting soil from a pile by the door.

"Why didn't they tell us that when we booked this place?" asks Kailey Lopez. "The lady we talked to never mentioned it."

"If she's a volunteer, then I'm not sure she would know," Truman answers. "I dug through a year's worth of council meeting minutes, and I think it's safe to say they don't want anyone knowing the details until it's too late to do anything about it."

"Prom's only a few weeks away. They can't get everything done before then, can they?"

"There's a final hearing and a vote coming up soon. Unless something is done to stop it, the odds don't look good."

The group goes silent.

"So . . . ," I say. "Should we find another place to have prom?"

"I don't want to have prom somewhere else," Jordan insists. "The only other option is the cheesy banquet hall where everybody and their dog has their weddings."

"I've got a plan to stop it," Truman says.

Jordan gestures toward Truman like, *Great. Somebody's actually going to do something.*

"So who will help Truman with his plan?" she asks.

Crickets. Surprise, surprise—nobody wants to work with Truman.

Jordan shoots me a look. I mouth a *No way.* I am the only person here who knows him on more than a purely superficial level, so I am the most likely suspect to team up, but no. Not going to happen.

Her eyes narrow, and there's something hard in them: the frustration I've been sensing lately concentrated into a stare that tells me I'd better play along or else.

Or else what?

Jordan is my best friend, so why am I feeling anything close to an *or else* from her?

Just do it. It's not worth getting into a fight over.

I decide to obey the voice in my head and give in. I flash Jordan a *you owe me* look, and her face lights up again.

Great.

I get up and trudge after Truman, who's already disappeared down a nearby path. I follow it to a koi pond ringed with big rocks, under a tree just starting to bud out. Truman sits on one of the rocks, obviously expecting me to have a seat next to him.

Not so fast.

"Before I work on anything with you, I want to make one thing perfectly clear. I don't know what you've been trying to accomplish these past couple of days, but I find it incredibly offensive."

"Is this the website you were talking about yesterday?" He pulls out a pen and a thick black notebook. "The only digital communication I've had with you recently is a text about debate. I get that you're not interested, and I won't ask again. But I'm confused why one three-word message would be so offensive, even one that came from me."

Is he messing with my mind, or is he serious? I plant my hands on my hips.

"It's all a little convenient, Truman. First the website, and now you here at prom committee. I have a date to prom already, okay? So if this is part of some elaborate promposal, you can call it off."

A smile, still tinged with confusion but infuriatingly smug, creeps across Truman's face.

"Now I really do think you have the wrong person. Even if I did want to take you to prom, I would not be doing a *promposal*. Even the name is ridiculous. No offense, but can you imagine?"

At any other time, I would be taking major offense to his prom snobbery. All I can feel now, though, is the fading of my hope for a rational explanation.

"You're telling me you didn't send me a link? From Jordan's Instagram?"

"How would I get into Jordan's Instagram?"

He looks genuinely baffled now. But if Truman didn't create it, who did? I scroll through a mental file of everyone I know, and no one else pops up as a prime suspect. The crumbling of that option leaves few others left. I plop down onto one of the boulders by the pond, staring into space.

"Skyler? Are you okay?"

His voice is soft—caring, even. Definitely not what I'm used to hearing from Truman Alexander.

"It's just, weird things have been happening. You really only sent me that one text? Nothing else?"

"After the way you responded, I didn't think it'd be wise to try anything else. You've made it clear you have no desire to join debate."

Something about the way he says that—like it hurt to get shot down a second time—makes me feel bad. It's true I've wished Truman a host of unpleasant fates over the years, but it's easy to wish those things on someone who's behaving like a cartoonishly awful douchebag, and cartoonish doesn't even begin to describe how awful Truman can be sometimes. But I don't enjoy kicking puppies, and right now Truman reminds me of a slightly dejected shelter dog.

"It just bothered me how you went about asking," I tell him. "And then you were an ass about my activities. I don't need to be lectured."

"I've always had this thing about saying what I think is the truth, even if it gets me in trouble. It gets me in trouble a lot."

I can't help smiling. "I can tell you've done the required Ms. Laramie reading, because you sound alarmingly Darcy-esque right now."

"Does that make you Bennet-ish? Or Elizabethan perhaps?"

Amused by the play on words, I feel my smile growing. "Was that an attempt at a compliment?"

"I guess it was. I don't always agree with you. Actually, I pretty much almost never agree with you. But I have to respect you. You aren't afraid to stand up for what you believe in and you have a natural talent for making a compelling argument, which is why I thought you'd be good at debate."

Truman is looking at me with that unblinking stare I've always found so creepy. Only it's not creepy now. It's intense, but there's a sincerity in his expression that is hard to deny or dislike. I've spent so little time with Truman outside of school, close-up, that I never really noticed the details of what makes Truman Truman. His complexion is clear, with ruddy patches at the apples of his cheeks. His hair has an endearingly shaggy quality. Then there are those eyes. Up close they are an almost shockingly vibrant shade of green.

The corner of his mouth quirks up. And suddenly I'm thinking about how things ended for Elizabeth and Mr. Darcy—about the reunion website and what it shows for Truman and me.

I spring to my feet. "I need to go."

He holds up the black notebook. "But we need to go over my plan."

I pick up my bag, reminding myself that (1) I have a boyfriend, and (2) I find Truman repulsive.

"Text me and tell me what you want me to do. I'm good at handing out fliers and stuff."

"But it's more than—"

"Seriously, just put it in writing. I forgot I have to pick my dad up from work. His car's in the shop."

Truman's voice follows me back up the path, still protesting. I escape into the courtyard just as the meeting is breaking up.

"I'm sorry I did that to you," Jordan says. "I know you hate him and things are weird, but nobody else would help, and . . . What's wrong?"

My phone buzzes. I pull it out, thinking it's Truman texting me his plan. Instead, it's an email—and it looks like it's from the reunion site.

Thanks for registering—you can now access all albums, download photos, comment, and take advantage of the full reunion experience.

"What in the hell is this?"

I hand the phone to Jordan, who squeals.

"I was going to ask if you'd checked it today. Get Harper over here, I want to show her how great my hair looks." She opens the reunion site and starts scrolling. "Ooh! It's even better now. Those extensions are *so* good!"

"Wait, what? It's different?" I snatch the phone back to find that she's right. Not only does Future Jordan have a different hairstyle, but the site itself has more features, including bios and fun facts about Alton High School. I search for photos of Truman and me. We're still together, but my hair is darker and he's wearing a hat.

"I was just with Truman, though. He didn't have his phone out at all. And when I looked at this right before I got here, your hair was still short. So that means it just changed within the last hour."

Jordan looks at me, puzzled. "So that means Truman can't be the one who's doing it."

"Ugh." I shove my phone back into my bag and head for the exit. "I can't handle this on an empty stomach. I need food."

CHAPTER FOUR

We head to Donor's Square, where people from school hang out pretty much anytime it's not freezing or raining. Donor's Square is right in the middle of what passes for a downtown in our dinky little corner of the Midwest, and part of what makes it so popular is that there are take-out places all around. You can get everything from pizza to burgers to burritos, and everybody eats under the monument at the top of the steps. The monument is a stone pillar that narrows to a peak at the top, with these sort of rounded things at the base that are supposed to represent waves, or arches, but just make the whole thing look like a giant penis. Donor's Square was named in honor of the people who gave money to create the park across the street. But we all call it Boner's Square.

Since it's Friday afternoon, the steps to the monument are crowded. Jordan and I get wraps and fries from Buddy's, then stake out a spot, saving room for Harper, who's getting a ride from one of the other volunteers once they finish their shift. Next to us sit Brynn and McKinley with Anna Larkin tagging along and a few of our other mutual friends. Brynn says hi. McKinley sort of nods. We all eat and talk, sometimes to each other, and I can't help picturing

43

the two of them as I saw them last night on the reunion site—adults in the real world, not just the queens of our tiny universe.

When you think about it, high school social life is like the rings of a planet you see in pictures. Everybody's circling the center, and the closer you go in, the more popular you are. You can't see the rings clearly from close-up. But when you look from a distance, they are definitely there. Sometimes a meteor hits—parents get laid off; parties and trips and expensive clothes drift out of reach in some places, while staying fixed in others. The ripples create new spots for everyone in the rings. And like a lot of people, I'm still figuring out where I fit. My parents are both working again, so that puts me in a better position than, say, Harper, whose dad is still job hunting. But we both have Jordan. So for now at least, I am somewhat comfortably in the mid- to near-center.

And thank goodness Truman is in a constellation clear across the Milky Way. He never hangs out at Boner's Square, so he won't see me eating fries when I told him I was picking my dad up at his office.

"So Truman thinks promposals are ridiculous?" Jordan says when I tell her about our conversation. "I always thought you were being a little extra about him, but now I'm reconsidering."

"I keep thinking there has to be an answer, though—something or somebody we're missing."

"Well, whoever's doing the site, at least we have bios now." She's got my phone again and has started exploring the bullets under both our names. "These are stupidly limited, but I guess they're better than nothing. Look at you, Sky. You're in marketing research. And look at me. I'm"—she reads from the screen—"'an entertainment industry executive.' Not too shabby!"

I take back my phone, wondering what in the heck a marketing researcher does, and more than a little jealous of Future Jordan's fabulous career. "It's probably not even real," I say. "Didn't you take philosophy? Occam's razor? When in doubt, the most obvious explanation is the correct one—this is a prank, and you're getting pulled into it too."

"But you have to admit . . . whoa!" She smacks me in the chest with one hand and points with the other. She's looking up, along with everybody else in the square. I follow their gazes to see a drone gliding over from the park. A few feet away, Agnes Shull is screaming with delight. Her boyfriend, Darius, holds the drone's controls and is squinting into the setting sun while his friend Ramesh tries to guide him.

Trailing underneath the drone is a banner.

AGNES + DARIUS = PROM?

Jordan gets her own phone out and starts recording for the promposal contest. I have to hand it to Darius; he's doing a pretty good job flying that drone. But the sun is sort of blinding right now. The drone buzzes too close to the monument. Darius and Ramesh try to steer it away, but it's too late. The banner gets hooked.

The crowd gasps. For a minute it looks like the drone is broken, but then it disconnects and flies away, leaving the banner hanging from the monument's pointy top.

"Oh damn," says Jordan. The paint on the banner isn't completely dry. The banner starts to slide down the monument, leaving a trail of red and black as it goes. The police officer who sits in his cruiser every day making sure we don't act like savages springs into action, thrilled to finally have something to do. We see him taking down Darius's information as Harper comes across the square with a box of salad from Alton's lone organic grocer.

45

She sits down as Jordan posts the video of everything that just happened, minus the collision and the subsequent, inadvertent, vandalism.

"That one might beat you and Eli," Harper tells me. "Take out the monument fail, and it was pretty spectacular."

"Skyler, give me back your phone," Jordan commands. "Now that Harper's here, I want to show her the reunion site."

"Is this that thing you guys were talking about last night?" says Harper. "It sounds creepy."

"It's amazing," says Jordan. "Check this out. . . ."

"No! I don't want to see." Harper scoots up a step, trying to get away from us. "Looking at yourself in the future can't be good for the space-time continuum. What if you open up some kind of wormhole and we all disappear into it?"

"Believe me, I've looked at this thing enough times that if a wormhole was going to happen, it would have by now," I tell her. "It's not real. There's no way."

"Whatever," Harper says. "Leave me out of it. I want to keep my future a mystery."

"I don't," Jordan says. "Every time I open this thing, my future gets better and better."

"Jordan." Now I'm starting to get angry. "It's not really real."

"Um . . ."

Her face looks like all the blood has drained out of it as she studies my screen. She hands the phone back to me, and I see that the site has changed again. Now a big class picture stretches across the top, all of our older selves lined up here in the square. The monument points toward the sky behind us, looking as phallic as ever. But if you look closely you can see streaks coming from

46

the top that match the ones that were just left by Darius's banner. They're faint, but they are definitely there.

Jordan and I look at the sculpture in the photo. We look at each other.

"Oh. My. God."

"What are we going to do? What are *you* going to do?"

Jordan's eyes are massive brown circles as she stares at me in shock. I, meanwhile, am staring at the monument on my phone. I don't want to believe, but it's right there in front of me—remnants of paint from a promposal I *just saw happen.* There is no possible way someone could have taken the picture I'm looking at and doctored it up. Not in that short a time. It's Occam's razor in the other direction. Given this latest update, the most obvious answer is also the craziest.

The reunion site is real.

It's really, really real.

"Now I really am going to throw up." I start pacing, trying to calm the churning in my stomach.

"This is unbelievable!" Jordan has the giggles, she's so freaked out. Meanwhile Harper is just sitting, watching us. "So that means all of it's true. You can see the freaking future, Sky!"

"Shh!" I hiss. Brynn and McKinley are looking at us funny, and other people have started to notice too. We sit down, quiet down, and slowly start to calm down.

"But seriously," Jordan says. "What are you going to do?"

"I don't know. Harper, you don't want to see it?"

"No. I really don't."

"There's nothing to be scared of," Jordan reassures her. "You look great. If you check your bio, it looks like you're—"

"Seriously, I don't want to know. If you say I look great and everything's great, then that's fine." She closes her salad box and stands up. "Sky, I need to get home. Can you take me?"

She's different somehow from when she first got here—flatter and edgier. She's already started down the steps, so I scurry after her, looking back to see if Jordan's noticed the change too.

"I'm coming over later," Jordan calls after us. "I want to check out my future reunion-planning skills some more!"

In the car, Harper puts on music and cranks up the heat. Now that we're alone, the other parts of the day bubble back into my mind: The prom committee meeting. Truman's news about Everest . . . No wonder Harper seems down.

"I'm sorry about the garden. That really sucks that they want to tear it out."

"Yeah," she says. "Everybody over there is pissed."

We drive, and I'm not sure what else to say. Harper started volunteering at the garden about a year ago, and it was the first place besides home that she went after the hospital. Even before she came back to school, she spent an afternoon over there, helping out.

"It's like, I find this thing that I really like that's fun and makes me feel good, and then it just gets taken away." She stares out the window. "Story of my life."

"You have other things you like. Your singing, show choir . . ."

"I know." I wait for her to say something else, but she stays silent. I don't hear that silence very often, but when I do, it puts everything inside me on high alert. Not long ago, we didn't really listen to Harper's silences. Now they bring up memories so loud they scream: Harper's mom on the phone, asking if I have any idea why she would cut her wrist with the blade of a pair of kitchen scissors. Jordan and me huddled in the ER waiting room, comparing notes. In hindsight, we should have paid more attention to Harper's plummeting mood, her interest in things she usually loves starting to fade. Her family was going through a hard time; it seemed understandable that she'd be sad. But sitting there that night at the hospital, we could clearly see that our friend was dealing with more than just a little sadness.

When we asked Harper about it, she told us she'd tried to hide the worst of what she'd been going through because she didn't want us to worry. She said she was getting help and feeling better, so why not focus on that? And we said okay, because for the most part, she did seem better. She told us she was fine.

But I know now that sometimes *fine* can mask a lot of *not-fine* underneath.

We've come to the part of town where I can either turn toward Harper's house or toward my own neighborhood. I slow down as we near the intersection.

"You want to come over? It sounds like Jordan's coming too."

She shakes her head. "I'm tired. I'm going to veg out with some movies. Maybe go to bed early."

"Okay." I make the turn toward her house. "Hey. Are you okay, really?"

"Yes."

"Are you sure?"

She smiles. It's obvious why I'm asking.

"Yes," she says. "This week's homework is all about my triggers and core beliefs and it's a ton of boxes and flow charts. I can't wait to get to work on that."

"You're picking flow charts over me? I see how it is."

"No way you could compete with a worksheet, Sky. I'm sorry."

"Well, call if you get bored. This whole thing on my phone has got Jordan stuck on her fabulous self, and I'm not sure if I can deal with that by myself tonight."

"Jordan *is* fabulous," Harper says as she gathers her stuff. "And so are you, Sky. You just never let yourself see it."

An hour later, Jordan lies on my bed, swiping and scrolling through my phone.

"There's not a lot here that's new," she says. "Your Insta is still pretty much the same too. This is the weirdest feeling: I'm looking at the actual, honest-to-God future, and I'm getting kind of bored."

Knotting my hair on top of my head, I plop into bed next to her.

"How nice for you. Your life turns out amazing, while I get stuck marrying Truman Alexander!" I cover my face with a pillow and scream into it. "Whyyyyyy? Seriously why? That's the part I don't understand. Why would I do that?"

"Maybe you don't have to do that. Now that you've seen how things *could* turn out, you can make them turn out differently."

Hope flickers in the back of my mind.

"So this isn't predestination? It's not fate?"

"Every action has a reaction. If you can see the future, I'll bet anything you can change it."

What she's saying makes sense. I've already seen small things change on the site. If small things can change, then I should be able to make bigger changes too. I don't want to go overboard. Like Harper said, it's probably not smart to mess with this stuff too much. My future life looks pretty good overall. I just don't want to marry Truman.

So that's what I'll focus on. Everything else can stay the same, I'll just do what I have to do to get Truman out of my future. And then? I'll stop.

CHAPTER FIVE

"So. Prom. Mitch is good for dinner. My parents are lining up a limo. Obviously, we go to the dance. But instead of the after-party, I wanted to run something by you."

Eli grins at me over his scrambled eggs during our weekly brunch at the Big Sky Diner. Our first date was here at Big Sky, before the Sunday matinee of the school musical because we were both too busy with him onstage and me in the pit to free up a Friday or Saturday night. We had such a great time that we almost missed the show, which would have been a disaster, since Eli was the star. So we hurried the two blocks to school, holding hands, and brunch at Big Sky has been our thing ever since. We sit and watch other people coming in after church, meeting up with their families, getting together with friends. It's a great place to people-watch. And eat waffles. Big Sky has the most delicious waffles ever.

This morning, though, I'm having trouble focusing on Eli *or* my waffles. Because the reunion site is real. Oh my God, it's real. I spent almost all day Saturday looking at it. I dug through my IG, too, peering as far into my Future Past as I could. Future Me doesn't seem to be as into posting pics of her daily life as Present-Day Me is, so between that and my super-basic bio, I can just make out the broad lines of what my life will be like: decent job doing some kind of research. Lots of hiking and nature-y stuff. Dog. Definitely with Truman.

Except not. That part is going to change.

". . . hotel room, just the two of us. But only if you're cool with it."

I snap back to the moment, just in time to catch the tail end of Eli's sentence. I might have missed the first part, but the blush in his cheeks, and the words *hotel room*, tell me exactly what he's talking about. Eli and I have been discussing taking things to the next level, and prom seems like the natural time to do that. I know it's cliché, but I don't care. It's special. It's romantic. Up until this very second, I liked talking and thinking about it. But now, it feels weird to be planning on sleeping with one person when my future is with someone else.

No. It's not. I'm going to fix that.

"You okay?" Eli looks scared he's gone too far. "I didn't book the room yet. It's okay if you want to wait. We don't have to decide anything right away."

"No, it's not that." I search for some way to explain how fuzzy I am today. The TV behind Eli's head shows a morning news reporter in front of the Blessing place. The ticker along the bottom reads: HISTORIC GARDEN TARGETED FOR BULLDOZERS IN EVEREST OUTFITTERS DEAL.

"There's drama around prom," I say. "Jordan's freaking out because the garden might get torn down. We're supposed to be trying to save it."

Eli turns, following my gaze to the TV. He swivels back around and digs into his eggs. "My dad's team's been working with Everest for months. He says it's pretty much a done deal."

I frown. I knew Eli's dad had some involvement, but I didn't know the details.

"Your dad's trying to get the garden torn out?"

"You make it sound like he's some evil garden hater. It's just business."

"It still sucks."

"I know. But Jordan could put on a killer prom in a garbage dump. And it doesn't matter where prom is anyway, as long as we're together."

The way he looks at me makes my insides melt like the butter on the fresh stack of waffles that just got delivered to our table. Eli is so sunny and fun. How could I ever choose dark, uptight, passive-aggressive Truman over him? Future Me had a lapse in judgement, clearly. Somewhere along the line, my taste in guys got corrupted. But now that I know this, I can avoid it. Starting now, I am on a mission.

Task #1: Make myself as unattractive to Truman as possible.

"You stink, Skyler." Harper wrinkles her nose and leans as far away from me as she can without falling out of show choir formation. "Why do you smell like you took a bath in a piña colada?"

"It's not that bad, is it?" I sniff my own arm; after smelling like this for three days straight, I've sort of gotten used to it.

"It's bad," Harper assures me.

"Good. Last year in APUSH, Truman let it slip that the smell of coconut makes him violently ill. So I bought all the coconut things—shampoo, lotion, body spritz, anything coconutty—and drenched myself in it. I'm trying to make him dislike me."

She coughs. "Nobody's going to like you if they can't get near you without gagging."

It's true I've noticed people giving me extra distance in the halls. Even Eli looks pained around me, although he hasn't said anything. Yet. I don't have a plan for how I'll explain this to him; I only know I need to be unappealing to Truman. And so, every day this week, I have worn State sweatshirts, State T-shirts, State shorts—any State swag that I can get my hands on to remind him of my inferior college choice. I have also been chewing gum in English class, loudly and grossly, because that is also something that I know Truman hates. Yesterday, during our *Jane Eyre* discussion, I put forward the sappiest, most obnoxious theory I could think of about Jane's telepathic communication with Rochester. And when Truman tried to waylay me after class, I pretended to be on my phone, ordering a pizza with extra onions, while I bolted for the door.

You would think I'd done enough to make him never want to get near me again, but he continues to text, reminding me that we are supposed to be working on his plan for saving prom. And the reunion website hasn't changed at all. It still shows the two of us together.

Something better happen soon, because at this rate, he'll be all I have. Harper makes a point of sitting across the table from me at lunch, and since Jordan's interviewing DJs and Eli has third lunch, we make up a somewhat sad-looking party of two.

"Can I get a ride home today?" Harper asks. She pushes her spoon through her yogurt without taking a bite.

"Sure. But don't you volunteer on Thursdays?"

"I'm not going. Everybody's so down over there. I don't need to be around that kind of energy."

"Is this seat taken?" I look up to see Truman looming beside me. He gestures toward the obviously empty expanse of bench to the right of my butt. Harper raises an eyebrow. I could do something odd to continue my campaign of getting him to hate me, but there are too many people around. I'd rather not have everyone thinking I'm obnoxious.

I scooch over a couple of inches. "You can sit if you want to."

He does, and I comfort myself that I still have my coconut-scented shield to protect me. Maybe if he gets close enough to smell me, it will be the thing that dooms us forever.

"Did you get my texts?" he says. "I wanted to ask if you could meet after school to go over my plan."

"I'm driving Harper home."

"Harper can come." He turns to her. "We're strategizing to save the Blessing garden."

"I don't know why you're bothering," she says. "All they have to do is hold one more meeting. Then they can tear it out."

She pushes her yogurt away and a little alarm goes off inside me. The Harper I know is all cosmic que sera sera. That Harper would be holding forth right now about how we should all trust the magic and wisdom of the universe to take care of things, and if that means gardens getting torn out, then whatever will be will be.

Truman leans across the table and fixes her with one of his steady stares. "We're not going to let them have the garden," he tells her. "We're going to stop it."

It's weird, but Truman seems to be working some magic of his own. Harper's eyes regain a bit of their sparkle. And that voice— the one that has always made my skin crawl—now makes something else happen. I get chills, all the way down my spine.

"What time after school?" I say. "And where?"

56

But before I can meet Truman, there's trig.

While the rest of the class does warm-up problems, Mr. Bannister calls me into the hall for a chat.

"I wanted to check in and see how you're doing," he says. "I just finished updating grades, and I was a little concerned by how yours have been looking this quarter."

He pulls up the academic portal on his tablet and shows me what I already know—the D on Friday's quiz, the low Cs on daily assignments.

"I'm here to help," he says. "We have review night every Wednesday, and I'd be happy to set up personal time too."

He's a genuinely nice guy, Mr. Bannister; the kind you can tell isn't just putting in his seven hours every day, counting the minutes until he can get away and enjoy his nonschool life. He cares more than a lot of teachers, so I want to be appreciative of his offer. But I'm busy with show choir concerts and yearbook and now prom stuff—I don't want to stay after school for something like trig, not if I can figure it out on my own.

"It's okay," I tell him. "I was confused about a couple of things in the last unit, but I feel better about this one."

Because the thing is, I should be okay. Math has never been my best subject, but my grades are pretty good everywhere else. A C in trigonometry isn't going to keep me out of college, especially State.

And according to the reunion site, I'll have a good job when I get out of school, so it's all good.

"How do you feel about the test today?" Mr. Bannister presses. "Do you feel confident about the material?"

"Yes." I did study. And I ended up feeling pretty good about it. I might not ace the test, but I'm not going to fail it either.

"All right, then. Let's do this."

We head back into the classroom. Mr. Bannister hands out the tests, I take out my pencil, and I do the best I can.

After school, I drive to the Blessing place. Harper decided not to come, and instead went with Jordan to try out caterers. I would much rather be eating tasty finger food samples with them than talking with Truman about his garden-saving plan. But if we don't save the garden, then Jordan's DJ and caterer auditions will be in vain because prom will be ruined—at least according to her. No garden = "crap-assed prom I want nothing to do with," she told me just before I got in my car to come here. And I did promise to help. So here I am.

But first, I stopped in the bathroom and did my best to wash off the coconut stank. Truman was nice to Harper, so I feel like I should be nice to him—at least while we work on this one project together.

When I find him, he's on a bench in the gazebo, with his head bent over something small and whitish. One hand works over the top of the object, carving and scraping and chiseling with what appears to be a small knife. When he hears me coming, he puts the object in his pocket and sits straight.

In an effort to loosen things up, I grab a low branch and shake down some droplets from the rain we got earlier today. He looks at the water on the shoulder of his oxford; then he looks back at me. He doesn't seem any looser, so I start talking.

"I have to say, Truman, I never would have pegged you as a nature lover. I also wouldn't have thought you were a prom enthusiast."

"I have nothing against prom. Although I personally have never been to a school dance, I don't begrudge other people the chance to dress up and have a good time."

His point hits its mark. It's not my fault Truman and his debate friends don't go to many social events, but I can imagine that it sucks to be on the outside—especially lately, when everybody's got promposal fever. I feel a little guilty now that he brought it up. I try a softer tone.

"Well, I guess I should thank you for today at lunch with Harper. She's bummed about all this and you made her feel better. That meant a lot."

"Don't make me into a hero yet. To be honest, my reasons for getting involved are selfish."

"Ah, finally the truth comes out. What's in all this for Truman Alexander?"

He tilts his head, speaking down his nose in classic Truman style.

"I reviewed my résumé over the holidays and realized I'm low on community activism. Admission trends at Johns Hopkins, where I'm planning to go, have been trending toward students with strong volunteer and activism profiles. Saving a community garden, and helping plan prom, will boost my chances of success overall and early admission in particular."

Yep. Okay. Now it all makes sense.

"I knew you were calculating, Truman, but that takes mercenary to a new level."

"I do have a human side too," he says. "This place belongs to my grandfather—or rather, it did, before he left it to the city."

"Really?" I rack my brain, trying to remember a pint-size Truman running around with all the other kids at those old Christmas parties. I was so focused on my own friends that if Truman had been there, I'm not sure I would have noticed.

"I used to come here all the time," he continues. "But my mom and her sister were fighting over his money. Then, when he died, it turned out he didn't have as much as everybody thought. He arranged for everything to be maintained until the funds were depleted, and I guess that time is now. But he would never have wanted them to just rip it out."

I nod, trying to put the picture together.

"Why aren't your parents trying to save it?"

"Because they see all this as poetic justice. Those were my mother's exact words, in fact."

"So you *didn't* find out about it while you were doing debate research. You heard about it at home? That's pretty sneaky, Truman."

"That's why I wanted to talk with you."

He nods at the empty spot on the bench next to him, inviting me to sit. I don't want to, but there's no place else nearby. I lower myself to the far corner, and that simple act brings a pang, like picking at a half-healed scab; I remember the exact moment I started hating Truman Alexander.

First day of seventh grade, we were hit by a small flood of kids from the gifted school, which had just been closed. Somehow, Truman managed to be in all my classes. I liked his round face, his big red backpack, the way he sat so still and straight in his seat while everybody else goofed off like the first day of school was no big deal.

Then, in social studies, he spoke. It was a long-winded opus on economics, and I'm not even sure now that it made much sense.

But it *sounded* smart. I wanted to raise my hand and respond, but I didn't want to draw attention to myself.

Later in the lunchroom, I spotted him reading by himself. I gathered up my courage and went to sit beside him.

"Hi. I'm Skyler."

And Truman, whose opinionated jabbering would come to drive me crazy over the next five years, said nothing. He just looked at me.

"You came here from the gifted school, right? I almost went there. I mean, I could have gone there, but my parents decided against it."

I was babbling, but I hoped he'd be cool with it. I waited for him to pick up his end of the conversation and start a rhythm that would help us fall into a groove of friendship. Instead, Truman just said, "Why?"

"Why what?"

"Why did your parents not let you go to the gifted school?"

"Oh! Well, they didn't think it would be good for me to be separated from normal kids."

The more I talked, the more I realized I was working myself into a corner. I didn't want to get into the main reason I didn't go: I would have had to take remedial math while taking accelerated everything else, and the gifted school had been clear that they weren't thrilled about it. Nor did I feel like telling him that Piper *had* gone to the gifted school until deciding she wanted to be a cheerleader and enrolling at the regular high school in ninth grade. Everyone was impressed by how smoothly she made the transition. *Piper can do anything! So incredible! That's our girl!*

"They just thought I'd do better here," I finally said.

"Well, your parents were correct that it's different," Truman replied. "In fact, I've been worried we won't be challenged enough at this school, and from what I've seen so far, I was right. As for whether you would do better here versus there, your parents are probably right about that, too. The gifted school wasn't for just anybody."

He went back to his book while I sat there, insulted to the core. Truman thought he was too smart for our school. He thought he was too smart for me. I could not let that stand. The next day in class, I did raise my hand to speak. I challenged him. And he could not let *that* stand.

From then on, anything I said had to be debated, dismissed, or mansplained into the ground. I didn't like Truman anymore. I didn't want to be friends. Meanwhile, he worked his own brand of social sabotage, alienating other people with his obsessive need to showcase his smarts and win every argument, until he ended up with a circle of friends no bigger than the Alton High School debate team.

Up until a few days ago, that wasn't my concern. Then a website from the future showed me getting far closer to Truman than the rings in Alton's social circles would ever allow. And then Jordan decided she had to have prom at a garden that, I now find out, had been owned by Truman's grandfather.

So. Here we are.

"So this hearing coming up," Truman says. "Someone has to speak."

"Perfect. That's your thing. You'll be great."

"I want you to speak with me."

"You want me to give a speech when you're already the debate king? I don't get it."

"Well, given that I have a family connection, I may not be seen as one hundred percent objective. Your connection to this place is the same as everybody else's. Plus, you're likable."

I have to take a minute to let this sink in. Especially considering how awful I've been lately.

"You think I'm likable?"

"Absolutely." He looks at me with a matter-of-factness I have to both wonder at and admire.

"So here we are again. You asking me to debate."

"It's not debate, per se. It's more like persuasive speaking. When Jordan asked for someone to help and you stepped forward, I knew we had a chance. No one would be better for this than you."

My mind is racing ahead of him, picturing what all this means. I sing in the chorus; I don't take solos and starring roles.

"I just don't know if I'd feel comfortable getting up in front of all those people," I say.

"Isn't getting up in front of people what show choir is all about? What about orchestra?"

"Both of those things involve other people getting up with me."

"I'd be with you. Granted, I wouldn't be in a uniform—or maybe I would. If it will make you more comfortable, I'm willing to look into a sequined bow tie and cummerbund."

The vision of Truman in show choir garb is more endearing than I want to admit. I have to work at hiding just how sweet I think his offer is.

"It still doesn't change that I, at some point, would have to speak solo. There could be news cameras there. Plus all my friends. I'm sorry, but the idea is pretty terrifying."

I've been avoiding looking directly at Truman, but now I do and something crazy happens—he captures me with those green eyes.

"You don't have anything to be afraid of," he says. "You're fierce and fearless and, in my opinion, completely captivating when you feel strongly about something."

"I thought you found me *not very sophisticated*. I believe the term you used was *solipsistic*."

"I knew that got to you." He smiles slyly. "Sometimes I'll put things out there just to see if I can hook you into an argument."

"I knew you were doing that."

"It's a rush, right? Even when I agree with you, I try not to let it show, because I'd rather keep going. Most days I walk out of class feeling frustrated, pissed off and wanting more."

My brain and my mouth have become disconnected listening to Truman. For once he's made a point to which I have absolutely no response.

Who knew it could be so hot?

"So will you do it?" he asks.

"I think I have to. I'm not sure I can pass up a chance to piss you off."

"It'll be an honor. And maybe I won't mind so much when we win. Your passion is contagious."

Truman has moved in so close that when I finally rip my gaze from his, I realize his lips are just inches from mine.

"It's not passion," I tell him. "It's loathing."

"There's a fine line between the two."

I've learned a lot of new things about Truman Alexander today, but one thing hasn't changed: he always pulls me in. Wherever that line is between love and hate, I cross it when I bring my lips to his, without stopping to consider whether I'll ever be able to cross back.

CHAPTER SIX

I f you had told me a week ago that I'd be lying in bed at six-thirty in the morning, replaying a kiss with Truman Alexander in my head and working myself into a hot, bothered mess, I would have said you didn't know me at all.

Maybe *I* didn't know me at all.

So does this mean the reunion site was right? And if it is, what does that mean for the next eleven years of my life? Do I have a say in whether or not I spend them with Truman? Or now that the wheels are in motion, do I ride this train into the sunset with everything laid out on one straight track?

As if to add absurdity to an already surreal situation, the website has started sending me notifications. Whenever someone comments on a photo or leaves a note in the guest book, my phone pings. The first ones came in last night. I checked in to find messages from the future versions of Anna Larkin and Ryan Oard.

Awesome time seeing everybody again—Ryan

Amazing what a difference 10 years makes! Can't wait to see what the next 10 will bring—Anna

The notifications started again this morning. As I lie here in bed, listening to ping after ping, a wave of terror washes over me. It's Friday. I should get up, shower, and get myself to school, but I can't face Eli. Or Truman. I need a day—possibly the entire weekend—to hide and figure out what to do next.

Shuffling out of my room, I head downstairs. Dad's already at work, and Mom is in the kitchen on video chat, making coffee while Piper's voice crackles out of her phone.

"Well, hang in there," Mom is saying. "We're cheering you on over here. Oh wait! Here's Skyler! Skyler, say hi!"

"Hi, Piper." I lean into the camera frame and wave. She's got early-morning bedhead and mascara under her eyes, but she still manages to look studiously successful as she waves back.

"Hey, Sky. How's everything going?"

I almost respond with, *Well, Piper, it's going freaking unbelievably weird, to be honest. I can inexplicably see the future through my phone, which often refuses to send a simple text but somehow has no trouble letting me know what random people from my class are doing more than ten years from now. And on top of that, yesterday I kissed a guy I can't stand. If you think that sounds like a good time, then I'd say everything is going just awesome, thanks for asking.*

I do not say this. Obviously. I tell Piper everything's fine, and I try not to read anything into the way she says, "Oh, that's good to hear." Because I'm pretty sure neither of us is going to apologize for the things we said at Christmas. I think we're to the point where we just pretend the whole thing didn't happen and hope it doesn't come up again. But it's not easy to forget the message behind her words: *You can't coast by anymore. Step up and take more initiative.* What it really means, if we're being honest, is that I'm *not good enough.*

"I don't feel well," I tell Mom, quietly so Piper won't judge me for missing school. Mom doesn't press her hand to my forehead like she used to, or even ask about my symptoms. She's too busy getting her lunch together and trying to get out the door.

"Go back to bed and I'll call the attendance office from the car," she tells me. I tell Piper "bye," then I go back upstairs, where I spend the next couple of hours obsessively scrolling through the reunion site. It remains stubbornly unchanged. My Instagram is pretty much the same too, except oh, look, Future Me went to Seattle. That's one nice photo of a cup of coffee in front of a rain-spotted window. At least Future Me's filter game is on point.

Around lunchtime, my phone starts blowing up with texts— real texts from my Present-Day friends. Jordan and Harper say they hope I'm feeling all right. Eli wants to know if I'm up for a date tomorrow night.

I am not up for a date. Or a breakup. Because isn't that what's supposed to happen when you've kissed another guy?

I don't want to break up with Eli, though. I want to go back a day and stop myself from kissing Truman. If a website link can travel through time, then maybe time travel is possible for me too. Because right now the near future looks a lot scarier than the distant one: Eli will be beyond upset when he finds out what I've done.

Not sure how I'll be feeling tomorrow, I text back. Probably best to skip brunch too until I know I'm not contagious.

He sends me back a sad selfie, and I can't look at those pouty eyes for more than a second without massive guilt gnawing at my insides.

The guilt is so intense that I can't bring myself to go to school on Monday, either. I spend the day watching Hulu, trying to ignore my phone. Sometime in the late afternoon, I haul myself off the couch and decide to see if I can start dinner so Mom won't have as much to do when she gets home.

While I'm surveying the contents of the fridge, a new notification comes through from Future Harper, commenting on a photo of her with Jordan and me at the reunion:

Love you guys, love this place, love life!

That's when I notice where the reunion is taking place. The details on the homepage say "Blessing Memorial Garden." And when I look closely, I see the rose wall in the background, the trees, and the gazebo.

Magical nite, Harper says under another photo. **Perfect how everything turned out.**

Okay, I can't take much more of this. I know it's ridiculous, but I have to check one more time; maybe this whole thing really is a joke.

I call Harper. "So . . . did you post something just now?"

"Where?" she says. "Instagram?"

"No . . ." I try to keep it vague. "I mean like a comment. To an album on a website . . ."

"Seriously, Sky? Are you still looking at that thing?"

"Yes. Fine." I abandon all attempts at hiding. "I'm looking at something that was supposedly sent by you. It's about the garden, and it's got you and me and Jordan. . . ." I fumble with my phone. "Ugh, I want to screen grab this. . . ."

"Don't." Her voice is tense. "I told you I don't want to see it."

"I couldn't pull it up if I wanted to."

"Oh. Well, so . . ." I can hear her relaxing, trying to be helpful. "You say I'm posting comments about the garden?"

"Yes. It looks like the whole reunion is being held there."

"Well, that's good news! Maybe it won't get torn down after all."

"You're right, I guess. I mean, of course, you're right. But everything else about this is making me want to pull out my hair."

"Which is exactly my point. Nothing good can come from messing with something like that. Why don't you just delete the link? Block the notifications?"

"You really think I should?"

"Yes. Definitely."

Maybe she's right. Maybe it's best to just leave all this alone. It's freeing to think I could let go and forget it ever happened.

"Okay," I say. "Thanks, Harper."

And I almost do manage to forget. I block notifications on my phone. I trash the original message from Future Jordan. For a few glorious hours, I am blissfully free of all things reunion site.

Then, after dinner, Truman shows up at my front door.

"Is this a bad time?"

He stands at the edge of the step, like he's prepared to dash away if needed. His overstuffed backpack perches on his shoulder, and he clutches his omnipresent black notebook. He stares at me, unblinking, while I attempt to shift gears from what I thought was just going to be a two-second exchange with the UPS guy.

"Haven't you heard of calling ahead?" I ask, painfully aware that I am wearing a shapeless T-shirt and a pair of old leggings, and have bed-matted hair. "Calling ahead is a thing."

"Hey, Skyler, who's this?" Dad appears behind me, a mug of tea in his hands.

"Good evening, Mr. Finch. My name is Truman Alexander. I'm in several of Skyler's classes at school. She and I are working on a project together, and I came by to see if we could get something done on it. We're under a tight deadline."

This resonates with Dad, who never met a deadline-oriented person he didn't like.

"Ah, well, don't let me hold you up," he says. "Skyler, aren't you going to ask Truman inside?"

I step back to let Truman in. Dad closes the door behind him.

"I'm dealing with some tight deadlines myself," he tells us. "I'll be in my office if you need anything. Your mom had a long day and went to bed early. Nice meeting you, Truman."

Frowning, I lead Truman into the den, suddenly hyperaware of every clutter-strewn surface and every inch of carpet that needs vacuuming. We had to let our housekeeper go when Dad lost his job. The three of us do the cleaning now, and we lack both the time and skill to do it well. I hope Truman doesn't notice.

I show him how to work the TV, then announce that I'm going to change my clothes. I make it quick, but I'd be lying if I said I didn't take a little extra effort with my appearance. No reason to look like a complete slob just because I stayed home from school.

When I return, Truman's got his laptop fired up, the black notebook open in his lap. Dominating his screen is a massive spreadsheet. I notice too that his notebook has been divided and subdivided with color-coded tabs.

I sit in Dad's old leather chair, unsure what to say. All weekend, I've been trying not to think about Truman. Trying to remind myself that I don't *want* him to text or call, then trying not to wonder why he hasn't. Trying not to speculate on what he thinks about that kiss.

But the truth is, I'm dying to know. His voice keeps playing in my head, repeating over and over what he said just before: *You're fierce and fearless and completely captivating when you feel strongly about something.*

No one's ever called me fierce or captivating.

He types a few lines into his spreadsheet, then looks up. "We need to write our speeches for the council meeting. We don't have much time."

Irritation shoots through me. I'm cool with playing it cool, but this is ridiculous.

"Thanks for asking how I am, Truman. I missed two days of school, and for all you know I could have the plague."

"I didn't think there was anything to be too concerned about. And I can see now that my assessment was correct. You look very nice, by the way—not sick at all."

I cross my arms over the cute top I just put on, wishing I'd kept my face pale instead of wearing makeup.

"So what did you think I was doing all this time?"

"I thought you might be avoiding me because of what happened the other night."

"You've got a pretty high opinion of yourself if you think my health depends on you."

"I don't think that. Like I said, your health appears to be fine. But I didn't call ahead because I didn't want to give you a chance to back out when we have so much to do."

I can't tell if he's being an ass or just awkwardly honest. One thing he definitely is, though, is infuriatingly adorable in a polo and deck shoes, with a spot of hair on the side of his head that looks like he slept on it wrong. He looks like a nerdy country club valet.

"So you thought I'd flake out on my responsibilities. You

assumed I wouldn't be able to overlook my emotions and focus. You must really think I'm shallow."

"I think you don't like me," he replies. "I believe the exact word you used was *loathing.*"

Now I know he's being an ass. I even caught a hint of a smile as he started to flip through his notebook. This is classic Truman doing his classic Truman thing. And it's driving me crazy.

"I don't loathe you, Truman. Okay? Are you trying to get me to prove that or something?"

He shrugs. "I'm just trying to get these speeches written."

I have no other choice but to wipe the smug expression off his face. I crash into him, grabbing his shirt, pressing my lips to his.

And that's how we spend the rest of the evening: Arguing. Making out. Jumping apart and pretending to work whenever Dad leaves his office. Something happens when Truman and I touch that I can't figure out. The second our lips meet I get this buzzing way down to my toes, along with the feeling that I'm riding in a fast car, knowing I should probably be scared but loving the way my stomach flips over all the little hills. The part of my brain that remembers current boyfriends and past insults and the fact that I am supposed to loathe Truman with every fiber of my being shuts off. He's either a really good kisser . . . or he's just really good at kissing me. Whichever one it is, time stops when I'm kissing Truman, and nothing exists but the delicious, thrilling now.

CHAPTER SEVEN

Tuesday morning dawns with everything inside me screaming to look at the reunion site. But I don't really need to. I know what it's going to show. After last night, I might as well have put that ring on my own finger. Truman and I are probably written in stone now.

Except now, as in today-now, I have an actual boyfriend who has no idea that his girlfriend is a Cheating Cheater. Eli meets me at our bench in the commons with a bottle of OJ and a box of old-fashioned cherry cough drops. It's millions of times more thoughtful than I deserve, and it actually makes me tear up. The only positive is that my red eyes and nose make me look sick enough that Eli doesn't even try for a kiss out of fear that I might be contagious.

He goes on to show choir, but before following him there I stop in the bathroom to hyperventilate a little. Up until now, my relationships have been black-and-white: Love Eli, hate Truman. Then came that stupid reunion site. And I can't stop wondering why it was sent to me. Did the universe or fate or some other higher power decide I needed to see my future so I could become a better person, like Scrooge in *A Christmas Carol*? If that's it, then why isn't the site showing some sort of warning, like evidence of some looming catastrophe only I can prevent? And if the looming catastrophe involves marrying Truman, then why does Present-Day Me seem unable to stop doing things that are destined to make that catastrophe come true?

Wherever it came from, the site now sits at the center of a seesaw in my mind. I definitely don't hate Truman Alexander anymore—but do I want to spend the rest of my life with him?

No. No, I do not. Eli is the guy who staged that amazing promposal, complete with barbershop quartet—the one who is right this very minute planning a fairy-tale prom for the two of us. He's the one who buys me waffles every Sunday and makes me feel included and loved. And he's the guy I'm talking about getting a hotel room with—the one I'm planning on giving everything to within a matter of weeks. All my friends love Eli. *I* love Eli. If I ended up with anyone from high school, it would be him.

"Get it together," I tell my reflection in the bathroom mirror. "You can fix this."

My phone pings. It's an update from the school portal. Mr. Bannister has finished grading our trig tests and just posted the results. My stomach clenches when I check it out.

I failed. Crap.

I studied. I thought I knew the material. And I still tanked it.

While I'm staring at the screen, my phone pings again. You updated your bio! This notification *is* from the reunion site. I want to ignore it like I've ignored everything all weekend, but something tells me that an update so close to the new grade posting can't be a coincidence.

My new bio is still pretty bare bones. I have to scrutinize it to find what's changed. Then I see it: Where "Head of Marketing

Research" used to be, it now says "Administrative Assistant." One bad grade in trig equals a demotion in my future career? I scroll through the albums, thinking I might find a bright spot—I'd *maybe* be willing to take a demotion if it meant no longer being with Truman. But no. We're still together, still wearing matching rings, except my hair doesn't have those nice highlights and Truman has a beard.

Damn!

I spend the rest of the day, and the day after, in a freaked-out haze. I can barely look at or speak to Eli. When Harper gets her promposal from Kiran Smith—a big stuffed goat on her seat in the cafeteria with a sign that says you're the Greatest Of All Time—will you go to prom with me?—I have to force myself to act as happy for her as I feel, because my face seems to be locked in a permanent frown. And sitting across from Truman in English makes me almost vomit all over my copy of *Mrs. Dalloway*. When class ends, I don't even try to make up an excuse for why I can't hang around. I bolt from my seat and push past him out of the room, making a mad dash to my car so I can get my rear end home.

Jordan video chats me after dinner.

"What's the deal?" she says. "And don't try to deny it. I can tell something is wrong."

"School," I tell her. It's partially true. "I tanked my trigonometry test."

"You've tanked tests before. Do some extra credit and make it up."

I don't want to bring up the reunion site and tell Jordan she's still super successful while my fortunes have dwindled. But I can't *not* talk about it, especially since I know it's only a matter of time before she asks.

"I wouldn't be worried, except now my future job has been downgraded to an assistant. I mean, not looking down on assistants or anything, but I definitely saw something a little more prestigious for myself."

"I can see where that's troubling," Jordan says. "But I feel like there's something else."

"Plus I'm still not feeling all that great."

"That would be called guilt. Harper says you are giving off major guilt vibes, and I agree. Come on, Sky. We deserve to know what's going on."

"It's just . . ." I know I can't keep this a secret. My friends would never forgive me, plus it's just too big. I need advice. I need moral support. I need a complete reboot of the past forty-eight hours. "Truman and I have been spending a lot of time together."

"And you hate him." She rolls her eyes. "So you really can't get over it? You guys are supposed to be working together on this garden thing. We need somebody else on it if you two can't figure out how to get along."

"That's the problem." I suck in air through my teeth. "We've been getting along a little too well."

She pauses.

"So you and Truman . . ."

"I don't know, Jordan. I really don't."

"But you and Truman . . ."

"Yeah. It's a mess."

"What about Eli?"

"Like I said, it's a mess."

"But Eli did that whole promposal."

"Not everything is about prom, Jordan."

"It actually is. Prom is a symbol of everything that's wrong with what you're telling me right now. You've got a guy who wrote a song to ask you *and* had it sung by a barbershop quartet, of all things, and you're thanking him by messing around with some other guy behind his back—a guy who, not to mention, you are trying not to freaking marry!"

An urge to defend Truman grips me—the sudden sense that he's been misunderstood by all of us.

"You make it sound like Eli's the only good guy here. Truman is doing a lot of good too—stuff he doesn't have to do, I might add—to save your prom from getting literally bulldozed to the ground." That came out meaner than I'd intended. But I wasn't prepared for the strength of Jordan's disapproval.

"You're basically making that website true," she informs me.

"Oh, really? I hadn't thought of that. But see, here's the thing: I didn't ask to see my future! How do you think it feels, seeing how fabulous all my friends are doing when I always end up with a guy I can't stand?"

"Well, it sounds like you're feeling that way about him less and less these days."

I pull off my glasses and slump over with my head in my hands. I hate fighting with my friends, especially Jordan, who lately feels like she is one argument away from ditching me.

When I retrace our steps to when all this tension started, I can go as far back as when Harper was in the hospital. It didn't just expose the pain in her life, it brought out cracks in everything. Like when snow melts, revealing potholes created by assaults of ice and water that you never saw because everything was so beautiful on the surface.

Jordan jumped into planning mode, collecting schoolwork, and organizing friends to come visit. I went into quality-time mode, spending every spare minute at Harper's side. You'd think Jordan and I would have made the perfect team, but that's not how it worked out. If Harper and I spent a day watching TV, Jordan would become antsy. And she became obsessed with getting Harper to do her schoolwork.

"You're getting behind, Har," she said one Saturday in the middle of a *Friends* marathon. "If you studied for chemistry, you could take the test when you get back and you'd be pretty much caught up."

"She has plenty of time for homework," I said. "Let her rest."

"If she doesn't get something done now, it's just going to be more painful later."

"This isn't helping, though."

"You aren't helping either by wallowing for days on end."

Harper threw us out then, and I never got to tell Jordan that if she saw my thoughtfulness as wallowing, then I saw her refusal to pamper Harper as just a little insensitive. We'd come to the edge of a fight that could have broken our friendship, only to back off at the last minute.

I'm not up for going all the way tonight, so I say, "I'm sorry. It's just a lot more complicated than it sounds."

"Then uncomplicate it. If you know you don't want to be with Eli, then break up. But do it now. I'm not going to watch you get caught up in some ridiculous love triangle, Sky."

Which is absolutely, 100 percent fair. This isn't some cringy Netflix drama, even if the existence of a website from the future feels more than vaguely out there. Jordan hangs up, and before I can chicken out, I text Eli.

> We need to talk

No sooner have I hit Send than I hear the front doorbell.

Truman stands on the porch, no backpack, no notebook. He looks at me with those intense green eyes and says, "We need to talk."

I take Truman to the kitchen. Sit him at the table. Pour sodas and open a bag of chips just to have something between us. This way there's less chance of ending up on the couch in the den or on the floor or anyplace else where we might be able to do anything other than talk.

Mom comes in to get a glass of wine. Truman greets her with the same formality he greeted my dad with Monday night, and she looks like she wants to crack up. My mother can smell BS a mile away. Nevertheless, she greets Truman with her usual warm Mom-ness.

Dad comes in next and appears pleased to see the two of us working toward our "deadline." Mom tells us she's going to her room to watch TV and decompress.

"We had protesters at the clinic today," she says. "The ignorance made my brain hurt."

Dad reminds her that ignorant people have First Amendment rights too; then he goes to his study to work.

I sit down across from Truman. He looks at his hands, then back at me with unnerving frankness.

"I guess it's stating the obvious to say we haven't accomplished much where that council meeting is concerned."

"You're not blaming me for that, are you?" I say. "Because it takes two to do . . . whatever this is we've been doing."

"There's no blame to place. If I'm going to not accomplish anything, then I'm not sure there's a more enjoyable way of doing it. I was more thinking about you. You don't seem to be enjoying it as much."

"Really?" I run a finger through the condensation on my soda glass. "Because I thought I was being pretty enthusiastic."

This brings a flush to his cheeks. "Yes. Yes, you have been. And believe me, I more than appreciate that. But at school, you were clearly uncomfortable. And I know you're officially with Eli, so that right there means we aren't being honest. I have a thing about honesty. It often gets me into trouble."

"Yes, you've said that."

"Anyway, I wanted to tell you that if this whole thing makes you as uncomfortable as it makes me, then maybe we should figure something out."

I think about how maddening Truman was, coming over and baiting me into kissing him. I think about all the grief I've gone through over the past few days trying to change my future. This is my chance to take care of it directly, cleanly, and finally.

"I say we quit right now. End it here."

"Really?" He frowns. "That's it? Just stop?"

"Yep." I let the silence sink in and, I hope, make its way into the future, to whatever space in time put the two of us together in the first place.

"Okay . . ." He slumps backward. "I won't lie. That's disappointing."

"It's what I think we should do."

"Okay."

"Okay."

He doesn't move. The next step would be to get up and show him to the door, but I'm stuck to my seat too. I slide my hand into the pocket of my hoodie and pull out my phone. I bring up the reunion website under the table, ready to see the change, feeling like once I've confirmed it I'll be able to move again, ready to get on with my life.

The first photo that comes up is me and Truman. Rings. Happy faces. Funny hats, because now the reunion apparently has some sort of Derby Day theme.

I drop my head into my free hand and groan.

"Hey." Truman leans in. "What's wrong?"

I set the phone on the table, screen down. I'm worried I might start crying.

"It's not because of Eli. Well, it partly is. Eli is . . ."

"Popular. And attractive. Not that I've noticed personally, but I can appreciate from the perspective of a member of the opposite sex that he's attractive. And popular."

The way Truman says *popular* twice shifts a lens into focus. I see myself in Alton's social rings again. And I see how the gravity of Eli's position has helped keep me where I am. Looking at it like this is like looking at that part of our relationship through a truth filter.

"You make me sound really shallow."

"I mean, the fact that I noticed Eli's popularity shows my own lack of depth," he replies. "But I think it's good to be honest about all aspects of each calculation."

"I don't see my relationships as *calculations*. Do you?"

"Maybe that's too cold of a word. Let's say I try to be aware."

When he puts it like that, I realize I've been woefully *unaware* of what goes on around me. I also find myself amazed that Truman, whose social skills have always seemed nonexistent, has been observing from the sidelines this whole time.

"So if we're being honest, then yes, Eli is popular," I say. "But he's also a great guy. I would never want to hurt him. That's not what's freaking me out, though. What's really freaking me out is too crazy to talk about."

Truman's hand moves across the table. Before I can move away, his fingers have twined with mine.

"It can't be that crazy."

"Believe me, this takes crazy to a whole new level."

"You don't trust me?"

"Actually, I do." I realize as I'm saying this how true it really is. Part of what I've always hated about Truman was his inability to be anything other than honest. Now, because of that honesty, I believe him when he says he'll believe me. And if we're telling truths, then maybe we should just get the whole truth out now.

I pick up my phone and say a quick prayer to whatever part of the universe is in charge of this little adventure in communing with the future. "Just trust me when I tell you that this is super weird. Trust me, and don't freak out."

I surrender the phone to Truman. He squints as he starts to scroll.

"What is this?"

"I keep thinking it's got to be a joke. It's supposed to be from our ten-year reunion."

"As in—" He does the math. "Eleven years from now?"

"Yes. It's creepy how realistic it is."

"Creepy is an understatement. Who sent this to you?"

"It came from an Instagram with Jordan's name on it, but she swears she didn't send it."

I want to look over his shoulder, but then I wouldn't be able to watch his face and see his reactions. He taps to open photos and thumbs things into the search bar.

"So this is that website you were talking about?"

"Yes."

"And I assume you've looked yourself up," he says. "Right?"

"That's the part that's really going to freak you out. I can't believe I'm showing you this, but . . ." I take the phone, enter both our names, then hand it back again. "Here."

He smiles faintly as he looks through the photos.

"So there are some of you and me together . . . Oh." He's noticed the rings. I watch his expression turn from bemused enjoyment to confusion and then alarm.

"You're freaking out."

"I'm just positive this is a joke," he says. "I mean, it's an impressive effort, but I'm sure if we look around a little more, we'll be able to figure out who's behind it."

He starts scrolling again, eyes scanning for clues.

He freezes. "Oh my God."

"What?" I can't resist jumping to his side. He's looking at one of the photos of himself with Harper and the woman with the red hair. When he speaks again, his voice sounds thick.

"That's my aunt Margaret. How would anybody get a photo of her?"

"Maybe someone knows your family?"

"She moved away years ago. And she hasn't talked to the rest of us since even before then. I looked for her awhile back and couldn't even find her on Facebook."

"Why would she be at our reunion?"

"It looks like it has something to do with the garden." Neither of us says anything else for what feels like a solid five minutes. The room might be quiet, but my thoughts are screaming. Nobody I know would care about Truman's aunt, let alone go to the trouble of putting her in a prank website. I can see the realization hit Truman, slowly at first, then with full force.

The website is real.

"I'm sorry," he says. "This is a lot to take in."

"I know. I have no idea how to explain it."

He puts my phone down and scoots his chair from the table. "I should go."

I stay in my seat, thrown suddenly off-kilter. "Why?" Of all the reactions I anticipated from Truman, getting up and walking out wasn't one of them. "Is something wrong? I mean, besides the obvious fact that some creepy stuff is going on here? Why do you need to leave?"

For once, Truman is at a loss for words. "I just wasn't prepared for *this*." He gestures from me to himself and back to me again.

"This *what*?"

"The whole you and me thing. Being married. I don't know what to do with that."

Regret and defensiveness create a combustible cocktail inside me. Part of me is pissed at myself for showing Truman the website. The other part is offended that my honesty has been rewarded with awkwardness.

"So . . . what? Am I somehow suddenly repulsive to you?"

"No! Not at all."

"Then what's wrong?"

"What if the site really is for our ten-year reunion?"

"Say it is. Is the idea of being with me that horrible?"

"I just . . . I've already planned out my future, and that isn't it. I intend to be nowhere near Alton once I leave for college. And I haven't even thought about how marriage fits into all that. What if I want to have a lot of different girlfriends after high school?"

I can't help myself. I burst out laughing, because the thought of Truman Alexander having a lot of different girlfriends is hysterical.

"What's so funny?" he says.

"Just that if you think you're going to have lots of girlfriends, it's no contest compared to how many boyfriends I plan to have. I plan to date a ton in college. A TON!"

"Fine," he says. "Have fun with that."

"Oh, I plan to. And another thing: How misogynistic is it of you to assume that just because I'm a girl, I'm already planning out my wedding?"

He tilts his head, looks down his nose. His voice takes on that self-righteous, debating-in-class tone.

"I don't know what you're planning. You once informed me about your talent for living in the now. I assumed that meant you couldn't be bothered to look more than a few weeks ahead of anything."

"Right, well . . ." I falter, unable to decide whether that insult works to bolster my argument or not. "Let's just say I haven't exactly been going around writing my name with your last name, drawing hearts all over my homework, Truman. When I first saw what was on that site, I thought there was no way in hell I'd be with you in the next month, let alone the next however many years."

Truman looks offended. "Thanks a lot."

"And now you're insulted by something that's not even supposed to happen for a freaking decade. Do you see how messed up that is?"

"This whole thing is messed up, Skyler. It's too much."

I'm close to tears again. My throat feels raw and sandpapery. "You asked me what was wrong. I didn't have to show you this."

"To be honest, I wish you hadn't. I'm not sure anything will be the same between us again."

"No, you know what? It will be the same. It will be the same as always, because I have absolutely no problem going back to hating you, Truman. Forget anything ever happened between us. I'm in charge of my future, and it will *not* be with you."

The flood of tears I worried about earlier has been replaced by an avalanche of angry words. I keep on talking, stabbing around for whatever will hurt most.

"I don't want to put up with your hyperfocused, overachieving nonsense. I don't want to be a part of your family, which sounds like a perfectly awful mess of money-grubbing snobs. And most of all, I don't want to listen to your soul-crushingly self-important voice for the rest of my life."

I wait for him to lob something equally as hurtful back. I'm prepared for whatever he might say. I'd welcome it, even, because arguing might help us get back to something that feels like normal.

Instead, he walks out of the room. I hear him make his way down the hall; then the front door opens and closes.

I go to the sink and splash water on my face. I put the soda glasses in the sink and the chips back in the pantry; then I shuffle into the den and curl up on the couch. Picking up the remote, I hover a finger over the keypad. So many choices in a day: What to watch, what to wear, what to do when a guy you might like reacts the wrong way to something you shared out of a mistaken sense of trust . . . My phone still sits on the kitchen table. I leave it there until I can't stand it any longer. I go get it, open my Instagram, and the first thing I notice is that there are no more dog photos. There aren't as many hiking ones either, but there are as many—if not more—shots of food.

The fact that my IG has changed makes me hurry to open the reunion site to see what might have changed there, too. I search my name, and every photo that pops up shows me with Jordan or Harper, or both. I search Truman, and all that comes up is a year-book photo in a section titled *Wish You Were Here:*

Know how to reach this classmate? Please contact the moderator so we can make sure they're included in invitations to upcoming reunions.

When I search for Eli, I find him in a bunch of photos with Mitch. That's it.

Something twinges inside me as I look through this updated site—something that feels remarkably like regret. First of all, I miss the dog, which is weird because I never really knew him. And second of all . . . no. There is no second of all. I'm glad Truman's gone. I didn't want him anyway.

But there is where the problem lies. It's one thing to not want someone in your future. Finding out they don't want you in theirs? That's one of the loneliest feelings I've ever had.

CHAPTER EIGHT

"So you said we needed to talk?" Eli settles in across the table from me at Big Sky. The diner is in full breakfast bustle with people grabbing coffee and donuts before school and work, which I'd hoped would be a good distraction but only ups my anxiety. I debated not even having this conversation after what happened with Truman last night. Now that I've killed that future, I can pretend the whole thing never happened.

Except I can't.

Even though it was tempting to tell Eli that all I wanted to talk about this morning was prom, I have to be honest.

Eli doesn't seem to anticipate any incoming bombshells. He's digging into his omelet, eyebrow raised like he's awaiting an update on how my dress shopping is going.

I pick at my toast, pinching off tiny bits I can't bring myself to eat.

"A lot has been going on lately. I need to let you know about it."

He puts down his fork. "Sounds serious."

"Yes. It's about me and you."

"Did I do something wrong?"

"No! You've done everything right. I don't deserve all the things you've done for me. I'm the one who's screwed up."

He waits while I dump sugar into my coffee, then watches as I start shredding the packet into tiny strips. My phone buzzes in my pocket, probably Harper or Jordan texting, but it reminds me to quit messing around. I put the sugar packet down.

"Do you know Truman Alexander?"

"That guy you hate? Dude looks like he's got a stick up his butt all the time?"

In spite of everything that's happened between Truman and me, I fight back the compulsion to defend him and inform Eli that he doesn't really have a stick up his butt. Except he sort of does. Even with my recently acquired appreciation for Truman's better qualities, I have to acknowledge that he is not the most chill person around.

"I don't hate him. At least, not anymore."

I peek at Eli, hoping this tiny seed will take root so I won't have to spell it out.

"Okay, so the guy is no longer your archenemy," he says. "So what about him?"

I go back to pulverizing my toast. "We've been working together on some prom things for Jordan. Believe me, I have no idea how it happened, but we got closer than I ever meant to."

Eli's face freezes mid-chew.

"So you and this Truman guy . . ."

"Yes. God, it sucks admitting that."

"How long has this been going on?"

"Only a couple of days. I feel terrible."

He swallows, sits back, and looks at me. I can see the gears turning in his mind, and I both want and dread to know what he's thinking. We've never had a real argument, so I don't know what to expect.

Silence, that's what. Apparently Eli gets deadly quiet when he's unhappy.

After a few painfully long seconds, he says, "So what does that mean? Did you guys . . ."

"No! Not even close. I haven't even considered doing that with anybody but you."

"And what's the deal now? Are you together?"

"No." I say this with certainty. After yesterday's scene in my kitchen, there's no way Truman and I will be repeating the past week ever again. "We're not together. We never really were, and whatever happened between us is over now."

Eli nods. Dreading another silence, I keep talking.

"It's probably wishful thinking that you wouldn't want to break up. I'd completely understand if you did."

"You're the one who's telling me there's someone else."

"There isn't, though. But I wouldn't blame you if you never wanted to talk to me again."

"I don't never want to talk to you again."

"Really?"

He stares out the window at cars creeping past the monument in Donor's Square, which still has the black and red paint streaks on it from Darius's promposal. Then he studies the ceiling as if seeking an answer in the dirty gray tiles. He looks hurt, but also sort of cute with his sleepy eyes and sandy hair. Sitting here, right this very minute, I feel like what happened with Truman happened to someone else. No way was that me.

"We've been together seven months," Eli says, finally. "We're supposed to be going to prom together."

"There's still time to ask someone else if you want to." There are probably a dozen girls who would leap at the chance to go with him. I can feel my chin start to wobble.

Eli shakes his head.

"Who else would I go with after I did that big production with you? We're probably going to win the promposal contest. This sucks, Skyler."

"I know. I'm so, so, so sorry."

He picks at his eggs, mashing his omelet into a scrambled mess before putting the fork down and looking me in the eye. "But it really is over?"

"Completely."

He nods slowly. I allow myself a glimmer of hope.

"So we aren't breaking up?"

"Not today, it looks like."

I know I shouldn't press my luck. I was prepared to be tossed into the dumpster of cheating ex-girlfriends, now here I am with a second chance.

I reach across the table to grab his hand.

"You're the one I want. I promise." A hint of sunshine peeks through the gloom. The warmth of it prompts me to squeeze his fingers. "And prom is going to be amazing. Especially after."

Now a genuine smile lights up his face.

"So you're cool with the hotel room?"

"Yes," I say. "Go ahead and get it."

The rest of the morning flies by like a dream. When Eli and I walk into show choir, Harper is happier than I've seen her in days.

"I had a feeling when I woke up that today was going to have positive energy in it," she tells me. "And I was right. My dad got that job he interviewed for!"

Harper's in such a good mood that she and Jordan and I make dress-shopping plans for the Galleria. Just when I'm starting to feel stressed about money, I get a text asking me to babysit for my neighbors after school a couple of days this week, which will net me a nice wad of cash. And in our show choir mash-up of '90s boy band songs, Eli sings the opening solo of "I Want It That Way" directly to me.

Best of all, both the reunion website and my future Instagram are frozen. When I try to check them, they load halfway, then refuse to load any further. Apparently killing my future with Truman was the key to stopping the whole thing in its tracks. Everything is going my way now. I've got funds for prom. My friends are feeling good. And I've got the guy I want—the one I was meant to be with all along.

Four hours later, I'm walking to lunch with Harper when my phone gives a massive shudder. A window pops up with a notification that I've left a comment.

To the reunion site.

"Oh no . . . seriously?" Somehow, somewhere, Future Me is online and posting.

"What's the matter?" Harper peers over my shoulder. "Is that—"

"No." I shove the phone into my pocket. "Just my mom."

When we've taken our place in the food line and she's busy talking to Kiran, I open the site to see what Future Me has to say.

Loved seeing everybody! Let's do it again soon—
just need to plan ahead so I can get a sitter for my
10-year-old 😊 😊 😊!!!

I freeze as I'm reaching for a tray, nearly forcing the people behind me into a mini pileup. I might not be great at math, but I can definitely subtract. If I've got a ten-year-old at my ten-year reunion, that means I got pregnant at seventeen.

I feel like I might pass out.

More mental math tells me that agreeing to an after-prom hotel room with Eli + website update showing me with a ten-year-old = not a coincidence.

No. Nope. Uh-uh. If I do end up with Eli, it is not going to be because I got pregnant in high school. I refuse to be *that* girl at the reunion.

And when I check out the bio for myself on the updated site, I see that I'm not even with Eli in this new future. My marital status says "divorced."

A small cry escapes my lips. I look frantically around, checking the clock on the wall for the time. Eli has third lunch, but sometimes I can catch him coming into the cafeteria. I have to catch him. I have to fix this.

"I forgot I need to turn something in for Spanish," I tell Harper. "I'll see you after school."

Out in the commons, I scan the crowd of people going to and from the lunchroom. I spot Eli coming down the stairs from C Hall, rush over, and grab him before he can get away.

The words spill out of me all at once.

"I have bad news about the hotel room for prom. I sent a text about it to you, but my stupid phone sent it to my mom instead.

Now she's freaking out and she told my dad, and they're saying it's a no-go."

"Crap." Eli looks disappointed, but also panicked. He hates looking bad to adults. "Are they mad at me?"

"No, they're mad at me. I told them it was my idea. You didn't get the room already, did you?"

"No." The look of panic fades into chagrin, as if someone pulled a rug out from underneath him. I feel terrible because I am the puller. And there's no way I can tell him the truth—not about this.

"I'm sorry. But at least now we can go to the after-party."

"Yeah." He still looks dazed. I stand on my tiptoes to give him a kiss.

"We'll figure something out," I say, making a million mental notes that if Eli and I do come this close to sex again, I need to double up on birth control methods—triple up if possible.

The bell sounds, signaling the end of second lunch.

"We'll still have a great prom," I tell him. "I promise."

He walks away, and I frantically check the website to make sure I've erased Teen Mom from my future. The site is frozen again. I hope that's a good sign. I go to my next class feeling like I've dodged an oncoming car but could still get hit by a truck.

In English, Truman refuses to look at me.

I stride to my own desk before class starts, sticking to the perimeter of the room, but he only looks up from the note cards in his hands to speak to some imaginary audience. He doesn't care that the people around him are giving him odd looks. He's practicing for some upcoming debate tournament. He's also avoiding me. I confirm this by staring at him from across the aisle until it becomes clear he's avoiding any form of eye contact. Any normal person would have at least glanced over, but Truman, who never used to pass up an opportunity to engage, now acts as if I'm not there. And when Ms. Laramie opens up the floor for discussion, he refuses to offer even the blandest of opinions, even when I throw out a couple that would have gotten his passive-aggressive motor revving just a few days ago.

So that's it. We're back to being enemies. And that's fine. No really, it is. I tell myself it's for the best that Truman and I aren't speaking, and by the end of class I've pretty much managed to make peace with the chilly distance. He and I don't have to be friends, or even adversaries. We can be nothing to each other. That's how I wanted it all along.

Except Jordan is out for blood when we meet up after school.

"I got a call from the people at the Blessing place, and they're telling me they might not be able to honor our deposit." Her eyes flash. "They said it depends on how things go at this city council meeting. The garden could be torn out by prom!"

My stomach drops. I forgot about the council meeting.

We stop at my locker, and Jordan whirls on Harper. "Have you heard anything about it when you've been over there? What do they think is going to happen?"

Harper's voice sounds small. "Nobody's saying anything to the volunteers. We only know what's been on the news."

"But, Sky, you and Truman are on it, right?" Jordan says. "We don't have anything to worry about."

Clearing my throat, I say, "Yes . . ." Except no. I reach for the top shelf, attempting to hide my scorching cheeks. I told them both about breakfast with Eli, but they don't know about the fight between Truman and me. I was saving the details for when we could spend some time actually talking. That time was supposed to be now. Only if I tell them how badly things ended, I might have to admit how little Truman and I got done while we were conducting our failed experiment in not hating one another.

"Okay," Jordan says, calming down a little. "We're just going to relax and trust Truman and Skyler to save the day."

"You got this, Sky," Harper says.

"Totally," Jordan agrees. "We're counting on you!"

I choke out a "Great!" while dying a little inside.

Dread follows me home. It grows stronger when I walk into the house to find a sheet of paper on top of the stack of mail on the counter. It's a printout from the school's academic portal with a big fat D in the trig column, circled in red pen. Next to it is my dad's handwriting: *Checked in at lunch and found this. I'm concerned. Let's discuss tonight.*

I need water. Just as I'm getting a glass from the dishwasher, my phone pings next to my grade card. I creep back over and can tell immediately it's another website update.

"Oh my God, stop!" I shout to the universe, as if it's even listening. I pick up the phone and pull up the site. Have I been demoted again? Am I now an unemployed loser living in my parents' basement, thanks to one lousy quarter of math?

When the site finally comes up, I sit at the table to study it more closely.

The design isn't as colorful and sparkly. There are fewer gal-

leries than there were, fewer pictures overall. And I can tell immediately that the location is different. There are no twinkle-lighted
trees, no rose wall, no gazebo. Unlike the previous version, there's
nothing to say where this reunion was held. I start clicking through
photos, scouring the background for hints. It could be a hotel, but
it's hard to tell if it's the Harrington, where most big events in town
take place, or some other hotel that looks like any other that could
spring up over the next decade or so. One thing is clear, though:
this reunion is not at our garden.

The site looks so different that I start searching names to see if
this is even our class at all. Maybe things have gone back to normal,
and now some other group of people is using this domain for a reunion that actually happened last month. Except there's Ryan Oard
again with his sun-aged skin. There's Anna Larkin, looking just as
multimillionaire-ish.

My heart thuds as I thumb in my own name. Only one photo
comes up, in the *Wish You Were Here* section. It's a simple, empty-
eyed headshot. The caption reads: "Skyler Finch, Cincinnati" and
underneath is a message that I guess was written by Future Me:

Have a great time. Sorry to miss it.

Truman's name appears a couple of entries underneath with
no photo at all.

My search for Jordan turns up better results. In most of the
photos, she poses with a doughy faced man—a Dr. Moessner, according to the captions. Jordan shares his last name, and in each
photo, she looks stylish but tired. She still looks like my best friend,
but more than a bit of her "Jordan-ness" has been rubbed away.

At first, I can't put my finger on what bothers me so much

about this new website, beyond the obvious and constant fact that viewing the future is incredibly strange. I realize what it is as I reach the end of Jordan's photos: Harper appears in none of them.

I enter her name, wait an excruciating several seconds, then watch as what looks like Harper's senior photo fills the screen. Above it, the header glows in eerie script:

In Memoriam

Underneath are messages submitted by our classmates.

I will always remember your smile.

Remembering the happy times—fly high, friend.

I hope you are finally at peace, dear Harper. The world isn't the same without you.

Choking on a gasp, I jump out of my chair. Every muscle in my body wants to move, to help, to *do something*. I can't believe what I'm seeing. It's unreal. Except I know that it *is* real. Because the reunion site is real. I've seen that it is.

I flatten my hands against the kitchen counter, forcing myself to focus. For some reason, I was given access to the reunion site. I've been looking for that reason, now maybe I've found it. Maybe this is the looming catastrophe only I can stop.

But how can I, Present-Day Skyler, help keep Future Harper's spark from going out? I grab my phone again and start backtracking, searching for clues. Photo after photo . . . I see people with drinks, people in pairs, in groups, alone, all in the same nondescript hotel.

It comes to me slowly at first, then hits like a smack to the face—the one major thing that is different on this site than on all the ones before it.

My hands shake as I pull up Truman's number. "Truman," I say before he can even get out a hello. "We have to get to work. Right now. We can't let them tear out the garden."

CHAPTER NINE

Truman lives in the nicest part of the nice part of town, where the super-wealthy Altonites live, not to be confused with the merely well-off Altonites, like my family used to be. Eli lives there too, which concerns me as I drive through the neighborhood. I promised him Truman and I were over, so how would it look if he saw me driving to Truman's house? I sink down into the seat and drive as fast as I can without speeding.

Truman waits in front of a huge house at the end of a cul de sac. Impeccable lawn, terrace with super-tasteful furniture, gleamingly clean windows—the house is perfectly manicured and stiff, just like him.

"Skyler," he says as I come up the walk. "What's going on?"

"The hearing is next week," I tell him. The humiliation from yesterday's argument has nowhere near worn off, and the last thing I want to do is bring up the reunion site. If Truman knew what was motivating me right now, he'd probably abandon me right here on his front doorstep. "We don't have anything done."

"I know."

"So shouldn't we get moving? We've wasted a lot of time."

Why and how that time got wasted hangs between us. For a

moment, I think he might actually acknowledge what happened yesterday in my kitchen. Part of me wants to talk it out, clear the air, come to some kind of agreement about what we are to each other now. The other part wants to never speak about it again.

"I personally don't care," I say, which is so obviously a lie that I cover up by adding, "But Jordan is freaking out about it. Also, I thought you needed this for your college applications. So shouldn't we get going?"

Appealing to his drive for success works. He leads me across the porch and motions for me to sit in a wicker chair, while he sits in a matching one on the opposite side of a round glass table, as far away from me as possible. This is a pride-smarting turn, Truman Alexander avoiding me instead of the other way around. But I can't get pulled into another fight.

Maybe I'm crazy for thinking it, but Truman and I working together just might be a matter of life and death.

"So you're the public-speaking expert. Do we just get up to the podium and launch in? What's our opening statement?"

"Whoa." He rears backward, throwing up his hands. "Before we think about where to stand and who says what, we need to do research. You can't just barge in and start talking."

"I'm not going to *barge*. I'm going to speak from the heart. You have to capture people's emotions."

"You also have to be able to back up what you say with facts and evidence. We need more in our arsenal than puppy dog eyes and a line about how gardens are pretty and people like them."

Classic pompous Truman is in full effect, I see. It takes everything inside me not to rip into him, because I need Truman on my side. If that means doing things his way, then so be it.

"Fine. Let's discuss our arsenal."

"Wait here." He goes inside and comes back with his black notebook. He starts taking down notes.

"I'll research how many jobs are projected to be created by building where the mansion sits now and whether that gets affected if they chose another location. Everest is saying they need that spot because it's close to the highway. We need to look at other areas that are within the same three-to-five-mile radius to show that this site isn't essential to their plans."

I interrupt with an exaggerated slow gag. "That's going to be gripping. Where are the feels? They need to understand exactly how much this place means to people."

"So how do you respond when they ask about tax revenue? Taxes don't pull anybody's heartstrings but they pay for things like firefighters, which matter just as much—probably even more—to people than a garden."

I let my shoulders drop, feeling the full weight of how ill-prepared we are. "You don't have to talk to me like I'm five."

A woman's face appears from behind the big front door, moon-shaped like Truman's but slightly pinched. This woman would be beautiful if she didn't look so much like the headmistress of a very old-fashioned school.

"Truman, it's almost time for dinner."

I jump to my feet. "Hi, Mrs. Alexander. I'm Skyler Finch. I'm in English class with Truman." She studies me with disapproval, and I'm suddenly ultraconscious of the hoodie I threw on as I rushed out the door, my messy ponytail, and my old running shoes. I get the distinct impression I should have worn something nicer.

"We won't be very long," I say. "We're just figuring out some-thing for a project we're working on together, and we're really behind on it, otherwise I wouldn't be here when you're trying to have dinner. We just really, really need to get this done."

I glance over at Truman, who is on his feet now. "Skyler and I are just finishing up," he says.

She purses her lips as if I've done something inexcusable, like belch or fart or announce that my parents vote Democrat. "Skyler, I'm afraid you'll have to leave. We're sitting down to the table in five minutes."

One more withering look, then she retreats, leaving me feeling about three feet tall.

"So . . ." I clear my throat. "That was . . ."

"My mother. Yes." Truman flips to a blank page in his notebook. He writes a list, then pulls out the page. He rips the list in half, keeping one piece for himself. "These are the points I'm certain they'll bring up. Research as many responses as you can. But make sure they're data-driven. And whatever you do, don't get flustered."

"I don't get flustered."

He tilts his head like, *Really?* I force myself to take the paper from him gently. I do not hit him over the head with it.

"So when are we getting back together?" I ask. "I mean, to work on this. Not as in . . . anything else."

So much for not getting flustered.

"What about Saturday? Can you get your questions done by then?"

Tomorrow is Friday. I'm supposed to go for dinner and a movie with Eli. We agreed on it as we walked to school from Big Sky this morning, right after I made my big confession and he decided not to break up with me. If Truman and I are meeting Saturday, and if I have to get all this stuff done before, then I'm going to need to work on it tomorrow. Factor in school, and I've got just the afternoon before Eli picks me up tomorrow night. I wanted to get dressed up and make it special, not rush to get ready.

But this is for Harper. I have to make it work.

"Saturday's okay. Do you want me to come back here?"

"I'll come to your house. Will nine a.m. work?"

Even if my answer had been no, he probably wouldn't have heard it, because he's started to usher me off his porch as the front door swings open and his mother reappears to order him inside. I scurry down the walk, back stinging with the knowledge that they are both getting a full view of me in all my hoodie-wearing, messy-ponytailed glory. As I get into my car, it occurs to me that I should probably be a little more concerned about what Truman's parents think. I'm working with their son to save a garden they'd be more than happy to see razed to the ground.

But instead, I'm worried about someone else.

How am I going to explain this to Eli?

Answer: gingerly, and not very successfully.

I did everything I could to get my work done quickly. When last bell rang I headed straight for the library, where I fired up my laptop and dove into my research. But when I checked the time after what I thought was just an hour, it was already six o'clock—barely enough time to get home, let alone make myself look nice. And if I did go out, even if I got up early tomorrow to start working again, I'd never get it all done before Truman came over.

So that's how I ended up on my phone in the library bathroom, listening to Eli express his displeasure about my need to cancel.

"Nobody does homework on Friday night," he says. "You've got the whole weekend for that."

"This isn't for school. It's for the city council meeting. The one with Everest on Thursday."

"What are you doing for that?"

I swipe the back of my hand across my forehead, feeling gross and grimy from the long day.

"I'm one of the speakers."

"I told you my dad is working with Everest."

"And I told you we were trying to stop them from getting the garden. I promised my friends I'd help."

"You promised me we'd go out."

"We will. Just let me get this done and then I'll make it up to you. Please. It's just one night."

Silence—the same as yesterday at the diner. "I thought we were starting over," Eli says. "This isn't a very good start."

"I know." It's past seven now, and the library closes at eight. I need to get moving if I'm going to gather everything I need for what looks like a possible all-nighter. "Just let me figure out how to get through the next few days and then everything will get back to normal. Believe me, after the week I've had, normal is all I want."

He finally agrees and lets me off the phone. I hurry back to my computer, back to cutting, pasting, and downloading as much as I can before the head librarian shoos me out at closing time. At home, I shut myself in my room and dig in again. I try to get excited about traffic patterns and economic development. I draft my own lists in one of Dad's legal pads, pushing chunks of information around but failing to make them stack up into anything solid. There's no way I'll be able to stand in front of all those people and spout this stuff.

I rip the lists out of the pad and swap my wishy-washy pencil for a no-turning-back-now pen. This time I'll focus not on what I think or know, but on what I feel.

I start to write.

CHAPTER TEN

"How'd your research go?"

Truman plops his backpack onto the table, pulls up a kitchen chair, and starts unpacking his laptop and stacks of folders like an attorney ready to defend a death-row inmate. He ignores the mug of coffee I've poured for him as he fires up the computer, opens his ever-present black notebook, and produces an official-looking lethally fine-tip Sharpie that he proceeds to flip repeatedly over his thumb, helicopter-style, while he consults what appears to be a foldout spreadsheet. He's so laser-focused that I'm unsure whether he really wants me to answer the question. But then he looks up with an expression that more than implies I've kept him waiting.

I'm actually quite proud of where I ended up. I finished my speech draft just as my parents were shuffling to their bedroom at midnight; then I read it again this morning after a good night's sleep. It expresses what's in my heart and in the hearts of my friends.

"Just sent it to you." I add milk to my coffee and sit back, enjoying a donut from Big Sky while Truman reads. I watch his face, waiting for the *aha!* when he recognizes my genius.

He looks up, brow furrowed. "What is this?"

"My part of the presentation. It's just a draft. There's always room for improvement, but I think it's pretty close, don't you?"

"No. Where's the data you were supposed to get?"

I put down my donut, still half basking in an expectation of praise, not quite caught up with the idea that I'm on the defensive again.

"It's there—mostly. I made it emotionally engaging."

"You made it a lightweight nonstarter. I told you, you can't just go in there with a sappy story. The council won't take you seriously."

The back of my neck starts to itch. My pulse jumps with the urge to fight back. At the same time, a switch flips in my brain and I realize Truman is right. A little bit. He's also a lot wrong, but I'm not going to scream it into his face this time. Instead, I speak calmly and, though it takes effort, not unkindly.

"What you don't seem to understand is that nobody is going to take you seriously either—not with all this." I sweep my hand over the folders, the notebook exploding with color-coded tabs. "If all you have are data points about taxes and traffic, people's eyes are going to glaze over. Worse, they'll see you as some obnoxious kid."

Truman's voice takes on that good old down-the-nose gravitas.

"Being well-prepared is not obnoxious. Do you have a better alternative?"

"Maybe we could trade. You give me what you've got, and I'll try to jazz it up. Then you can go through my stuff and tell me where it needs more backup."

Truman agrees to this plan and we get to work at opposite ends of the table. I find a storyline in his talking points. He beefs up my stories with facts. We drink a lot of coffee. I eat a lot of donuts. And when it's time to share our progress, we're both surprised to find a convincing argument starting to take shape.

"Now, this is getting somewhere." He looks at me, and I finally see the appreciation I've been hoping for in his eyes. "You're really talented, Skyler."

I've been told I'm pretty, that I'm fun, that I'm somebody people want to hang around with. But no one's ever told me I'm talented. Part of it, I'm sure, is that I don't go out of my way to show off whatever talent I might have. But listening to Truman, I can see why people seek a little specialness for themselves. Everything inside me warms up and my mind starts clicking with possibilities. If I can do this, what else can I do?

He tilts his head as he reads my laptop screen, and his cheek comes close enough to mine that I feel the warmth of his skin. I catch myself leaning in a little closer. Something in my body has disconnected from my brain and wants to push right up against Truman. Maybe it's the fact that he smells amazing—like he took a shower with expensive soap, then ate a stack of pancakes for breakfast. Maybe getting complimented on my talent is a major turn-on. Or maybe my body is a big old traitor in need of a good smackdown from the part of me that knows every single reason why I should *not* be wanting to get close to Truman Alexander right now.

Lucky for me, he turns away to pick up his notebook.

"I found an article about how Everest is known for firing people as soon as their stock price dips. Let me find it."

He opens the notebook, and the profusion of colored charts and tabs assaults my eyes.

"Hold up." I snatch the book from his hands. "Let me see that."

The pages feel softly worn as I turn them, and every one is filled to the margins with stuff: Stuff hastily scrawled. Stuff written with a neat, squarish hand. Stuff marked up with a fluorescent rainbow of highlighters.

"Holy cow, Truman. What is all this?"

"It's my life."

He says this as if everyone carries around a book bulging with the minutia of their daily existence. One section is dedicated to his schedule. Every minute is accounted for, and each completed activity has been struck through with a color-coordinated line. With so much detail, I'm surprised Truman's bathroom time isn't also included. Or maybe it is, and I'm just not seeing it immediately—thank God.

"This isn't your life, this is your DNA profile," I tell him. "I'm pretty sure there are actual pathological diagnoses for this kind of thing."

He takes back the notebook. "The contents of this book are responsible for where I am today, which is not too shabby, if we'd like to be honest about it. And they'll get me where I'm going too."

"Right. Johns Hopkins." I roll my eyes because everybody has heard about Truman's college plans.

"That's just the start. After that I'll get a masters in global affairs at Harvard Kennedy School. Summers will be internships and work in DC with Senator Stevens if he's still in office, which according to my projections, he should be. I'll go on to work as a lobbyist for the aerospace industry. Then, after I've made some good money, I'll get a PhD and join the faculty back at Hopkins or go on to a think tank, whichever is more lucrative."

"Wow, you really do have it all planned out."

"Everything I do is designed to get me toward those goals."

This is the part where I usually get that creepy skin-crawly, can't-handle-Truman's-voice sensation, coupled with an irresistible urge to take him down a few notches. But I don't feel like that now. When Truman talks about his lofty goals and superior intellect at school, it's easy to see an arrogant jerk. Sitting next to him in my kitchen right now, all I see is an overworked kid who's going to plan himself to exhaustion.

"Truman. Do you mind if I ask what you do for fun?"

"Debate is fun."

"Okay, but I'm thinking things like hobbies. Embarrassing Internet fandoms. Things you just sort of end up doing because they're relaxing or interesting, or maybe even a guilty pleasure."

He stares at me.

"Oh, come on. You're telling me you don't take a break from all that hyperscheduling to daydream, even a little?"

"I'm not *that* hyper-scheduled. I actually had another commitment this morning, which I shuffled so I could work on this with you."

"Lucky me." I tug his collar, forcing him to stand. "But that's not what I meant. Come on, we're getting out of here."

I pull him into the hallway, grabbing our jackets while racking my brain for the most frivolous thing two people can do on a Saturday afternoon. Inspiration strikes in the driveway as we're getting into my car.

"Hey, have you ever been bowling?"

Turns out there's a reason Truman has never been bowling. He's terrible at it. Whatever the reason, he rolls so many gutter balls that the manager comes over and offers to put in the kiddie bumpers. This wounds Truman's *win at all costs* pride, but he doesn't quit. He refuses the bumpers, sticks it out, and continues to royally stink the place up.

And yet today I suck even worse, which does a lot to repair Truman's ego. I let him rub it in as repayment for all the terrible things I said after showing him the reunion site the other night.

However, I do have limits.

"The way you throw the ball is disturbingly graceful," I tell him after the first throw of his last turn. "You remind me of a bowling ballerina."

He drops the ball, sending it scuttering down the lane to take out one lone pin.

"I studied fencing until the age of thirteen," he tells me. "It's the only sport I've ever participated in. I guess I never got it out of my system."

The image of young Truman in a white jumpsuit with a long sword cracks me up, especially since he doesn't seem to find any humor in it at all. He retrieves his ball from the machine, continuing to look far more sober than I would have anticipated for this line of conversation. His last self-conscious throw results in only two more pins picked off.

"Ha!" I crow. "Did I beat you? I think I beat you!"

"How could you have beaten me? You were only up by one, and mine was the last shot."

I look down at my phone, up at the scoreboard, then at my phone again, distracted. Two things just came in at the same time. One is a text from Jordan: a photo of Eli jogging down a sidewalk near her house.

Just saw your boy. Working it out for dat tux

Seeing Eli sends a twinge of guilt through me, but I can barely register it before my screen starts to fill with reunion site notifcations. I tried to turn them off yesterday at the library, because I needed to focus on my work, and because they upset me. For a while, my phone obeyed. But now it looks like everything I missed in the past twelve hours is getting vomited out in one big stream of pings.

Ping!
Lischer-Dunlap, Brynn—
WISH WE'D HAD A BETTER TURNOUT . . .

Ping!
Peterson-Butte, McKinley—
I VOLUNTEER TO ORGANIZE THE 20TH . . .

Ping!
Larkin, Anna—
REALLY MISSED THOSE WHO WEREN'T THERE . . .

"Skyler?" Truman stands by the ball return, waiting.

"Okay, so you won." I push out what I hope is a lighthearted laugh. "Far be it from me to deny you your first sports-related victory since fencing. Bowling is so much more lowbrow, though. Are you sure your parents would approve?"

He deposits his ball on the rack with a sullen *smack*.

"My parents made me take fencing because they thought it would help me focus."

"You mean you weren't always Mr. Eyes on the Prize?"

"Let's just say I spent a large portion of my childhood feeling like a disappointment."

I flash back to Truman's mom with her disapproving glare and icy voice. If the seven minutes I spent in her presence were painful, I can only imagine what seventeen years must have been like. Thinking about it brings to the surface a familiar ache.

"I can relate. I could win the Nobel Peace Prize and my sister would have done something even more impressive for people to ooh and ahh over."

Truman sits beside me and takes a sip of his soda. "I didn't know you had a sister."

"Piper Finch. I thought everyone knew about her. She went to Duke, now she's in law school at Baldwin. She's brilliant. You'd probably love her."

"Sounds like sibling rivalry."

"It's not even that." I pluck the straw from my own drink and twist it around my finger. "She's not competing with me. And I'm not really competing with her. She just likes to assume she's the expert on everything, and . . . Hey, what's this?"

On the table next to my cup sits a figurine the size of my thumb. It's a little boy. Or maybe it's a man. Maybe both, because its face is wrinkled and worn while the eyes are huge and childlike. It's made out of a smooth kind of wood, and the whole thing has been varnished with a milky substance. The body isn't really a body, just the suggestion of one, rendered in a sinewy wave of gray and blue. It's eerie and earthy and unlike anything I've ever seen before.

"You asked what I do for fun," Truman says.

"You made this?" I pick the sculpture up, turning it between my fingers. It's dense and weighty for something so small. And those eyes. They're creamy, dreamy saucers that look up at me as if asking the world's most innocent and profound question.

"I'm still working on it," he tells me. "I did the first glaze too soon, before I decided the face wasn't quite right."

I remember Truman carving something when I saw him in the garden a few days ago. This must have been it. "Truman. It's beautiful."

"They take me a long time to do," he says. "I'm kind of a perfectionist about getting them just the way I want them."

"Do you have more?"

"Not with me. But if you want, I can show you pictures."

"Yes, please!"

He takes out his phone and starts flipping through photos of more tiny people, all with the same wide eyes, the same old-young features, but different hair, different expressions, and different clothing, although the outfits are little more than hints since the bodies are all done in that wavy, unformed style. Then there are sculptures that are nothing but waves—small curving spires reaching upward for the ceiling. Everything has that glazed, warm glow.

"They're incredible. You must be burning it up in art class."

"I don't take art."

"That's such a waste! Forget debate, Truman. This is what you should be doing."

My heart skips an extra beat. I always thought I knew exactly who Truman was and what made him tick. But all this time, there was this whole other version.

"I had no idea you were a sculptor," I say.

"I don't show them to many people."

"Thank you for showing them to me."

A chuckle drifts over from a neighboring lane—two women telling each other how adorable they think we are. Truman's gaze

115

flicks down to my mouth. It's only when his eyes leave mine that I see how close we've gotten. We're inches apart, lips a breath away from meeting. The buzzing has already started inside me, my brain switching off, then on again, just in time to realize what I'm doing. Truman realizes it too, and we move apart in unison. All around us, the bowling alley is filling with senior citizens meeting up for their afternoon leagues. People smile when they see Truman and me, and I want to tell them they shouldn't get the wrong idea: we're just project partners. I was not two seconds away from kissing him. He was not looking at me with an expression mixing heat and surprise and a *what the hell* readiness to become a hell of a lot more.

He reaches for the laces of his bowling shoes. With his long shorts and preppy fleece, they make him look like an overgrown schoolboy.

"Before we go, I need a picture to commemorate your bowling debut." I say, whipping out my phone. "Those saddle shoes really make the outfit."

This, finally, notches me a win. Grinning, Truman strikes a pose. Then, just as I'm about to take the photo, my phone pings again. The preview window descends. I glance at it and nearly choke.

Alexander, Truman—
SORRY I MISSED THE REUNION . . .

"How does it look? Are you getting the shot you wanted?" Truman sticks out his hip in a seductive pose that I would find hilarious if I weren't so preoccupied by a message from him from the future. The fact that I'm no longer just seeing messages from

116

random classmates is something I can't ignore. I have to see what Future Truman is saying, and I can't let him see that I'm seeing it.

"Hold on. I have to go to the bathroom."

I make it as far as the shoe cubbies before I can't stand the curiosity any longer. Hiding between the cubbies and the concession stand, I pull up the site.

Sorry I missed the reunion. I was in Barcelona completing the second leg of my European sabbatical. Next stop: Greece. Then I'm on to Vietnam for vacation. The sights are beautiful, but I find myself missing home. I will try to make the next one—Truman

Jealousy scorches my very being as I read about Truman's fantastic, world-traveling future. I pull up his new, just-updated bio and don't even bother reading the inches upon inches listing all his many jobs and honors and accomplishments. I look myself up again, and there's nothing but that short, sad sentence in the *Wish You Were Here* section, along with one new word in my bio: *homemaker*. I've also checked the box for married, but nowhere does it say to whom.

And still, on the *In Memoriam* page, is Harper.

I shuffle back over to where Truman stands with his bowling shoes in his hand and his jacket on. Then I stalk toward the parking lot, and he follows. If he notices a change in my attitude, he doesn't show it.

"I'm starving," he groans as we get into the car.

"Me too. Let's get a burrito."

"I watched you consume an entire plate of nachos before that last game, not to mention all those donuts back at your house. How could you possibly have room for a burrito?"

"I'm a stress eater." I navigate out of the lot and start off toward the one and only burrito place in Alton. "When I'm worried, I eat."

"What are you worried about?"

What am I not worried about? I want to say. The reunion site now shows me as a going-nowhere loser while Truman jet-sets across the globe. Jordan will be beyond pissed if she has to have her prom anyplace other than the Blessing garden. And then there's Harper—most of all Harper. But the website is unmentionable between Truman and me. He seems to be pretending he never saw it.

"I'm only getting ready to stand up in front of a roomful of city officials to try and save a place that means a lot to some pretty important people in my life," I tell him. "Harper is going to be especially upset if we can't keep them from ripping it out."

"I heard she was having a hard time," Truman says. "Is she okay?"

"I think so. It's just funny, you know? One of the things I love most about her is that you always know what she's feeling. Whatever this thing is that wants to eat her up has sort of stolen that."

"So she's not okay."

"She is. I guess I just worry that she won't be."

"And you think you can stop that?"

"I don't know. Before, when things were bad, I didn't do anything. If you thought there was something you could do to help a friend, wouldn't you do it?"

"I would if I thought it would really help."

My phone vibrates in my lap. I glance down to see a notification from Jordan Moessner—Future Jordan. I don't read it; I have no desire to end up wrapped around a utility pole thanks to texting and driving. But it's another reminder of the future I'd do anything to avoid.

"I think it will help," I tell Truman. "Maybe. I don't know. Either way, I have to try."

When we get to Javier's, I let Truman order first. I need a minute to process the past hour. It's almost too much: nearly kissing Truman, his sculptures, seeing him on the reunion site in all his high-achieving glory. Because of that, I don't immediately notice when the door opens and in walks Mitch, Eli's best friend and our double date for prom. I don't catch a clue until the door opens again, and I'm face to face with Eli himself.

"Skyler! Hey!" He looks thrilled to see me. "I've been trying to text you. Wanted to see if you were up for a burrito, and it looks like you were. Great minds, right?"

I nod awkwardly, letting him pull me in for a kiss.

"I'm having phone issues again." A strange, high-pitched laugh escapes my throat. "But we're definitely on the same wavelength. I've been craving Javier's all day."

Right at this moment, Truman can be heard telling the guy behind the counter, "Put whatever she's having on my bill." He turns to me and says, "I owe you since you paid for bowling. Is that okay?"

Ugh. Fail. Truman sees Eli the same time Eli sees Truman. Eli's eyes narrow. Truman's head tilts backward in shock.

"You don't have to do that," I say, scooting closer to Eli. "In fact, I'm sort of not hungry any—"

"Bowling?" Eli says. "So did you guys just run into each other, or are you coming from somewhere else?"

"We're not here together," Truman tells him, and for a split second, I think we might be safe. Until Truman's ridiculous honesty kicks in. "I mean, we are technically, but we're just taking a break from a project we're working on."

Double fail. Eli doesn't know Truman is part of the council meeting. And Truman doesn't know that Eli knows about all our non-garden-related activities.

Eli goes silent. Mitch is suddenly engrossed in his phone. Meanwhile, the guy behind the counter waits for me to order a burrito for which I no longer have any appetite. I get mine to go and pay my own way. Truman makes a hasty escape out to the car, and I wait for Eli, suddenly freezing in the dress I put on this morning because it was cute rather than practical for early spring. Of course, I didn't admit that to myself while getting dressed. But now my skin goose-pimples with the truth. *Maybe Eli won't notice,* I tell myself. He turns and gives me a once-over. Who am I kidding? Eli notices everything.

He pays for his burrito, then pushes past me.

"Eli! Can we talk?"

Wordlessly, he veers to the side door. I follow him out to a patio stacked with chairs waiting to be used once the weather turns warm for good.

"I was going to call you," I tell him.

"When you fixed your phone?" He nods sarcastically. "I was going to see if you wanted to go out tonight since we didn't get to last night. But apparently you have plans. Again."

"I don't have plans. I'm only busy this afternoon."

"Busy bowling?"

"It was just a quick break. We worked all morning and we needed a change of scenery."

"What I'm trying to figure out is what you could have been doing all morning that was so intense you needed a bowling break."

"Truman is working with me on the Blessing garden. We're speaking together at that meeting on Thursday."

He crosses his arms now, thoroughly pissed.

"You kind of have a habit of failing to mention things, because I don't remember ever getting that bit of information."

"I didn't leave it out on purpose. I just . . . didn't tell you all the details."

Until this moment, I hadn't articulated even for myself why I was keeping Truman's involvement with the garden a secret from Eli. Of course, the cheating would have been enough of a reason. But the truth is that I'd hoped to sneak by, fix the future, then get my present life back to normal.

That was back when I could fool myself that normal existed. Before my phone started blowing up with comments from thirty-year-old versions of my current friends. Before my best friend showed up on a memorial page right around the time I flaked out on helping to save a garden she loves. When a website can appear out of nowhere and give you a glimpse of what's to come, it's hard to expect anything to be normal again.

"The garden belonged to Truman's family," I explain. "We thought we'd do better if we teamed up, that's all. If it *was* a project for school would you be so mad right now?"

"I think it's pretty clear that it's more than a project. And what's this crap about his family owning it? More like he's trying to get you to feel sorry for him. Seems like it's working."

"Nothing else has happened between Truman and me. I promised it wouldn't."

"But how does it look? You and I are together and you're out bowling with someone else."

I squint, not certain I heard him correctly. "Is that what you're worried about? How it looks?"

"I'm pretty sure most guys would be."

"Well, it's stupid. I can bowl with whoever I want. I'm with *you*. All I'm doing is helping my friends. This means a lot to Jordan and Harper."

Eli softens when I mention them, but he isn't done being mad. "Look, about tonight," he says. "Me and some guys are going to go to a movie, okay? Maybe you should just focus on getting your project done."

I huff out an exasperated sigh. "Fine. Whatever. Are we still having brunch tomorrow?"

"Sure, if you're free. Text and let me know. Assuming you aren't still having phone problems."

With that he walks away, leaving me clutching a cold burrito and wondering whether this day could possibly get any more messed up.

Back in my car, I find out that the answer is yes, yes, it could. Because Truman is now in a craptastic mood.

"You told Eli about us?" he demands. "Why would you do that?"

"Because honesty," I shoot back. "You're the one who's always talking about how it's best to tell the truth, even if it gets you in trouble."

There are so many things I want to say—that Eli is my boyfriend and Truman isn't. That Truman and I are supposed to be enemies, so why does he care what happens with Eli anyway? But

I can't deny that something almost happened again between us at the bowling alley, and I can't deny that things were painful with Eli just now.

Calm down, Skyler. Calm down and change the subject.

I ease my grip on the steering wheel, watching my knuckles regain their color.

"So I was thinking we should probably create a cheat sheet for Thursday," I say. "Like a list of FAQs to help keep us organized . . ."

"I need to get home." Truman's voice has taken on the same distant tone as the other night, after I showed him the reunion site and he acted like I was trying to lure him to Vegas for a quickie wedding.

God. Boys. I don't have the time or the sanity for this. I should tell them both to take a hike, declare celibacy, and go on to live a fabulous, solitary life. Or maybe I'll just stay single until after the reunion is over. I'll have my whole life ahead of me after that. Unless I die before then without ever experiencing true love, which would really suck.

I throw the car into reverse and start backing out, taking some satisfaction when I pop over a curb and seat belt–less Truman nearly whacks his enormous head against the ceiling.

"Whatever weirded-out thing you're tempted to do right now, just don't," I tell him. "All I'm interested in is being ready next week and not making any more of a fool out of myself than I already have. I think you'll agree we are nowhere near ready."

"I'll upload my stuff so we can both edit it," he says. "You'll have it by tomorrow night."

"Great."

Steering toward home, I put on music so Truman won't think

I'm expecting him to make conversation. My phone pings and I glance at the screen, thinking it might be Eli calling to apologize.

Oard, Ryan—ANYONE STILL IN TOWN UP FOR GOLF?

"Your phone's been blowing up all day," says Truman. "Do you want me to answer that for you since you're driving?"

"Nope." I shove my phone into my bag, then step on the gas. "I don't give a crap what's on my phone right now, and believe me, you shouldn't either."

CHAPTER ELEVEN

Saturday night, Mom makes a roast and the three of us eat dinner as a family for the first time in a long time. Sitting down at the table, passing around platters of real food instead of take-out or one of Mom's slow-cooker experiments feels so good. I'd almost forgotten what it was like.

While we're eating, I fill them in on everything that's happening with the hearing—everything I *can* tell them without sounding like I've lost my mind, and they go into problem-solving mode.

"I'm willing to bet some open-records laws were broken while this land deal was coming together," Dad says through a mouthful of potatoes. "Do you want me to look into it? Pro bono, of course." He winks.

"I don't know. I'm already getting a reputation as a troublemaker. I probably don't need my whole family getting in on it too."

"Hmmm, well, let me know. I rather enjoy making trouble." He butters a fresh piece of bread, and I can tell he's relishing the idea. Dad really has been happier since he left Eagle Mills. We may be broke, and I may never see them these days, but he loves his job at Legal Aid, and the same with Mom at Planned Parenthood. Maybe that's the point. Whatever I end up doing in my future, I want it to be something I love, not something I do just because it makes me a lot of money or because I didn't have any other choice.

I want to have a choice. First thing Monday I'm going to the counseling office to see about a math tutor.

"Well, if you do manage to get them to turn it all around, it will look good on your résumé," Mom says. "Piper was telling me that even schools like State are demanding more from applicants these days. Better grades, more leadership activities . . . You can't just assume you'll get in anymore."

Talking about Piper and college applications makes my stomach hurt. All those uplifting emails from her that I've sent to spam feel like fingers pointing at me through the ether, ganging up with the reunion site to tell me, *See? Coasting has consequences. Avoid it all you want, but it will catch up to you eventually.*

After dinner, I sack out in the den with my homework, determined to get more serious. When Jordan and Harper call asking if I want to go to a party at Fia Reyes's house, I tell them I'm not feeling well. With the week I've got coming up, I need a few hours of alone time. I might also need a good cry. I spread out my books, then alternate between spurts of studying and bawling my eyes out.

Sunday morning, I wash my tear-crusted face, put on a cute sweater, and get ready to start over with Eli.

His smile when I walk into Big Sky says he wants a do-over too.

"Sorry about yesterday," I tell him.

"I'm sorry too." He slips his hand into mine. "You look nice. I like when you wear your hair like that."

I look around, noticing the diner is a lot more crowded than usual. On any other Sunday, he'd be waiting at our usual table. Today, all the tables are occupied, with a big chunk of them taken up by people from school. Brynn Lischer spots us and drifts over to where we're standing.

"We have room with us if you don't want to wait," she says. I can't help noticing that she says it more to Eli than to me.

"What is everybody doing here?" I ask, more to Eli than to Brynn. But Brynn jumps in to answer.

"It's our church group. Eli was telling me about brunch last night at Fia's party. It made me crave pancakes, so we got our youth leader to let us move our meeting over here." She looks around, clearly satisfied with herself. "I'd forgotten how cute this place is."

Eli smiles one of his sunny smiles and starts following Brynn in her adorable skirt and ballet flats over to where her group has crowded into several pushed-together tables. Apparently everybody was at the party, including Eli, where he spent God knows how much time talking with Brynn. Now, instead of our usual, just-the-two-of-us brunch, we get brunch with the A-listers. Any other time, I might have been thrilled. But I sense something sour in the air.

As I'm sitting, I catch McKinley looking at me.

"Cute sweater," she says, her nose wrinkled with distaste.

"Thanks." I fold my arms across the top I thought was cute earlier but am now aware screams SO LAST SEASON, picturing grown-up McKinley all leathery and orange with a smoker's cough and stinking like an ashtray. That's one perk of getting to see the future, I guess. I can silently gloat about jerks like her getting up close and personal with karma later on.

"So, Skyler!" says Brynn. "Where are you getting your hair done for prom?"

"Oh . . ." I try to look like I haven't thought about it yet. "I'll probably let my mom do it. She lives for that kind of thing."

"You should come with us to Bella. We're doing the full makeup, mani-pedi, and hair treatment."

It's a flattering invitation. Brynn looks super sweet for asking. But I'm pretty sure this sweet has a poison center. Brynn doesn't have a date to prom since she and Elliott Minhaj broke up, and everybody else is pretty much paired off at this point. Although no one can believe it, it looks like Brynn Lischer will be going solo. But from the way she looks at Eli, and the fact that a conversation with him at a party led to her crashing my brunch date, I'm starting to suspect she's hoping I'll be the one who ends up alone at the dance.

"You should go," Eli says to me. "Bella is supposed to be amazing."

I look sideways, marveling at his cluelessness. He's either completely in the dark about what Brynn is doing, or he's tone-deaf to the fact that I don't have hundreds of dollars to throw around on hair and makeup after buying a dress and shoes and everything else for prom.

Brynn's eyes go wide, like she's just had a great idea.

"You could be our eighth person! If we sign up with eight, then we all get a twenty percent discount, plus a cheese and fruit plate to share."

"Sounds like fun!" says Eli.

"So should I book you?" Brynn pulls out her phone and looks at me, waiting.

"Um . . ." I'm stuck. "Okay."

She thumbs in the reservation, lightning fast. "It's done. You'll be there, right? Because if not, we'll all lose our discount, and no appetizers. That would suck."

I assure Brynn I won't let her down; then I sit miserably while we wait for the waiter to take our order. Everybody else already has their food. They're talking, happy, oblivious—including Eli, who's recounting the plot of the movie he saw before the party last night, complete with impersonations and special effects. I can hear Truman's voice in my head, the way he made me feel so shallow for buying into the whole popularity thing, and now I can't unhear it. I'm Lily Bart from *The House of Mirth,* gambling herself ever deeper into debt, afraid to stand up to the people whose position in the social order is safely fixed, for fear of getting kicked out or left behind.

I have no plans to end up dead like Lily, but I also don't feel like enduring a long slide into social oblivion. I don't want a *House of Mirth* ending.

When it becomes clear we won't be eating anytime soon, I lean in to Eli. "I should go. There's a prom committee meeting and I'll be late if I stick around here."

"Okay," he answers cheerfully. "Tell Jordan hi for me."

At the door, I look back to see him head to head with Brynn, and know I have no right to be mad about it. It's probably what I deserve. But that doesn't mean I want to watch it happen. So I lied. The prom meeting is actually in an hour. I have time to kill, but I don't want to go home.

I text Jordan.

Heading over now. Can you meet me?

Already there. Measuring stuff.

When I get to the Blessing place, I find her on the sidewalk, criss-crossing the garden wall and door with a tape measure for twinkle lights. "What's the matter?" she says when she sees my face.

"Everything."

The caretaker unlocks the gate, and we step inside. I wait until he goes into the shed before saying, "So some really freaky stuff has been happening with the reunion site."

"Uh-oh. Freaky weird or freaky bad?"

"Bad. I'll show you."

We sit at a little wrought-iron table and she looks over my shoulder. When a photo of her pops up, she stops me from scrolling.

"Ew, that *is* bad. Look at me. I'm an old-lady mess here. And who is that dude I'm with? Just no."

"Jordan—"

"I mean, I guess I should be happy he's a doctor, but my last name is really going to be Moessner? It's a literal mess all around."

"Jordan! This isn't about you. Look."

I pull up the *In Memoriam* and show her Harper's photo. I wait for the horror, the tears, the freaking out. Jordan's expression hardens. She hands the phone back to me.

"Just because it's that way now doesn't mean it will stay like that," she says.

"What if it does?"

"That site has changed so many times already. It'll change again."

"But it changed because of something I did. And this came up after Truman and I started fighting instead of working on our speeches."

"Not everything is about you, either, Sky. Anything could happen between now and then."

"So you're cool with the website when it shows what you want to see, but when it shows something you don't like, you want to blow it off and say it's not important?"

Her head snaps back and her eyebrows shoot up, telling me I need to *watch it*.

"You know what? I thought that thing was cool when it first showed up. But I'm starting to think Harper was right." She jabs her finger at the phone in my hand. "It's not healthy. You're starting to be obsessed with it."

"If I'm obsessed, then I would hope you would be too. This is our best friend we're talking about."

"Freaking out isn't going to do her any good. And obsessing about the next eleven years right now is going to make us all crazy. I think the best thing to do is forget all this reunion stuff. Just forget about it and live your life. The future will take care of itself."

The more she talks, the more certain she sounds that she's right. And once Jordan is certain about something, nothing can change her mind.

"Fine. I'll forget about it." I make a show out of slipping my phone into my bag. And when Jordan doesn't look convinced, I give her my own *watch it* glare. She stands and goes back to her measuring. I get up and wander. It really is beautiful here, with the trees blooming and everything bursting out green and fresh. Over near a fountain are two angel figurines, each holding a heart in its arms. Normally, I wouldn't pay much attention, but something about them looks familiar.

I bend down and run my fingers over their smooth surfaces. They're much bigger than the sculptures Truman showed me yesterday, but they have the same look and that same milky glaze. Did he make them? Or did someone else in his family? One thing I've learned is that there's a lot more to Truman than he ever lets show. Maybe his connection to this place is about more than just beefing up his activities and accomplishments.

I take a photo of the angels as Harper's voice carries over from the garden door.

"Hey, Jordan? Sky?"

Jordan's head pops out from behind the rose wall.

"You're not going to show her the site, are you?" she whispers.

"What? No! I'm not an idiot."

She lets her gaze linger like she might just have doubts about that. I turn around to go find Harper.

She's hanging out with a couple of the volunteers in the shed while waiting for the other committee members to show up. She calls me over, hands me a trowel, and we plant herbs together in a long window box.

"What is it about this place that you love so much?" I ask while we work. "I mean beyond the fact that it's probably one of the most peaceful places ever."

"Oh, I can't answer that," she says. "It's embarrassing."

"I won't judge."

She pats soil over some basil seeds. "Things are always starting over here. It's like, no matter what happens, or how I feel on any given day, I come here and everything is still growing the way it's meant to. It's kind of like getting second chances all the time. Does that make sense?"

It does. A thought pops into my head.

"Instead of Truman, why don't you do the hearing with me?" The more I think about it, the more I like it. Harper might not have files full of factoids, but she's great in front of an audience. Truman could do his speech on his own, which would cut down on tension with Eli, and we could save the garden without having to team up.

"I love that idea," says Jordan, who's just popped her head in to see if we're ready. "Harper, you should definitely speak too."

"Nah, that's Truman's thing—at least for the actual meeting. But I'm definitely helping. I've been growing marigolds from seeds, and I'm putting them into little pots for the council members' podiums."

"Good, good, I like how you're thinking," says Jordan. "We need all the help we can get."

Harper nods, peering out the shed window at the other people arriving for the meeting.

"Speaking of Truman, is he coming?"

Her question sends a jolt of anxiety through me. Last night I received a folder with Truman's research in it. I added mine, too, but we still need to finalize who's going to say what. The fact that I am even thinking about saying anything in public is a huge deal. It might not be to Truman, but it definitely is to me. Considering I haven't heard anything else from him since he left my place yesterday afternoon, we need this meeting today to figure things out.

"He'd better be coming," I tell Harper. "We still have a ton of work to do."

CHAPTER TWELVE

Truman doesn't show up.

Monday morning while I'm eating breakfast, I get an email from city hall saying we've been placed on the agenda, which makes me so nervous that I text him to meet me after school.

When I arrive at the building, the first thing I do is go to the counseling office to set up a tutor for trig. I schedule the only free lunch meeting slot, then head off to first bell, noticing that Truman hasn't returned my breakfast text. I don't see him during morning passing period, and he isn't in the cafeteria at lunch. In English, I find myself staring at his empty seat across the aisle. I wait for Ms. Laramie to start her PowerPoint, then text under my desk.

> You OK?

> Are you sick?

> The hearing is Thursday. WTF?!

By the fourth unanswered text I'm starting to feel like an idiot as memories of the weekend drench me in skin-crawling regret. Truman's fingers touching mine. Truman and I almost kissing over the bowling alley's ball return. The scene with Eli at Javier's. Of course Truman is being weird. He's freaking out, just like he did after I showed him the reunion site, terrified I'm going to drag him to Diamond Emporium to pick out rings. He's worried I'm going to ruin his stellar future, so he's acting like a scared, stupid guy who is utterly unable to deal.

But he wouldn't leave me hanging where the council meeting is concerned . . . would he? When last bell rings, I step into the hallway, hoping to find him waiting. Instead, I'm met by three of his teammates.

"Are you Skyler Finch?" asks a tall guy in an Alton Debate sweatshirt.

"Yes," I say, though it's clear they already know who I am. "What do you want?"

The second guy speaks over his friend's shoulder. "Do you know where Truman is?"

"No. Why would I?"

The girl with them looks me up and down. "Because you seem to be the reason he's MIA lately. We thought if anybody knew where he was, it'd be you."

"We'd appreciate it if you'd give him a little space and let him fulfill his obligations," the guy in the sweatshirt adds.

"Hold on. I don't have any say in what Truman does or doesn't do."

They look at each other, smirking.

"Where is he now?" Sweatshirt Guy presses. "We've got practice in ten minutes and no one has seen him all day."

"Why are we even asking her?" the other guy says. "Ever since Truman started hanging out with her, he's been in hiding. I wouldn't trust her to tell us a thing."

"Did you know we had a mock tournament Saturday?" the girl asks. "It was supposed to be prep for Belleville this weekend."

Saturday, Truman was with me. So according to these guys, the whole time we were together, he had somewhere else to be. My first reaction to this news is relief. At least up until then, Truman was making our presentation a priority.

But something deeper nags at me. The Truman I know would never skip something as important as debate. If he'd really wanted to, he could have put me down as another line item in his hyper-scheduled notebook and made it to his mock tournament. I'm torn between feeling honored he chose me and wondering whether there's something going on that I've missed.

Truman's teammates continue to glare, clearly expecting me to either provide an explanation or magically produce Truman.

"Look, he and I are presenting together at the city council meeting on Thursday. I have no idea where he is now, but after that he's all yours."

"Really?" The girl raises an eyebrow. "Far be it from me to be-grudge Truman a relationship with whomever he chooses, but if he's going to continue to skip out on his commitments, then it affects us all."

The more this girl talks, the clearer it gets that she has a crush. And it bothers me more than I want it to. The longer I stand here, the more the whole situation bothers me—the fact that Truman is missing in action. The fact that he's skipping commitments he would never in a million years skip. And the fact that I'm feeling all sorts of bothersome things, not just when I think about other people thinking we're together but when I think about him together with someone else.

"Truman and I are not in a relationship," I tell them. "When

Thursday is over you can have him back, I promise. Now I have to go."

They don't look happy, but at least they let me leave. I start down the stairs to the commons, passing Brynn and Anna Larkin on their way up.

"Don't forget pre-prom at Bella!" Brynn calls to me.

"Can't wait!" I reply. But she's not the one who really has my attention; I can't stop looking at Anna. This mousy girl following Brynn off into C Hall is so different from the confident entrepreneur she's destined to become—at least according to the reunion site.

Then it hits me: the notifications have stopped.

I should be grateful I'm not getting tormented every five minutes. I definitely should *not* be opening that link again—at least not until after the hearing on Thursday.

Who am I kidding? Ducking into the nearest bathroom, I pull up my Instagram. It's super boring now, just photos of blandly decorated rooms and rainbows with nauseating inspirational quotes superimposed over the top. Future Housewife Me doesn't even have a dog?

I really miss the dog.

When I pull up the reunion site, it's changed again. Bare-bones design. Much smaller than last time. It's basically just one album of carelessly dumped photos. I flip through, scanning faces. There's the Brynn and McKinley squad, looking rich and gorgeous. There's Eli, looking especially preppy and decidedly single. And there are a few other people whose circles would never normally overlap with Brynn's, looking like they stumbled into the wrong event. This appears to be a future version of the kind of A-list party that is only fun for hard-core A-listers. No "Where Are They Now?" section for absentees. No "In Memoriam" for those who are no longer with us. Jordan would write this reunion site off as a half-assed disgrace.

Which sparks the next question: Where *are* all my friends?

I swipe through again and can't find myself in any of the photos. No Jordan or Truman, either. And no Harper. Clearly, we didn't attend this reunion, and clearly, no one cared to follow up on what became of us. I scan the backgrounds, and it appears the event is at a bar. There's also nothing to indicate who organized it, though from the sheer number of Brynn and McKinley photos, it's probably safe to assume that this is their shindig.

The biggest question is, what happened to make the site change? I was expecting a transformation after the hearing. But maybe that's the point: In this version of the future, the garden could be gone, and whatever effects that has had simply have not been noted by whoever created this website. Or the garden could still be open and going strong, and the rest of us are celebrating our own separate reunion over there, having a much better time and using a different URL.

It could go any which way, which is exactly how my life feels right now.

By Wednesday I'm a lot less philosophical. Now I'm just really pissed at Truman. I even drove to his house yesterday afternoon, where I sat at the curb debating whether to knock on his door and demand to know why he's suddenly disappeared. Then I pictured his mother answering, and it was enough to get me to drive off.

But this is getting ridiculous. He asked me for help with the council meeting. He got me to sign up against every one of my better instincts. We are on the agenda, and now he's disappeared.

So I'm here, staking out his locker before school. It's harder than I'd thought it would be, just hanging around, trying to look like I'm not on a stakeout. And I don't even want to think about what would happen if Eli were to walk by. Truman's locker isn't on the usual morning route to show choir, so those chances are slim. But still. Things are delicate.

Time ticks away toward first bell, and still no Truman. Then, he's there, shirt rumpled and shoulders slumping as he makes his way down the hall. I hang back, waiting for him to pass the drinking fountains before making my move.

"Where have you been?"

"Skyler." He startles when he sees me. "What are you doing here?"

"Oh, come on. I've been calling and texting for two days. What the hell, Truman? Why would you leave me hanging like this?"

He pulls his backpack off and tucks into it the study guide he'd been carrying, next to his notebook with all the color-coded tabs.

"I've been sick," he says. But Truman is a terrible liar.

"I think the correct answer is that you were avoiding me. And you know how I know that? Because I am the queen of that game." Admitting this isn't easy. Just a couple of weeks ago, I was the one faking sickness to avoid seeing Truman.

He lifts his chin, fixing me with that down-the-nose stare.

"I actually was also grounded from my phone. So I never got your texts or calls, which follows that I shouldn't be accused of quote/unquote 'leaving you hanging.' Believe me, I am well aware of my obligations."

Close up, I can see shadows under his eyes and a dullness in his complexion. The part of me that cares for Truman more than I want to admit is telling me to let up—maybe he really isn't feeling well. But the freaking-out, desperate-to-not-screw-up-in-front-of-everyone part finds his obvious attempts at having nothing to do with me crazy making.

"Meet me after school to run through what we're going to say," I plead. "Please. Just once and I'll feel better."

"I have debate. My coach called my parents and told them I've been skipping practices. That's why I was grounded."

"Why have you been skipping?"

His face goes even more pale as he surveys the hallway. People are staring at us and whispering. I become aware that I'm leaning in a little too close and straighten up, stepping backward.

"I know things are weird. Okay? I get that. All I want is to be prepared."

"Fine," he says. "Can you meet me in the morning? I'll tell my parents I've got an early appointment with the college counselor."

"Yes. Thank you." But my lighter mood lasts only a moment. Over Truman's shoulder, I spy the girl from his debate team. She's coming toward us but stops when she sees me. Truman notices her a split second after I do. For a painful beat, no one moves. We are a Bermuda Triangle of awkwardness.

"All right then, I'm leaving. Wouldn't want you to be seen with me any more than you absolutely have to."

"Skyler, that's not—"

"No, it's okay. Once Thursday is over we can both get back to our regularly scheduled lives." I push past the girl, calling over my shoulder, "I'll see you tomorrow morning, Truman. Be there. No excuses!"

CHAPTER THIRTEEN

This is it.

In a little more than an hour, I'll be in the spotlight, front and center at city hall with all eyes on me.

Sitting in my car on the street outside the building, I pull the rearview mirror over to take one last look at myself. Mom loaned me one of her cashmere sweaters to wear with my black skirt and boots. She flat-ironed my hair and put it in a half updo. I even put on lipstick. The only thing about me that doesn't look on point is my forehead and chin, which have broken out in the kind of stress pimples that resist all attempts at concealer. It's the best I can do.

I close my eyes and fold my hands in my lap to keep from picking at the clear-polish manicure I gave myself an hour ago. This morning Truman met me before school like he said he would. We were both all business. We worked out what to say; then we went on to class. And after that I forced myself to stop worrying. I quit obsessing over the reunion site. I stopped thinking about Debate Girl and her crush on Truman. I blocked out memories of Eli and Brynn and the complicated reality that relationships are complicated. I put everything on pause to focus on the hearing. And as the hours went by, I found myself feeling more and more confident—even a little excited. I felt that way until two seconds ago, when I pulled up to find the parking lot clogged by news trucks.

I open my door to a jumble of voices. Two cameramen and two reporters, a guy in a suit and a woman with a helmet of blond hair, are strutting through the quickly growing crowd like they've mistaken a small town council meeting for some overseas war zone. As I look around to see what's causing so much excitement, a familiar voice rises above all the others.

"Hell no, let it grow!"

Standing on a bench off the front walk is Harper with a flower crown in her hair. In one hand she holds a hand-painted sign declaring, THIS PARADISE ISN'T YOUR PARKING LOT. In her other she wields a bullhorn. She chants into the bullhorn, lowering it just long enough to wave at me and give a thumbs-up.

The sight of her rattles me. When we talked about speaking, this wasn't exactly what I envisioned.

I'm heading over when Truman appears at my side.

"Did you know she was going to do this?" he demands. "Did you drive her here?"

He fidgets one foot to the other, like he's getting ready to run a race for which he's overtrained. I resist the temptation to reach out and force him to be still.

"First of all, Truman, hello. Second, no, I did not know Harper was planning on doing this."

"Wake up, people!" she shouts. "If Everest doesn't care enough to save a hundred-year-old garden, what makes you think they care about you? We need to protect the garden against corporate interests that are out to murder our history."

"What is she talking about?" Truman drops his head into his hands. "This isn't helping."

"You freaking out isn't helping either," I inform him just as Jordan emerges from around the side of the building.

"Wow," she says. "What happened here?"

"I was going to ask you the same thing," says Truman. "You didn't coordinate this?"

She flashes him a look of annoyance. "I don't coordinate *everything*, Truman. And I have no idea how Harper got here."

"Well, someone needs to stop her."

He makes a move toward the bench, and this time I do reach out. I clasp his arm and pull him toward me. "Hey, wait," I say, close to his ear so we can keep this between us. "She's fine. Leave her alone."

Our eyes meet; then we both turn back around, and I let out a groan as the situation veers from painful to personal. Eli is standing across the sidewalk, watching me. I drop my hand from Truman's arm and move away, but it's too late. I know how it looked.

"Can someone help me out?" The reporter in the suit approaches, consulting his phone. "I've got an agenda here, and it looks like two students are in the lineup. Who are Skyler Finch and Truman Alexander?"

I step forward, only to be nudged aside by Truman.

"I'm Truman Alexander. How can I help?"

The skin on my arms starts to prickle. It's impossible to miss that Truman didn't say *How can we help?*

"You two are speaking?" the reporter asks. "Can you share a bit about what you're planning to say?"

Before I can utter a sound, Truman has launched into a

highlights reel, speaking in that sanctimonious tone I'd kind-of sort-of pushed out of my memory because it's been awhile since I've been on the receiving end of it. There he is with that unblinking stare and that ridiculously convoluted vocab that makes him sound like a parody of some bow-tied college professor. And there's that creepy feeling down the back of my neck, served up with a side of wondering when the hell Truman is going to let me get a word in edgewise.

The reporter lets him talk for a couple of moments, then says, "Weren't your friends also planning to have the junior-senior prom at the Blessing garden? How much does that factor into your objections?"

"Prom is a trivial concern," Truman says.

Oh, hell no.

"Prom is far from trivial," I say. "It's an example of the kinds of celebrations that need a place like the Blessing garden."

"So you don't want Everest here?" the reporter asks.

"That's not what I said."

"What Skyler means is that we want an intelligent and thoughtful review of the options." Truman is talking over me again. At first, I think he's not aware he's doing it; then I realize it's 100 percent on purpose. Ultra-competitive Truman Alexander is suited up and on the field.

The female reporter scurries over. "I've got a counterpoint. When do you want him?"

"Now would be great," says the male reporter. The woman beckons to someone behind her, and a new person steps into the mix.

Eli.

I gape at him, mouthing a silent "What. The. F . . ." But he's glaring at Truman.

"This surge of interest in the Blessing property appears to be student-led," says the male reporter. "But not everyone supports the effort to save it. I understand you're on the other side?"

Eli's gaze never leaves Truman's as he says, "I just think we have somebody coming in that is going to give a lot of people jobs, so I'm confused why it's all of a sudden so important to potentially mess that up."

"There's nothing sudden about it," says Truman. "Some people simply don't want to see our history bulldozed without a fight."

"Whose history?" Eli looks around dramatically. "The only person I know who has any real history with the place is you. Didn't your family own it?"

Now Truman is glaring at me, while the reporter practically licks his lips at this new layer of drama. Behind him, people are making their way inside, and it's my dad who comes to the rescue.

"Did you get a release to interview these kids?" he asks. "They're minors, so by law their parents need to grant permission before you put them on air or online."

The reporter slinks away, sputtering about the "free press." Meanwhile, I can see Mom coaxing Harper down from her perch, and I find myself getting swept into the building along with Truman, Eli, and Jordan.

Eli bumps Truman's shoulder, hard. "You need to watch it, bro."

"Is that a threat?" says Truman.

"Take it however you want, since you seem to love fighting so much."

"You know what would be great?" Jordan breaks in. "It would be great, Eli, if you weren't trying to destroy my prom."

"Sorry, Jordan, but it's kind of hard to care about prom when I've got Debate Geek messing with my girlfriend behind my back."

Jordan turns to me like, *Yeah, Skyler,* and now they're all glaring at me, like this whole fiasco started with that damned promposal, when it really began with Truman dropping his bombshell about Everest taking the garden, which wouldn't have happened if he wasn't trying to add "community activist" to his college applications.

So technically this is all Truman's fault. Or maybe it's the fault of that stupid website, which took everything I thought I knew about my friends and my future and scrambled it up like a Big Sky omelet. I can't believe I'm actually standing here watching Truman Alexander, my maybe future husband, and Eli, my probably soon-to-be ex-boyfriend, go at it.

"Your love life isn't my problem," Truman informs Eli.

"Oh yeah? How about we talk about whose problem it is?"

Eli squares up, ready to fight. Truman backs up like this isn't his circus or his monkeys. Jordan is glaring at me like I've finally screwed things up just as badly as she always thought I would.

Harper turns and starts back for the door.

"If all you're going to accomplish is yelling at each other, then I'm going back outside," she says. "They can't stop me from demonstrating. It's my right as an American citizen."

With one alarmingly swift movement, Truman snatches away her bullhorn.

"Can I be honest, Harper? Your demonstration is not helpful in the slightest."

Harper freezes, as if she'd been slapped. "Whatever," she says. "I'm trying to raise awareness. I can shout louder anyway."

Truman plants himself in front of the door, blocking her path.

"Seriously, Harper. The best thing you can do right now is just sit down and be quiet."

"Okay, that's enough," I say. "Come with me."

I grab him by the shirtsleeve and drag him deeper into the lobby, searching for someplace private. I try the first door I find, only to encounter a janitor's closet. The next one opens into a dark conference room. I pull him in, turn on the light, and let everything out.

"What is your problem, Truman? You're acting like a complete asshole!"

"I'm trying to prevent Harper from sabotaging us."

"She's passionate about this. Let her be passionate."

"It's too much. Carrying on like she's at some anti-war protest? Talking about murdering history? The last thing we need is to look overemotional. This is my future we're talking about!"

"*Your* future? I might believe you were that self-centered if I didn't think you had other reasons for being here tonight."

He squints at me. "I don't know what you mean."

I pull out my phone and pull up the photo I took of the angel sculptures in the garden. I thrust the screen into his face.

"I saw these at the prom committee meeting you missed."

"What do they have to do with anything?"

"I have a feeling a lot more than you want to admit. Whether we win or not tonight, you can still put this whole garden-saving project on your applications. So why are you being so intense? Are you sure there aren't other reasons you want to save it?"

"This isn't an exercise in sentimentality," he says. "I'm in this to win it."

"Oh, okay. So you're *this* worked up about one extra line item on your résumé. Got it."

He unpuffs a bit. "Not that my family issues are your business, but fine. Yes, I have memories of my grandfather that make me

147

want to preserve it. *Real* memories that mean something, not just some warm fuzzies about Christmas parties with my friends."

There's a tightness at the edge of his voice. I put my phone away and regroup.

"Fine, Harper needs to cool it. But you didn't have to humiliate her like that."

"I was just being honest."

"No, that's not an excuse. You can't hurt people, then say you were *just being honest*. You're so in love with the sound of your own voice that you barely let anybody else get a word out. Like with that reporter just now."

"He was trying to trap you."

"And I could have handled it. You talked me into speaking tonight, but then it's like you have no intention of actually letting me speak. Are you going to talk over me once we're up at the podium too?"

"You seem to think I deliberately set out to be hurtful," he says.

"Whether you intend it or not, that's the effect. The first day we met, you all but told me I wasn't smart enough for the gifted school. You might not think I'm as brilliant as you are, Truman, but I at least try to consider other peoples' feelings."

He lowers his nose until he's no longer looking down, but right at me. There's anger in his eyes now, and hurt.

"I have never disputed your intelligence. And I'm all too aware how considerate you are. I remember you telling me you could have gone to the gifted school but didn't because you didn't want to be a freak. You assume to know me, but you have no idea how much a friendly gesture would have meant back then. Or even just a second chance."

"It's difficult to give someone a second chance when they

seem to be set on making everything about them. This is about way more than your list of achievements. If we lose tonight, things could happen to people I love—things that can't even be a possibility."

"I have no idea why you're so convinced of that," he says. "When we started, you were nowhere near as emotional as you are now. So what's different?"

I pull myself up taller, preparing to enter forbidden territory.

"The last time I brought this up, you couldn't handle it."

"This isn't about that website is it?"

"Don't look at me like that. I know you think about it too. If you hadn't seen the two of us together there, we could have saved ourselves a massive amount of awkwardness."

"I guess I was hoping it had gone away. Or that you'd stopped checking it." Truman peers at me from under a shock of dark hair. "Why would you keep checking it?"

"Because I'm human? Because the thing keeps sending me notifications? And because it keeps changing from when I first showed it to you. It's showing bad things for Harper now—things I'm worried could be more likely if we lose tonight."

"This is crazy." He runs a hand through his hair. "I don't want to talk about this."

"I sort of have to wonder why, though. You're the one with the color-coded notebook, planning everything in your life out to the nth degree. I would think you'd be happy to have one more item out of the way."

"It's one thing to plan for academic success. It's another thing entirely to know you're looking at the person you're going to be stuck with for the rest of your life."

Everything inside me freezes—my breath, my blood, the part

of my brain that has become expert at arguing with Truman. For a moment, I'm back on his porch, painfully aware of my clothes, my hair, the way the entirety of me seems to meet with utter disapproval, not just from his mother but from him, too.

"So I'm not good enough?"

"No," he says. "I mean, yes. You are. . . . I just . . . I don't know how to talk about this, Skyler. I plan all these things out for a reason: So I can get into the right school, lay the groundwork for my career . . ."

"And I'm not worthy to be a part of all that. I'm not ambitious enough, or accomplished enough, or *enough* enough for you. And I bet your parents agree. Don't they?"

Any other person would come up with an excuse about how their mom and dad are old-fashioned or not good at first impressions, even if it was a lie. Because normal people don't prize some idealized concept of honesty over the feelings of their friends. But Truman doesn't even try to deny that his parents dislike me. Instead, he says, "You don't want to be a part of my family anyway. You said as much. So why does it matter what they think?"

"Because you think it too. Why else would you pick a time to work with me when you were supposed to have debate?"

He blinks. "How did you know that?"

"Your friends told me about the mock tournament. They think it's my fault you skipped it, and I guess it is. Because if your parents thought you were at debate, then they wouldn't know you were at my house. You said once that I was captivating. Well, apparently I'm captivating enough to hook up with, just as long as it's a secret."

"That's nice coming from someone who for years has acted like it would be social suicide to be seen with me." His voice drips venom, but I catch the slightest hint of a flush in his cheeks. "I didn't see you rushing out to acknowledge quote/unquote 'hooking up' with me either."

"Right, because I'm so very shallow and superficial. You know what? We talked about this already, and you couldn't handle it. I was stupid for ever showing you that website."

"Let the record show that it was you who used that word, not me."

A sharp ache twists in my stomach. I bury my face in my hands.

"This is a disaster. How are we going to work together if we can't stop hurting each other?"

"I don't know. Since you're so big on seeing into the future, maybe you could consult a Magic Eight Ball for the answer?"

He lets the words hang between us. I could fill the space with another, more cutting remark. When we used to argue in class, when things would start veering into personal territory, I would sometimes wonder how far it could go. If I really wanted, I could find out now. But something inside of me has collapsed. Truman and I have pushed too far. I don't want to do it anymore.

"You're right," I tell him. "Showing you that website was a mistake, and so was everything else that's happened between us. Tonight, say whatever you want, and I'll do the same. But alone. We're not a team, no matter what some website says—not now, not ever."

CHAPTER FOURTEEN

Swiping away tears before they can ruin my makeup, I walk out of the meeting room and make my way into the council chambers. The room is nearly packed. I spot Eli's dad in the corner with a group of people in business suits, all of them super polished and surprisingly young. They must be the Everest team. Eli sits a few rows over with some other people from school. And then there's Jordan's social media brigade. They're easy to spot, with their TEAM GARDEN: BE A BLESSING buttons.

I wade through the third row to the seat Jordan and Harper have saved for me.

"Everything okay?" Mom leans up from where she and Dad are sitting in the row just behind. "What was all that about with Truman?"

I shake off the urge to flinch at the sound of his name and shrug. "It was just Truman being Truman. I told him to try behaving more like a human being for once."

"You don't have to punish him just for my sake," Harper says. She tugs at the sleeves of her sweater, then checks the basket of marigolds under her seat. "I don't feel like he meant to be mean. You can go sit with him if you want."

This is classic Harper, able to feel sorry even for someone who hurt her. But she doesn't know how petrified I am right now, not just by the idea of what I'm about to do, but by what I've just done: fired my partner and ensured that when I step into the spotlight I'll be doing it alone.

"Trust me," I tell her. "I'll do a better job if I'm not with Truman."

I look over my shoulder at my parents, and their smiles give me confidence. Behind them, at the very back, stands Truman, silently mouthing his speech. No one stands with him, and when I scan the crowd, I don't see his parents. Sympathy pokes at me in spite of everything, and I'm almost grateful when seven people file onto the stage at the front of the room. One of the council members is Fia Reyes's dad, and he starts thumbing through a stack of papers as if prepping for his own personal courtroom drama. The mayor comes in last, smiling like it's utterly normal for this many people to pack a Thursday night hearing. She bangs her gavel and we all stand for the Pledge of Allegiance.

Thus begins what must be the most deadly dull forty-five minutes I've ever lived through. First up on the agenda: a shopping center wants to expand its parking lot. Some guy from the city drones on about easements and flood plains. Some guy with a house behind the development is concerned about his property value. Some of the council members think the improvements are overdue. Others want more information. As I listen to the blah blah of engineer's reports and asphalt contracts, I tell myself that fighting with Truman could have affected the near future, too. Maybe it's all been resolved and the garden isn't even on the agenda anymore.

Just when I've started to think that's actually what's happened,

the mayor says, "Our final piece of business is the zoning and imminent domain request by Everest Outfitters."

The room wakes up as the Everest people gather at the podium. Their presentation is a bunch of corporate BS with bad
PowerPoint.

Okay. I know I can do better than that.

Next up is one of the volunteers, a woman with stooped shoulders and a voice scratchy with age. She talks about knowing Mr.
Blessing, about how much he loved the garden, and how she'd
committed to working there after he died because it made her
happy and she knew it would make other people happy too.

Out of the four others who speak, only one is anti-garden. It's
clear that the place is loved. And it makes me think Truman and I
might not have to speak after all.

I can't resist checking, just to be sure. I try to pull up the reunion site on my phone.

Internal Error

I try again. The browser takes less time to load but still pulls up
the same black screen. Same error message.

Refresh. Reload. No change.

Damn.

"What are you doing?" Jordan whispers.

"Nothing," I say. It'd be easy to blame the error on my phone
being in a slow death spiral, or crappy Wi-Fi; we are in the bowels
of city hall, after all. But what if the reunion site is spinning in
some sci-fi void like a held breath, ready to update after Truman
and I have made our speeches?

The mayor beams out at the crowd.

"Last but certainly not least, Truman Alexander and Skyler Finch."

Jordan glances at me, and everybody realizes at once that we never really figured out how this was going to work. I force myself to stay put as Truman walks up the aisle. Harper rises to join him, and there's a moment where they meet and it's clear Truman's not sure what to do. Harper scurries past to place a marigold in front of each of the council members. They thank her; then everyone waits while she makes her way back to her seat.

Truman stands at the microphone with his notebook. He clears his throat.

"Lack of thorough and thoughtful planning in urban development has detrimental impacts on communities that might not be felt immediately, but should be considered before decisions are made that permanently remove assets which have proven beneficial for decades."

My heart sinks. This is not the presentation we agreed to. If I listen closely, I can maaaaaybe hear a bit of what we worked on in there, but it's getting buried alive under a mess of esoteric crap. Truman is talking a mile a minute, spitting out vocab bombs like he ate a thesaurus for dinner, talking with his nose at a forty-five-degree angle to the ceiling. And his voice. Oh my God, his voice is so *Truman Alexander* that I have to fight the urge to scratch at the millions of tiny insects now crawling up and down my arms.

I'm afraid to look at the council members, terrified to see their reactions. I force myself anyway and am surprised to see them actually listening. Maybe it's just me who's not connecting because Truman and I have all this history, and I'm obviously not objective, so perhaps I should calm down and let him do his thing.

Except one of the council members just checked his phone.

Another is watching a video of baby otters. Still Truman keeps talking. The smiles on the other council members are wearing thin. One woman starts to nod off.

"In conclusion," Truman says, "many factors are at play where the Blessing property is concerned, and there are many alternatives to consider. We should not be so shortsighted in the quest for economic improvement that we overlook a better solution. Thank you."

As he leaves the podium, the only sound is the rasp of someone with a stubborn cough. I stand and wipe my palms on my skirt while Mom gives my arm one last squeeze.

My shoulder brushes Truman's in the narrow aisle. I should give him the courtesy of a "good job" or even a polite nod, but I'm afraid it will signal to the council that I'm going to be just as disastrous. Every person up there looks like they've been through one root canal and are dreading round two.

I fold the speech I'd prepared into a tiny square and tuck it inside the palm of my hand. I pull the microphone down to my height and begin.

"Do you remember me? Do you remember my friends? If you went to the Christmas parties at the Blessing mansion, then you saw us when we were just learning to walk. You watched us playing as grade schoolers, and you may have even seen one or two of us experiencing our first kisses. Those parties were more than just parties, they were magic.

"So much has changed since Mr. Blessing died and Eagle Mills left, but that garden has stayed the same. And for some of us, it's offered a real reason to hang on. If you're looking for a place to build our future, don't tear down our past. We need both."

I'm speaking from the heart, taking the time to look each council member in the eye, and the difference between now and three minutes ago is stark in the best possible way. No one checks their phone. No one yawns. They're sitting forward in their seats. Some are even taking notes. I'm rocking the room, and even though I know this, the applause that erupts at the end hits like a massive wave, bringing with it an almost euphoric giddiness as the adrenaline my body had been storing up gets released all at once. From out in the audience, Dad gives a thumbs-up. Mom beams. Jordan and Harper hug each other with excitement.

I'm ready to ride the wave back to my seat, when a voice stops me.

"Miss Finch, would you remain at the podium, please?"

It's Fia's dad. As I pivot back around, my heart starts to pound. Mr. Reyes thanks the Everest people for their "diligent, comprehensive work." He thanks everyone else for their "dedication to the community." He says he wants to "engage in further dialogue about this issue." Then he looks right at me.

"Miss Finch, the city has experienced a decrease in revenue due to unemployment and falling property values. What are your ideas for replacing the funds we're projected to lose if we don't go ahead with the plan as it was described tonight?"

"I . . . I don't . . ." I feel like someone cracked my brains into a bowl and started going at them with a whisk. *This right here is exactly why I don't put myself out there. I fooled everybody for a minute, but now they're going to know I really have no idea what I'm doing.*

All I can do is stand in front of all these people and stammer. Until Truman appears at my side.

"We've calculated at least two scenarios where Everest could do everything they say they want to do without tearing out the Blessing garden," he says.

When Mr. Reyes takes his eyes off me, it's like getting released from a choke hold. Truman proceeds to break apart Everest's arguments, point by point, in that self-important voice I've hated for the past five years.

If I could hug him right now, I would.

Mr. Reyes looks annoyed. "But it's awfully late in the game for objections. There isn't any money left. And the volunteers, including the groundskeeper, are all in their . . . ahem . . . later years."

"I'm a volunteer!" Harper stands up. "I bet I could get at least ten other people from school to volunteer too!"

The determination on her face gives me hope. Maybe Harper will be the one who convinces them, after all. Back up on the dais, the other council members are nodding at this new idea: maybe it could be a community garden.

"It's too late for that," snaps Mr. Reyes. "The way Mr. Blessing's final wishes were arranged, when funds run out for the mansion and garden, they go to the city."

"He was trusting you to take care of them," Truman says. "Not tear them out."

"So why didn't he trust them to his own family? Does anyone have any plans to buy it?"

Truman's back stiffens. Years of arguing have taught me to recognize when he's backed into a corner. Truman may be a maddening know-it-all, but no one should have to explain their family's dirty laundry to a roomful of strangers.

The mayor finally comes to his rescue.

"For whatever reason, Mr. Blessing decided to take those decisions out of his family's hands." She checks her watch, letting her gavel hover. "And I don't know about all of you, but I'd like to get home to my own family. Can we have a vote?"

It happens almost insultingly fast. Next to me, Truman stands

158

like a stone, while one by one, these people who seemed like they might actually have been ready to give us a win, vote the exact opposite way.

"I do want to add that I know the high school has been planning its prom at the garden," the mayor says. "Is there a need to break ground right away?"

"We'd be happy to wait until after prom to start demolition," says someone from the Everest team.

The mayor smiles warmly at me. "See? You can still have your party there. Make sure to make it extra special, okay? Maybe the city can send over a cake."

If I weren't in public, I'd let loose a string of choice words to express exactly how I feel about her stupid cake. People are getting to their feet to leave, but I refuse to move. If I stay right here, maybe the last two hours will somehow have a different outcome—or the outcome that did happen won't become reality. If I'm frozen, maybe I can freeze time.

Truman glares at the city seal on the wall at the front of the room. The notebook he'd been clutching has taken on a slightly warped look.

I turn to him. "Well, that was . . . insulting?"

Truman purses his lips. He uses both hands to straighten out his notebook.

"I appreciated your help tonight, Skyler. Your speech was very good."

"Obviously not good enough."

"Maybe if you'd had a few more facts?"

"Maybe if you'd had a few more feels?"

His jaw twitches and his expression closes off, like shutters snapping over a window.

"Well, you were right about one thing. I can still put this on my résumé, so it's a success in the long run. Now I have a debate tournament to prepare for. I'll see you in school."

Without another word, he walks out of the room. I watch him leave, then face the front again. All but one of the council members left the marigolds Harper gave them behind. The one person who took his was the one who spent the hearing on his phone. I want to race after him, grab the pot away, and break it over his head.

I walk back into the gallery, which is now a jumble of empty seats. Harper sits in her chair, head low, pulling apart a seed pod from one of her transplanted flowers. Jordan sits next to her with an arm around her shoulders.

"I'm sorry," I say, grabbing Harper's hands. "We were so close. This whole thing is completely unfair."

"It's not your fault," she says. Marigold seeds spill through our fingers into her lap, forming a small pile in her skirt.

"I'm just . . ." I can't think of anything else to say. I don't want to think that this whole night was a waste, but what other conclusion is there? In the end, Truman and I worked as a team and it still didn't do any good. "I'm just really sorry."

I wait for her to tell me about the wisdom of the universe— that some things just aren't meant to be. Instead, she stands and brushes the seeds off onto the floor.

"I'm tired. And I have a lot of homework to do."

"I can take you," I say.

"Or I can," Jordan adds.

"Sky's mom and dad already offered," says Harper. "Thanks, and no offense, but I don't feel like talking. I just want to go home."

CHAPTER FIFTEEN

"I am really starting to regret that I ever thought up this promposal contest," Jordan says in the yearbook office after school. "Mr. Kimura told me he wants to make sure we're being 'safe and respectful of others' property.' I guess the people who built Donor's Square are mad about Darius's banner fail on their giant penis. Hello, have they looked at that thing? A little paint should be the least of their worries."

I adjust the layout on the page I'm editing, only partly listening. Last night I barely slept because I kept running the council meeting over and over in my head. Then this morning Eli spent show choir at the opposite end of the room, and Harper didn't even show up until halfway through class. She sat on her phone all through lunch, hunched over and irritable. And in English, Truman greeted me with a curt "Skyler" that didn't even include one of his super-formal head nods. I dragged myself to last bell and would love to go home, but we're behind deadline, so I agreed to put in extra hours with Jordan, making sure the sports section gets done.

"And then there's drama about the judging," she continues. "I keep telling people I'm not part of it, but they're complaining that you and Eli are probably going to win because we're friends."

"Oh no. Damn!" I sit back in my chair and cover my face with my hands.

"It's not that big a deal. People will get over it."

"No, it's not that. I saved the wrong version and lost all the work I just did. Ugh . . ." I pull off my glasses and rub my eyes, feeling close to tears for the millionth time this week.

"Hey." Jordan puts an arm around my shoulder. "What's wrong?"

"I mean, isn't it obvious? We lost last night."

"No, we didn't. We get to have prom over there. That's all you, Sky. You were amazing."

"But prom isn't the problem. It's after. They're going to tear it all out."

"We did the best we could. You can't beat yourself up."

"But what about Harper? She was so quiet today."

"Harper is allowed to be upset."

"I know, but the reunion site . . ."

Jordan shakes her head. "You have to forget about that thing. It's not good for you to be thinking about it all the time."

"Well, then why was I shown it at all? In some version of the future, Harper is gone and so is the garden. Maybe those two things aren't related. But if there's even the slightest chance that they are, and if there's a chance I can help, then I have to try."

"Having a garden isn't going to magically change her brain chemistry," Jordan tells me.

"But what happens around her can make things worse. And when I first opened up the site we were all there, so I'm thinking it has to be connected, and—"

"Skyler, listen to yourself. You really are obsessed now."

I want to protest that I am not obsessed, except I've been checking the site every ten minutes all day long. The new future I see there shows the reunion at a swanky restaurant, everyone mingling with cocktails. In this future, Alton High is now Everest Academy; apparently all those promises of economic success came true, and people were grateful enough to rename our school. Like the website before it, this one doesn't have information on individuals, just a gallery of photos. So all I can do is scour one after the other, searching for hints of what happened to me and my friends. A back of the head here, a mostly obscured side view there, of someone who could or could not be Jordan or Harper or Truman . . . that's all there is. Which is not reassuring in the least. In fact, it's the perfect recipe for obsessing, which only makes me more frustrated with Jordan.

"I wasn't aware that wanting to help a friend equals obsessing," I say. "Excuse me for being worried."

"Are you sure that's what it is? Or are you just upset you didn't win?"

"I don't understand the question."

"In case you hadn't noticed, you can be pretty competitive. I swear, sometimes you make even Truman look laid-back."

"It's not competitiveness, it's concern."

"Mm-hmm." She gets up and goes back to her own computer.

Once again, I've stepped wrong on the eggshell floor of Jordan's patience. Normally, I'd take a step backward—try to tread lighter. But this time I don't.

"What if something bad happens? We've already seen it once. If it happens again and we didn't do everything we could to help, I'd never forgive myself. Or you. Because if we're being honest here, Jordan, it looks to me like you don't care."

And that? Turns out that was the absolute wrong thing to say. Jordan whirls around in her seat.

"Screw you, Skyler. I care, which is why I'm not getting stuck in the past or the future. It's not good for any of us. You have to make the best of whatever happens now."

"But . . ."

"No. We could all get hit by a semi tomorrow. The roof of this school could cave in and wipe everybody out. The next time you open that link, we could all be gone. Now is all we have."

"And right now you still have your prom the way you want it, so you're happy. I get it."

She keeps her eyes on her computer screen. "I'm going to pretend you didn't say that. We are going dress shopping tomorrow and I want to still like you, Sky."

"Fine." I put my glasses back on and return to my layout, shocked by the way both of us just behaved. How did I get to the point where my best friend is threatening to not like me anymore?

We work in silence until we become aware of a third person in the room. Harper is over in the corner in her show choir dress, flipping through old yearbooks. When she sees I've noticed her, she waves.

"You ready?"

"Oh, right." I'd almost forgotten we have a performance at the nursing home—it's something we do once a month for community service hours. Harper and I had planned to go over together. "Let me go change."

I duck into the bathroom and put on the purple dress with its sequined bodice, balancing against the sink to buckle up my regulation nude jazz heels. Jordan is still at her computer when Harper and I head out for the parking lot.

"See you guys tomorrow," she calls after us. "I'm picking you up at nine, so be ready!"

Harper turns to me once we're on the road.

"The vibes between you and Jordan back there were super tense. Are you guys okay?"

I sigh as I switch lanes. Harper's always been the peacemaker, but we were talking about her so I can't really go into details.

"Eli is giving me the silent treatment," I say, instead.

She nods. "I thought something felt off in first bell."

"He's mad about last night, and we're supposed to shop for dresses tomorrow, but I don't know if I even have a prom date anymore."

"Eli wouldn't ditch you for prom."

"You're right, he wouldn't. It would look bad, and if there's anything Eli hates, it's looking less than amazing."

"Well, if you do need someone to go with, you can come with me and Kiran."

"Thanks."

We ride a ways, and while I don't want to talk about last night specifically, there are so many things I *do* want to talk about. So much with my friends has been on the surface—I can see that now. And some things we've avoided altogether.

"I've been wanting to ask you something for a long time," I say. "But I've been scared."

"Why?"

"I guess I didn't want to upset you. I maybe even kind of didn't want to hear the answer. I didn't know if it was my business or if it was too private."

"You can ask. I'll tell you if it's too private."

"Okay, well . . . when you went to the hospital . . . when you

165

cut yourself badly enough that you had to go, why did you do that?"

For a minute, I'm not sure she's going to answer. She runs the hem of her dress between her fingers, bunching it up, then smoothing it back out again. I'm about to tell her to forget I asked, it's not important, when she says, "Remember when you used to say I was all woo-woo about everything? You were like, 'I don't know how you can be so happy all the time.' And I didn't know either. It was just easy, maybe because I had all these good things in my life. But then things started to get taken away—my dad's job, my family the way it used to be before my brother screwed up. I felt like all the good things were disappearing. And the me that knew how to be happy all the time started to disappear too. I had to psych myself up every day, first to find that version of me, and eventually to even just do regular things like get out of bed and brush my teeth. After a while, I started to feel like I just wanted to be gone completely."

"But you're better now, right? You don't want to be gone anymore?"

She pushes her skirt down over her knees and tugs her hair away from her face before letting it fall down her back.

"How am I supposed to answer that? If I say I can't promise I won't feel that way again, everybody will freak out and assume that I *will*. All I can tell you is that I'm working on it. And I don't feel that way now."

"Would you tell me if you do again? Please?"

"Would it keep you from worrying so much?"

"If we're being honest, probably not."

This makes her laugh, which makes me laugh too. Laughing feels good after a day of being tense and watchful and annoyed with idiot politicians who would rather bow down to some big company than save something special for their community. This is one of Harper's best gifts: making everything seem a little lighter, and now that I have her back, I realize how much I've missed it.

When we get to the nursing home, we meet up with the rest of the show choir in the dining hall. Eli is here, being his usual sunny self—just not to me. He doesn't seem to want to acknowledge me at all, and he doesn't have to, really, since he's in the front row and I'm in back with the chorus. Today, being in the back gives me a good look at how everything he does is just a little over-the-top. Eli is a born performer—that's obvious. But then so is Harper. And while Harper gives herself to the audience, Eli feeds off them. It's entertaining for sure. It's also a little exhausting.

Twenty minutes into a half-hour set, we finally end up next to each other, and he utters the first words he's said to me in twenty-four hours.

"Skyler, smile."

I keep my jazz hands up while the audience applauds. "What?" I say through my teeth.

"Seriously," he whispers before dancing away, "you need to smile more."

Afterward, everyone gathers in the nursing home foyer to mingle with the residents. And Eli is the star once again, handing out hugs and basking in praise. I flash back to his promposal—how it felt like some sort of Broadway production. Then I flash forward to what a future with Eli could look like. I see the two of us, popular and pretty, the perfect couple with a perfect life. I also see constant pressure to stay popular, pretty, and perfect.

All that, plus nonstop barbershop quartet.

I don't need a magic website to tell me: That's another girl's future. It's not mine.

CHAPTER SIXTEEN

" Let's color coordinate."

Jordan flips through a rack of gowns, considering and rejecting in rapid-fire rhythm. We drove an hour to the Galleria because Alton has nothing but a couple of old-lady clothing stores and a bridal shop, and nobody wants to look like a bridesmaid at prom. So now we are crammed into the Schöne Boutique with tons of other people from school, practically drowning in chiffon, sequins, and satin.

Jordan selects an ice-blue dress with crystal straps and holds it up to me. "Or we could do a theme. Maybe jewels? You could be diamonds."

I put the dress back. It's beautiful, but I'm just not feeling it. "Maybe we should wear trash bags instead. That would fit the mood."

"No, we're doing this right." She moves to a rack with more dramatic options. "I know some people are upset about the garden, but we're going to have a good time. It'll be like prom and a farewell party all rolled up in one."

"More like a funeral."

"If that's the attitude you want, then enjoy your misery. But we are way behind if we need alterations or whatever, so if you don't find something today, that trash bag might be your only choice. Harper, how about this one?" Jordan holds up a deep-green gown with a layered skirt. "It would look great with your hair."

Harper looks up from her phone. "It's strapless."

"Oh . . . right." Jordan puts the dress back.

At the last shop we went to, Harper tried on a dress that exposed a noticeable scar on her shoulder. But that's not what really has her down. She told us her doctors are working on finding the right medications for her, and the one she's been on has made her gain weight. She never used to be body conscious, but with dress after dress not fitting the way she wants because things are shaped differently than she's used to, her mood has been steadily deteriorating. Now her Harper spark is nowhere to be found.

Jordan walks past a couple more racks, then stops with her hands on her hips. "Well, I'm trying something on." She grabs a red dress in one hand, Harper in the another. "Come on, you're going to help zip up. Sky, you wait here and tell us what you think."

While the two of them disappear into a dressing room, I check out a sale rack. There's nothing good on it, so I wander, looking at price tags and trying not to cringe. Mom told me not to worry too much when she handed me her credit card, but still. I don't want to give her a heart attack when she sees the bill.

The bell on the front door of the shop sounds like it's attached to the collar of a manic cat thanks to so many people going in and out. Everybody we know is at the Galleria today, so I guess it shouldn't be a surprise when I almost run right into Brynn.

She's picking up her dress from the alterations counter, the clerk handing her a fuchsia gown so stunning that I can tell it's stunning even when it's in a clear garment bag. Brynn's feet are buried in a pile of other bags—bags from the shoe store, bags from the luxury-brand makeup place, bags from some of the most expensive shops in the mall, and she and McKinley are chatting loudly about their spring break plans.

I freeze and start backing up, praying they won't see me. I can practically hear all the things Brynn will say if they do: *Don't forget about Bella! Do you have your dress yet? Can I see it? How's Eli?*

I creep backward until I've backed myself into a circular area surrounded by mirrors. There's a carpet-covered pedestal right in the middle, and I don't stop until I've backed right into whoever is standing on it.

"Ow! Hey!"

I turn around, and who should be there, rubbing her ribs where I accidentally elbowed her, but the girl from Truman's debate team—the one who cornered me after English. She's wearing a pink dress, and a woman kneels at her feet, pinning up the hem. Another woman stands nearby, supervising.

"Oh my gosh, I'm sorry," I say. The girl just stares at me. I give her what I hope looks like a friendly smile. "Hi?"

The woman standing next to her does that thing moms do, where she gets all delighted to see one of her daughter's friends but doesn't realize that the person she's talking to isn't really friends with her daughter at all.

"Hey there!" she says. "Are you one of Riley's friends?"

"Um . . ." I glance back at the girl—Riley, I guess her name is—and tilt my head in an extra apology before saying, "We go to the same school. I'm Skyler."

"Skyler." The woman shakes my hand. "Nice to meet you! I'm Riley's mom. Are you shopping for prom?"

"Yes. I'm here with some other friends. But I haven't found anything yet." I don't know why I'm volunteering this information. Maybe because I sort of wish I'd let my own mom come along. She wanted to, but it would have meant coming later because she had to work this morning at the clinic. Jordan wanted to leave right after breakfast, so that's what we did. Now here I am, chatting with the mom of someone who clearly doesn't like me very much.

I spot a navy dress on a nearby display. It has lace along the neckline and cutouts that show a little skin, but not too much. The skirt is great too. It's got this sort of 1950s retro thing going on.

I point over Riley's shoulder. "I was actually coming over here to try on that one."

"That is beautiful," says Riley's mom. She plucks the dress from the rack and hands it to me. "I saw some shoes that would look perfect with it. Wait here."

She takes off toward the shoe section, and I'm left with Riley on her pedestal.

"That dress is really pretty," I tell her.

"Thanks," she says.

"So . . . how is debate going? Is Truman going to practices again? When's your next tournament?"

"Next week."

"Oh. Great."

She raises an eyebrow. "You know he's taking me to prom, right?"

I start stammering. "Um . . . well, see, I did not know that. Truman and I don't really talk anymore, so . . ."

171

It's true, at least as far as the last forty-eight hours are concerned. Yesterday in English, Truman was a man of very few words, even when Ms. Laramie opened the floor for discussion of whether Mary Shelley's Frankenstein was a cold-hearted God figure or a victim of his own obsessions. Truman left class as soon as the bell rang, and I haven't heard from him since.

Riley doesn't have much to say about the fact that Truman and I aren't talking, and thank goodness her mom comes back quickly. She hands me a pair of rockabilly heels. They are red with white polka dots. They are adorable.

"I guessed your size. But they have more if you need something bigger."

"Wow. Thank you!" I glance over at the register. Brynn has finally left. And across the shop, I see Jordan's head above the racks, searching for me. "Well!" I say to Riley. "I hope you have fun at prom with Truman. Tell him I said good luck on your tournament next week." Then I make my escape.

Jordan looks unspeakably elegant in a body-skimming red gown. And she's managed to get Harper into a dress too—a floral maxi with gauzy long sleeves. Harper twirls in the dress, laughing at her reflection in the mirror.

Jordan eyes the dress in my arms.

"I love it." She shoves me into a fitting room. "Put it on and get back out here, lady."

Slipping on the dress feels like slipping on a new outlook. The material against my skin, the act of getting dressed up, lifts my spirits. It needs a little taking in here and there, but Mom should be able to handle that. And Riley's mom was right, the shoes are perfect. Looking at myself, I see someone who doesn't need a date now, or ten years from now. I'll be fine on my own.

Back in the showroom, the three of us stand side by side to admire ourselves in the mirror. We look beautiful, and so much older than we did just minutes ago.

"We're going to have a great time," Jordan says to our reflection. She puts one arm around Harper, the other around me, pulling us both close. "Right? No matter what."

CHAPTER SEVENTEEN

"If this is your sine and this is your cosine, what is your hypotenuse?"

"Um . . ." I roll my neck to try and work out the kinks after spending my entire lunch hour cooped up in a music wing practice room being tutored by Lydia Hodge. Lydia is a sophomore math prodigy, and more than qualified to help me improve my trig scores. Still, none of it makes sense. Shapes and numbers are sliding all over the page, and I'm to the point where I can't even start a problem, let alone solve it.

"This really isn't that hard," Lydia tells me. "Maybe if you look it over on your own, it will start to come together?"

"Maybe . . ."

"Look, I need to go," she says. "Try more problems tonight. I can meet again tomorrow and go over them if you want."

I feel bad. It's not Lydia's fault I seem to have a complete mental block for trigonometry. And it's not her future on the line if we can't stop my grade from its crash-and-burn trajectory. I play a few ominous chords on the practice room piano as she leaves. We met here because it's quiet and private, now I am seriously considering hiding out in this tiny room and sneaking in a nap for the rest of the day.

I'm exhausted.

Lydia has left the door open. I'm reaching out to close it when a familiar figure appears at the end of the hall. It's Eli, and there's no way to pretend we didn't just make eye contact.

"Hey . . . ," he says, stopping.

"Hey . . ." I let go of the doorknob.

"I was just bringing some music for Mr. E."

"I was just getting tutored in math."

We are face to face now in a quiet hallway with no way to escape a conversation. He clears his throat.

"Sorry about missing brunch yesterday," he says. "I wasn't feeling well. You got my text, right?"

"I texted you back. I said okay."

"Oh yeah."

This is ridiculous. I hear myself saying, "I think we should talk" before I even know what I want to say. All I really know is that I can't keep on coasting, acting like everything is fine.

He looks around. "Right now?"

"Yes. I don't think it will take very long."

I step back into the practice room. He comes in too and sits on the piano bench.

I shut the door.

"Let's be honest. I think it's obvious this isn't working anymore between us."

As I'm talking, I become aware of how straight my back is. I notice the tilt of my head—how brave it makes me feel. I hear my words and realize they sound familiar. I'm channeling Truman, and holy cow, it helps.

"Okay . . ." Eli looks like he's been caught off guard.

"And I think you should go to prom with someone else."

He frowns.

"Before you ask, no I am not going with anybody else. I'm going to go with Harper and Kiran. Probably also Jordan if she's not too busy making sure everything is amazing."

"It sounds like you've already thought this through," Eli says.

"I'm just being truthful. And while I'm not going to say who I think you should go with, I think it's pretty clear who would be perfect. I'm also pretty sure she doesn't have a date."

He nods, clearly tracking but still surprised.

"This means you probably won't win the promposal contest. I still think it was a great promposal, by the way. I'm sorry it got wasted on me."

His expression softens, and I can see in it the Eli I used to think was so perfect. I used to think we were meant for each other because we were easy together. But now I think that was because nothing had ever challenged us. We were comfortable because nothing made us uncomfortable.

"It wasn't wasted," he says. "What about after prom?"

"If you're talking about *those* after-prom plans, then I think you'd probably agree that that would be weird." He laughs. I laugh too. "But seriously, in the long run, I think you can be with whoever you want."

He nods again, looking distinctly un-sunny.

"So this is it?" he says. "We're breaking up?"

"Looks like it. I'm sorry."

"I am too. But thanks, I guess, for being honest."

I've never broken up with anybody before. I always imagined it would be full of drama and heartbreak. Because of that, I might have been tempted to let things go on and on, no matter how not-right they were. Turns out honesty can be a great drama repellent.

The third lunch bell rang ages ago, but I no longer feel like hiding the afternoon away. I bend down, a little awkwardly, and give Eli a hug. He hugs me back, also a little awkwardly.

"I'll see you in show choir," I say.

He follows me out, then continues to the choir room. I watch him go—one more piece of the life I used to have breaking away. From the moment I saw Future Truman with Future Me on that ten-year-reunion site, everything in my present has been unraveling. I haven't checked the site since Friday after Jordan accused me of obsessing. But now I feel like I need to.

As I make my way to trig, I wake up my phone to find it's not the reunion site that's changed, it's my Instagram. Future Me has added to her quote collection. This new one appears over a photo of a blue sky:

In the process of letting go, you will lose many things from the past, but you will find yourself. —Deepak Chopra

I've been pretty salty about Future Me and her sappy quotes, but this one is oddly comforting. And it feels less than coincidental. Is Future Me trying to send a message to Present-Day Me? If so, I wonder if I can send some sort of message back. I've already looked for a way to DM myself with no success. Maybe if I try posting directly to Future Me's feed, it will work.

I stick out my tongue and snap a selfie.

I write, Hey, it's 17-year-old you. Are you aware of what's happening here? Are you doing this? Can you help me? Then I hit Post. But my phone just whirs and whirls, and then the screen goes blank.

CHAPTER EIGHTEEN

"You girls are absolute perfection!" Jordan's mom lowers her camera to dab at her eyes. "I don't think my heart can handle it."

Jordan glances apologetically at Harper and me while her mom and my mom gush about how beautiful we are. Harper's mom steps forward to push Harper's hair out of her eyes for a better view of her glittery eye shadow, while the dads stand off to the side, drinking beer and trying to pretend they didn't get bored ten poses ago.

I smooth back my skirt, checking to make sure my shoes aren't covered in lawn clippings from wandering back and forth in front of my house, following instructions to stand in front of the lilacs, sit on the porch swing, pose by the redbud trees. I still can't believe how everything turned out: Not long ago, I was the star of a once-in-a-lifetime promposal staged by a guy I thought was the love of my life. Now that guy is taking Brynn Lischer to the dance, and I am going dateless.

But Jordan said we need to make the best of it. So I'm looking at every bright side I can find. The best one was telling Brynn it'd be too awkward if I went to Bella with her and her crew. Is she mad at me for taking away their eighth person and making them lose their cheese plate? I don't care. She has a date because of me, so I'm pretty sure we're even. I went to Chez Finch salon instead, where Mom gave me a mani-pedi, and hair and makeup that look just as good as, if not better than, what I would have gotten at a fancy spa.

At least Harper is getting the full fairy-tale treatment; Kiran has been a champ, posing with us in his tux while our parents take photo after photo. And, best of all, she's nominated for prom queen. Jordan swears she had nothing to do with it—it was all people from school who knew she'd had a rough year. With Brynn and McKinley nominated too, there's no way she'll win, but it was a nice gesture.

"Hold on, I want to text this to Piper," Mom says after photo number ninety million. "She's at a study group so she can't video chat."

I'm not sure why she's bothering. I haven't heard a peep from Piper in weeks—not even when the city council hearing was going on. I sent her a link to one of the news stories; I wanted her to see that I was taking initiative, not coasting, putting myself out there. I thought for sure she'd jump at the chance to pat me on the back, but nope. Not a word.

"Skyler, Piper says she just sent you a Snapchat or whatever you call it," Mom tells me. "She wants you to check it."

I pick up my phone, but all the apps are grayed out. I do a quick restart. When it comes back to life, a little window pops up.

NEW FEATURE: Upload your own photos to the Alton High School Days album and share memories with your classmates!

I try to navigate away. I promised myself I'd make this a reunion-free evening. But the notification just sits there with a button next to it prompting me to open the album.

"Oh for God's sake." I tap the button.

Up pop five photos. Two are of Ryan Oard—Present Ryan, with the present-day golf team. I almost close the album without looking at anything else because, come on, Ryan, give it a rest with the golf already.

But wait. The most recent two photos show people in tuxes and gowns. I pull one up to see it closer. It's Kailey Lopez and Vanessa Halpern, hugging in front of a tree full of twinkle lights. In the background is a silver banner with blue script that reads, ALTON HIGH SCHOOL PROM, with the current year underneath it.

The second photo I pull up shows a packed dance floor. If I look closely at the crowd, I can make out Eli in a white tux, and the back of Brynn's stunning fuchsia dress. That might be the top of my head—I recognize the rhinestone clip Mom fastened into the curls at the back of my updo. And there is Harper, eyes closed, dancing with her arms above her head.

So now I can see the near future, too?

"Okay, enough pictures!" Jordan steps toward the limo her dad hired for the evening. "Let's go! I planned this thing, I don't want to miss any of it."

We join her in the back, wave to our parents, and we're off. I almost show her the prom photos on my phone—there are more of them now, and I know she'd love knowing that the whole thing is going to be a success. But a spiteful part of me holds back. She wanted me to stop checking the reunion site so much. She said I was *obsessed*. So fine. She didn't want to see the bad stuff, she won't get to see the good stuff, either.

Besides, she's got her own tech issues right now.

"Download this app," she says, sending me a link, then thumbing in her username and password. "It's for the king and queen voting. You and I are the only ones on the committee without dates, so I'm making you backup admin in case everybody else gets distracted. It's just for emergencies."

"I don't know why we even need prom kings and queens," says Harper. "The whole thing is a remnant of an antiquated caste system that reinforces socioeconomic and gender stereotypes."

"But wait till you see the crowns I got," says Jordan. "They are ah-mazing."

We ride in style through the sunset streets, sipping complimentary sparkling water and trying to spot other people on their way to the dance. Everybody's laughing, excited, happy, until the limo pulls onto the street in front of the Blessing place.

Across the street, where there used to be a vacant house, now sits a fleet of yellow bulldozers. They hulk on the torn-up lot with their clawlike arms and blunt steel plates, waiting for their chance to crawl over and start chewing up the garden.

Harper's smile freezes. I suck in a breath, trying to push away the sudden panicky feeling in my chest. Jordan scowls at the bulldozers, then sits forward and says, "I've got a surprise for you guys. Look over here."

We've pulled up to the garden door. Garlands of white flowers loop across it, and in the dusk, a warm glow is starting to spill over the top of the wall.

Jordan gets out and scurries ahead of us, holding out her arms.

"Close your eyes," she orders. "I want to make sure you get the full effect."

Harper obeys. I do too, grateful for the distraction. We grasp each other's hands as the three of us step together through the entryway.

"Okay," Jordan says. "Open."

Harper gasps as we get our first real view of Jordan's handiwork. In the photos I've seen tonight, I could only catch glimpses of what it looked like, but now I'm seeing the big picture. Crystals hang from the trees. Tinsel and twinkle lights entwine across branches, climb walls, and drape over statues. There are garlands of tulle, ice sculptures, foil snowflakes, and blue spotlights bathing everything in magic.

"I wanted to remind people of the old Christmas parties," Jordan says.

"It's beautiful," says Harper.

I work to find my voice, finally managing a quiet "It's perfect."

People are streaming in around us, and they all seem to agree. They're wandering the paths, marveling at the effect of hundreds of white lights glittering off faux crystal and silver foil. I turn just in time to see Eli enter with Brynn. He wears the white tux I saw him in earlier, and she seems to be enjoying the attention they're attracting as she twirls in the fuchsia gown that looks even more stunning in person.

You did the right thing, I tell myself. But watching Eli strut around, like this was what he really wanted all along, has tipped my mood toward a nosedive.

Not far behind Eli and Brynn are Truman and Riley. She looks smart and pretty in the pink dress from the Galleria. He looks handsome and a little sad—but that could just be me projecting, because misery loves company. I know from working on the debate team's yearbook page that Truman led them to the most qualifiers ever for the state championship. Together, he and Riley are the very picture of debate squad success.

Jordan goes off to check on the bubble machine. The DJ takes the courtyard stage, and the dance floor floods with people. Harper gets swept up, and we lose each other as the party swings into high gear. My last image is of her with her eyes closed, arms raised, swaying to the beat.

I do not join the dancing. I lurk around the food table, drowning my sorrows in dry-iced punch. I take out my phone to see if I can open Piper's message from earlier. This time it works, but only for a few seconds.

"Hey, Skyler," says Piper from under a kitty-cat filter. "Listen, don't tell Mom and Dad this, but . . ." The image freezes.

Jordan rushes up as I'm trying to refresh.

"A couple of seniors screwed around with the photo booth, now it's spitting out random pictures," she says. "The repair guy disappeared, and if I leave it unattended, people are going to start hooking up inside. I don't want to be responsible for whatever photos get spit out after *that*."

I follow her to the offending piece of machinery and look it over.

"What do you want me to do?"

"Guard it while I hunt down the stoner they sent with this thing. I'll be back in a minute."

She hurries away and I sit myself on a bench, blocking the entrance to the broken booth. It's calmer here off the main path, and I try and get the rest of Piper's message. No luck. I open the reunion site instead to see if there are any new prom photos in the new album.

There are four. The last one shows Eli and Brynn, onstage with the DJ. Matching sashes span their chests; Eli's says KING, Brynne's says QUEEN. Jordan was right: the crowns she picked out are, indeed, amazing.

It's fitting. No, actually, it is. Brynn and Eli getting crowned together will be the cherry on top of the crap sundae that this entire spring has become.

I close the album and decide to people-watch. I see couples hooking up, couples fighting, and tons of flasks coming out of pockets and purses. Brynn and McKinley stagger down the path with Anna Larkin on their heels, not even noticing that I am sitting less than two feet away.

"I thought we *were* going to the after-party," Anna is saying. "If we're going someplace else, I need to tell my parents."

Brynn's face crumples in a way that almost manages to appear apologetic. "Yeah, I was going to tell you. We *were* going to the after-party, but Eli's got this hotel room, so I think we're going to do that instead."

Anna balks. "My mom and dad aren't going to let me go to a hotel."

"That's okay," says McKinley. "There's only room for a few couples anyway. You and Marcus can take the limo home, we'll get a ride with someone else."

"It's nothing personal," Brynn adds. "I just can't stand much more baseball talk. And the after-party is mostly sports people anyway. You can fit a bunch of his teammates in the limo. Then he'll have someone to hang out with who actually cares."

"Speaking of Marcus," says McKinley, "there he is!"

Anna checks over her shoulder, and the other two use the distraction to slip away. I watch how Anna wilts at getting ditched, while fuming myself that the hotel room Eli had planned for the two of us is now going to be used for a party with Brynn and McKinley. The whole thing is so mean that I wouldn't have believed it if I hadn't witnessed it with my own eyes and ears.

But it doesn't have to be this way. According to the reunion site, at some point Anna is supposed to become the kind of badass who leaves the Brynns and McKinleys of this world in the dust. Future Anna is going to be fierce as hell. Even if nothing that showed up on the original website happens, she still has the *potential* to be fierce.

And even if *that* wasn't true, nobody should have to put up with Brynn Lischer's BS.

I stand up. "Hey, Anna."

"What?" She turns, startled.

"So I'm totally in the wrong place at the wrong time, but you were just talking with Brynn?"

"What are you doing back here? Are you spying or something?"

"No!" I point to the bench, the photo booth, the way both are tucked into a spot that's sort of hard to escape when three other people are standing on the path. "I'm . . . stuck. I'm helping Jordan. I wasn't trying to hear what you were talking about, but it was hard not to."

"So?" She widens her eyes, and I know I need to get to my point.

"So those guys were being jerks."

"Oh, they weren't." Anna's laugh is electric with tension. "Brynn was just saying there isn't room at the hotel."

"Which was super jerky, just saying."

"Okay . . ."

I'm not sure exactly where I expected this conversation to go, but it's definitely veering into awkward territory. I try spelling it out.

"What I'm trying to say is that you're better than their drama."

"I have no idea what you mean. I'm not better than anybody."

"Maybe not now, but I'm pretty sure you have some ideas about things you want to do in the future. Maybe think bigger than high school?"

Anna is now gaping as if I just landed in a spaceship and told her I wanted to take her back to my home planet and probe her brain. "How would you know that?" she asks.

The truth of how I know isn't much more bizarre than an alien encounter, which means I should probably shut up. Yet I continue talking.

"It's just a feeling. If I'm right, then you can chalk it up to ESP or something. And even if I'm wrong, it's not okay to treat people like that."

She scowls, which is not exactly the inspired encouragement I was hoping for. "I can take care of myself," she says. "And my friendships aren't your business."

Okay, fine. It's clear I wasn't shown the reunion site because I'm destined to motivate people into achieving their own best futures. I obviously suck at it. And I never wanted to be a shrink or a career counselor anyway. If Anna is destined for greatness, then she'll have to figure it out on her own.

But maybe I can stop Brynn, at least for one night.

"You're right," I tell Anna. "I'm sorry I said anything. Have fun at the after-party with Marcus."

She stalks off, and I pull out my phone. The battery's close to dying, so what I'm planning might not work. I shouldn't even be thinking about what I'm planning. If Harper's fears about messing with the space-time continuum are correct, it probably *will* open up a wormhole. And even if it doesn't, it will get Jordan in really big trouble if anybody finds out.

But I can't resist. I'm so tired of seeing Brynn get everything she wants while being terrible to everybody else, that it's overriding my rational side. My heartbeat hammers in my throat as I sign in to Jordan's voting app.

As suspected, Brynn is the top vote-getter for prom queen. But the margin between her and Harper isn't that big. I've been telling myself that if the difference was wide enough to set off any alarms, I'd abort my plan. But now I have a dilemma. The results are close enough that my plan is highly possible to get away with. And Harper deserves it; she's been through so much. Something happy and fun—an honor that lets her know how much everybody loves her—would really mean something.

Before I can talk myself out of it, I give Harper an extra seventy-five votes. Just enough to put her in the lead. If a bunch of new Brynn votes come in, they could overrule Harper's count, so there's still a chance of it going the other way. It's sort of a cosmic dice roll—a nudge in a direction that could get derailed if that's really how it's meant to be.

So now, I'll just have to wait.

Footsteps sound on the path. I shut the app, thinking it must be Jordan.

"Nobody's been inside the booth," I tell her. "I've guarded it well."

It's not Jordan. It's Truman. And he seems as surprised to see me as I am to see him. He's stopped just off the path, and he's looking down at something. When I venture closer, I see the two angels I noticed a few weeks ago—the ones that are so much like Truman's little sculptures.

"I thought those looked familiar," I say. "Did you make them?"

"No," he replies. "My grandfather did."

"They're beautiful."

"I know. He was a real artist."

"So are you."

Truman doesn't answer. He rocks on his heels with his hands behind his back, the very picture of elegance in his tux. Most of the guys here tonight are playing dress up, but Truman pulls off formal wear like he was born to it.

"Jordan did a great job," he says.

"She did. I'm blown away."

"And you look beautiful. That dress is stunning on you."

The compliment means a lot, because Truman has no reason to flatter me. He's not my boyfriend, but he's not really an enemy anymore either. I've stopped seeing him as my archnemesis; now I'm not sure what he is. Maybe someone who was almost a friend?

"Are you here with Eli?" he asks. "I thought I saw him with Brynn a little while ago."

"We broke up."

"Because of the hearing?" Truman's pale complexion gets even paler. "Because of me?"

"No. I just realized I wasn't being honest about whether we should really be together."

"Oh." He seems relieved. "I'm sorry it didn't work out."

"I mean, the hearing turned out to be a big old nothing. We're standing in the middle of what will soon be a big pile of rubble."

I shrug. "What's one more *womp womp* in the grand scheme of things?"

We're both looking at the angels again. Each one has a heart in her arms with a name on it: Marina and Margaret— Is that Truman's mom and her sister?

"You should take them," I say. "It would be a shame if they were destroyed."

"Maybe it would be better if they were," he says. "Maybe it's time to move on."

Move on. Why does that seem to be everybody's advice these days? I can buy it from Jordan, but not from Truman, not when we're talking about something that clearly meant a lot to him once. I can't believe he could throw all this away so easily.

"It's kind of hard to move on when you literally have a fleet of wreckers waiting for you to vacate the premises."

"We did the best we could," he says. And I want to respond with *But did we?* Because I've been haunted by the feeling that we didn't.

Actually, it's more than a feeling.

"I can't stop thinking that there should have been something else. The first time I saw the reunion site, the pictures were of us here. So if the website was right, then in some version of the future it was possible to save this place. If you and I didn't argue—if we did a million little things differently, would we have done better?"

His expression closes the way I've seen it do before, like a window shutting tight.

"I don't think it's productive to think about that now. I'm focusing on the future—the one I've been planning all along. Maybe this means you're free to do the same."

He sounds like the Truman Alexander I'd expect to hear a

month ago. Except I know now that there's more to him than this calculating person who only cares about what college he's going to, what career he's going to have, and what's next in his color-coded notebook.

Something inside of me snaps.

"It's big of you to think about my future, Truman. And how nice for you that you can just move on. But I think this place means more than you want to admit. Why can't you admit it?"

"Why do you care?" he says. "Why is it so important to you that I admit anything?"

"Because it sucks! And the more I think about it, the more I think we deserved to win. Everybody's walking around going, *You did the best you could,* but I have this feeling that's not true." A tinsel strand flutters down from overhead. I catch it and weave it between my fingers, the silver glittering against the blue of my dress. "I guess I was hoping you of all people would at least *get it.*"

For a moment I see a spark of understanding in those green eyes. Those dangerous eyes. As much as I hate to admit it, I can't look into them without feeling things I'm not supposed to feel.

He blinks. Then he says, "I honestly do appreciate how attached you've become to this place. It's a tribute to my grandfather, and—"

"Ugh, Truman. Did you really just use the word *tribute* in this conversation?" I let the tinsel fall to the ground and turn back toward the party.

I feel his hand on my arm, trying to pull me back around.

"Skyler . . ."

"Truman?" Riley appears at the other end of the path, scowling at the sight of me with her date. I brush Truman's hand away and nod at her.

"Hi, Riley. I love your dress, and these shoes your mom picked out are perfect. Tell her thanks for me." I wave my hand over my shoulder at the photo booth, where Jordan is now chewing out some guy in coveralls who's holding a screwdriver like he has no idea what to do with it. "I've just been helping out with this little drama, but clearly my help is no longer needed."

"Skyler . . . ," Truman says again.

"I'm glad you liked my tribute," I tell him. "Now I'm going to find Harper."

CHAPTER NINETEEN

Back in the courtyard, the party has hit the everybody-dancing-themselves-into-oblivion stage. Lights strobe. Bodies flail. Jordan joins me as I'm making my second trip around the dance floor, and Harper emerges between songs with flowers sticking out of her updo. She looks like an elegant scarecrow.

"Jordan! The whole thing is just magic," she gushes. "Everything is so beautiful! You made it into an absolute dream!"

Harper's always enthusiastic about stuff she loves, but this is a little much. She sounds like she's flitting over the surface. Not all there.

"Harper," says Jordan. "Are you all right? Where is Kiran?"

"Resting." She motions toward some chairs against the wall, and there he is, slumped and manspreading with his head back and his mouth open. The chaperone at the punch bowl appears to be debating whether to check if he's drunk or high, except Kiran is known for being one of the most laid-back people in the world. He sleeps through most of his classes and still makes the honor roll every semester, so if he wants to sleep through prom, too, I guess people figure it's not out of character.

"I'd rather dance with you guys," Harper says. She starts pulling Jordan toward the dance floor. "You're my best friends!"

"Okay . . ." Jordan looks like she doesn't know whether to laugh or be weirded out by Harper's spaciness. Before she can decide, Kailey Lopez rushes over.

"There's a clog in the chocolate fountain. We need you at the food table."

Jordan lets out a string of expletives as she rushes away. Harper reaches down to take one end of my skirt in each of her hands. She pulls, laughing when I stumble to keep up.

"Come on, Skyler. Dance with me!"

Another fast song turns the courtyard into a mass of bouncing bodies. Harper throws herself into the middle, arms thrashing, hair coming down, flowers dripping everywhere, while I bob awkwardly along. We dance and dance, and every new song lifts my spirits a little more. I look around and feel like everyone and everything is connected in a moment so perfectly *now* that nothing else exists outside these stone walls. Even Truman is dancing—or attempting to dance—while Riley shows off some impressive moves of her own. In such a perfect moment, I can almost forgive Truman for being so maddeningly obtuse. Almost.

The music ends. I smile at Harper, and she smiles back. Under the lights with her hair around her shoulders, she is the very heart of this evening.

"Are you ready to crown your prom king and queen?" The DJ has surrendered the mic to Mr. Kimura, who bellows at us from the stage.

I cheer along with everyone else, especially when Jordan gets onstage too, carrying three envelopes, two of which have silver around the edges.

Jordan hands the first envelope to Mr. Kimura.

"First, we have a contest to conclude," he announces. "I've been watching these past couple of months while you kids asked each other to prom in ways that ranged from impressively creative to, I won't lie, a little terrifying at times. Now our panel of faculty and peer judges has selected a winner to receive a year's supply of burritos from Javier's."

I crane my neck, looking for Eli. It's impossible to not feel a little bad that his barbershop extravaganza got disqualified.

"The winner for best promposal goes to . . ." Mr. Kimura opens the envelope. "Darius Johnson."

From somewhere in the crush of bodies, Agnes can be heard screaming, while Darius struts to the stage to get his prize. Everybody cracks up when he kisses his fingers and points them skyward in tribute to a rogue drone.

Harper stands oddly still next to me. She pulls her wrap around her shoulders and puffs a lock of hair out of her face.

Mr. Kimura takes the two silver-edged envelopes from Jordan. Nobody wants a speech, but he makes one anyway. He tells us this is a night to remember. He thanks Jordan and her committee for all their work. He talks about the decorations, the food, the music, but he doesn't say anything about the place—the fact that we are the last ones to experience the garden like this.

"They don't care," Harper says. "People are going to walk out of here tonight, it'll get torn out, and everything we did will be gone."

"I care," I tell her.

"And look at what good it did."

I start lacing and unlacing my fingers behind my back, mentally urging Mr. Kimura to finish his stupid speech already. I want to see if my plan worked—reboot Harper's mood and show her how many people *do* care.

Finally, he opens the first envelope.

"Your prom king is . . . Eli Wolfe."

The way Eli whoops in triumph, he's now easy to find. He may have lost the promposal contest, but he definitely got the bigger prize. He saunters to the stage, mugging for his fans, while Jordan puts the crown on his head. Out in the crowd, Brynn squeals with delight. She can't wait to join him up there.

I can't wait to see that smile get wiped off her face.

Mr. Kimura opens the last envelope, and I can barely hear over the blood rushing through my ears.

"Your prom queen is Harper Hanneford."

Over one sucked-in-breath moment, Jordan looks surprised, then happy, while Brynn looks like someone just took away all her Christmas presents. An ecstatic surge of energy races through me—a feeling of righteous power. *This* is the reason I was shown the future: so I can use it to correct injustice and restore balance to the universe. This might be the first time Brynn Lischer has ever been told no.

A path forms to the stage. Harper glances over at me.

"Go up there," I tell her. "You deserve this."

She starts to walk, past dozens of clapping classmates. I'm clapping too, thinking, *This is amazing. It was all worth it. Look how happy Harper looks.*

Except when Harper reaches the top of the steps, she doesn't exactly look happy. She looks like someone who thinks they *should* be happy but can't quite get their face to play along.

Jordan reaches out and pulls her into a hug. Harper hugs her back. Then she leans over so Jordan can pin the crown into her hair. She barely has a chance to stand straight again when Eli grabs her other shoulder and tries to crush her to him too. When she doesn't immediately step into his arms, he tugs.

"Oh no . . . ," I murmur as they turn to face the crowd. Eli shouts to his friends, drunk on all the attention he's getting, while Harper stands soberly beside him. I clearly have miscalculated her feelings by . . . oh, a few million miles.

A slow song starts for the king and queen's dance. Eli thrusts out his hand, just like in show choir. Harper looks at it and hugs herself, refusing to play along. He untangles her, throwing one of her arms over his shoulder. The other he holds straight out in front as he tangos them both down the steps to the dance floor.

Eli is clueless, as only Eli can be. To him, Harper's just another show choir sidekick—one more person to reflect back his sunniness. She rests her hands at the base of his neck and sways to the music, but her smile has gone slack.

One of Eli's friends whoops. Someone else whistles. Eli twirls Harper, making her stumble. When he attempts a dip, she lets go and takes a step backward. He prances around her in a ridiculous hat dance parody. It's a disaster. He's too high; she's too low. And I know now that putting her out in front of everyone was a mistake. I never should have messed with the voting app.

Eli tries another dip. This time Harper shoves him away. She rips the crown from her hair, then plunges into the crowd. For a few moments she's swallowed up. But then she breaks free on the other side, hair and skirt trailing as she flies through the garden door.

By the time I catch sight of her again she's across the street, heading for the bulldozers. She kicks the metal-toothed end of one with a loud *chunk* that unleashes a scream of pain. Racing toward her, I see blood starting to soak her shoe. She sinks to the ground, clutching her foot.

Truman reaches her first. Then Jordan. He sits with her in his lap while I kneel as people hold up their phones for light. I take off her shoe and find a deep cut.

"Do you think you could stand if we try and get you to the hospital?" Jordan asks.

She shakes her head.

"I'm sorry, I'm sorry, I'm sorry . . . ," she says, over and over.

Mr. Kimura breaks through the onlookers. Jordan fills him in on what happened, and when it becomes clear that none of us is going to be able to get Harper into a car, someone calls for an ambulance. While we wait, people start trickling back to the dance. Couple by couple, they fall away until I spot Eli at the edge of the lot. He holds his crown in one hand, Harper's in the other. I wait for him to come over, but he seems lost with nobody around to cheer him on. I guess it never occurred to him that too much sunshine can burn.

The paramedics arrive within minutes. When they lift Harper, I stand too, and my stomach starts to swirl. I stumble over to some bushes, trying not to throw up.

What if it's all happening again? None of us saw it coming the first time. But ever since then, I've been paying attention. I was looking for signs, and I still missed something. What if the awful things on that website come true? What if this sadness-that-is-more-than-sadness becomes too much for Harper to bear? What if she never makes it to our reunion? And what is the use of being shown the future if I can't do anything to change it?

"Skyler?"

Truman's voice is in my ear. I look up at the bulldozers, then at the stars over the Blessing mansion. I see the reunion site almost as if it were written across the sky—the very first version with Truman and me together. In that future we were all happy and whole, and we were all here, at the garden.

Somehow, I always end up back here. And then an image slams into my mind: Harper shaking hands with a woman—someone Truman knows.

"You said we did everything we could," I tell him. "But we didn't. There's something else."

Truman frowns. "What?"

"The reunion site. There was a picture of a woman. She had red hair. You said it was your aunt Margaret, and it freaked you out because nobody was supposed to know about her."

"What does she have to do with any of this?" Truman asks.

"We're going to find her."

CHAPTER TWENTY

"Hey, Harper. Can you please say something? Just let us know you're okay."

Harper lies in a bay of the ER with her skirt up around her knee and a bandage on her foot. Head turned, she stares at the wall. She hasn't uttered a word since we arrived, not even to her parents, who are outside talking with the doctors. Other than a cut requiring five stitches, there's nothing physically wrong with her. What's most concerning is the silence.

"Har, come on," says Jordan. "I know you're upset, but you have to talk sometime."

I squeeze Harper's hand. "If you don't say something, I'll be forced to tell that joke you hate about the duck who walks into a bar and asks if they've got any grapes. I'm sure the nurses would find it hilarious."

Jordan's eyes meet mine; then she hauls herself up out of her chair.

"I need a break," she says as she heads for the curtain separating us from the nurses' station. I follow her, through the waiting room and the main doors to the circle drive. She heads for the bench where the smokers hang out, stopping just outside their smog cloud. Her dress is wilted, her shoes are stained with dirt, and her makeup is smudged. It's the first time I've ever seen Jordan look not-amazing.

"This is all my fault," I say.

She gives a tired sigh. "How could it possibly be your fault?"

I tell her about the new album on the reunion site that let me see photos of near-future things, and about rigging the voting so Harper would win tonight instead of Brynn.

"I wanted to get back at Brynn, and I thought winning would make Harper happy. I didn't realize how on edge she was. This never would have happened if I hadn't put her out there like that."

Jordan looks angrier and angrier as she listens.

"I don't know what to say, Skyler," she says when I'm finished. "I'm furious with you right now, for a million different reasons."

"But I'm going to fix it."

"How? If you admit you rigged the voting, it will get me in trouble too."

"I was talking about saving the garden. On the reunion site . . ."

"Oh my God. You have to stop messing with things. Leave the future alone."

"You were the one who told me I should try and change it."

"I was talking about staying away from one certain guy, not messing around with other peoples' lives. I realized it was a mistake when you started bringing up all this life-and-death stuff. I told you to knock it off. And instead you went even more in."

"Because you won't go in at all. You can give up, but I'm not going to."

"It's called self-preservation. I have been working my ass off making things great for other people, and right now I'm exhausted."

She drags her fingertips across her face, leaving smudges of mascara that make her already dark eyes look like black holes under the hospital lights. For as long as I've known Jordan, she's thrived on being the social organizer.

"You don't have to do all this," I tell her.

"I sort of do. It's who I am."

"But you love it."

"Don't you think it's still stressful? And the last thing I needed was you messing around with my voting app. I should have known better than to trust you. You're incapable of not making a mess out of things."

I pull in a hiccuping breath. "You think I make a mess out of everything?"

"Maybe not everything, but it's a lot lately."

"So then why are you even still friends with me if I'm so terrible?"

She throws up her hands. "Did I say I didn't want to be friends anymore? Why do you have to take everything to the most extra conclusion, Sky?"

"Because you've been pissy with me forever, it seems like. What else am I supposed to think?"

"I have not been pissy, I've been real with you."

"But see, maybe I don't need that. Maybe I need someone to appreciate just how *unreal* things are right now."

"No, that is exactly why you need a reality check. Everybody would be better off if you focused less on things that don't matter and more on things that do."

"And obviously we disagree on what exactly those things are."

"I guess we do."

Through the waiting-room window, I can see that Truman has

arrived. He stands in front of the nurse's desk, looking around. Meanwhile, Jordan waits for me to respond, to back down, to let her win like always.

"Truman is here," I tell her. "The two of us are going to figure out what to do next. Don't worry, I won't mess it up. I might actually surprise everybody and succeed. But here's some realness for *you*, Jordan, and if you ask me, it really sucks: instead of succeeding with the support of my friends, I'll be doing it with someone who isn't a friend at all."

"I haven't seen Margaret in at least five years," Truman says. "I don't think anyone in the family has."

I refill his cup before topping off my own from the box of coffee I bought at the hospital's late-night cafeteria. Riley shakes her head and glares when I offer the same for her. She could have gone with the debate team to Big Sky; everybody is there now, eating post-prom pancakes and omelets. But she decided to stay with us—I guess to keep an eye on me. She doesn't have to worry, though. It's not Truman I'm after.

"Have you ever tried to see her?" I ask.

"She doesn't want to hear from me," Truman answers.

"How do you know?"

"I think it's a safe assumption. I told you she doesn't have a great relationship with any of us."

I gulp coffee, then shove a minimuffin into my mouth. It's nowhere near as good as a Big Sky waffle, but fighting with Jordan has given me a massive case of the munchies.

"Well, maybe things have changed. Maybe she's forgiven you

guys. Or maybe she decided she was the one who was wrong, and she's just waiting for you all to come back into her life."

Truman regards me wearily over his untouched granola bar. "I appreciate your optimism. But say we did find her and she was open to seeing me. Your idea of getting her to buy the garden is completely unrealistic. She's not going to buy it."

"She might."

"When are you going, anyway?" Riley asks. "We have school."

"Not on weekends." I flash her a *so there* look. She gets up to throw away her trash, and I lean in close to Truman. "Come on. Your aunt was on the reunion site originally. There has to be a reason. We have to get to her before it's too late."

"I thought we were done with that website. Now you want to make travel plans based on it?" he says. "Can you see how that's not exactly inspiring a lot of confidence here?"

"I could see it if I didn't think that you think it's real too. You've been weirded out by it from the very beginning."

He stirs sugar into his coffee, suddenly very intent on the swirling spoon.

"But you don't have to be weirded out anymore. Because you and I aren't even together on there now. So yay, right? No more worrying about being stuck with me for the rest of your life."

He blanches at the reminder of our fight in the city hall conference room. But it's not vindication I'm looking for.

"It's fine," I assure him. "Really. This isn't about me anymore. But it could be about you."

His head tilts. I've got his attention.

"You know this isn't what your grandfather would have wanted. If you could stop them from ripping out the garden—from taking such a big part of your family's heritage—wouldn't he be proud?"

Truman goes back to stirring. Clearly, appealing to his emotions won't take me to the finish line. If his better instincts aren't working, then I'll play to his worst ones.

"We both saw Eli acting like an idiot tonight. Remember how smug he was at the hearing? He won, or he thinks he did."

Truman's eyes flash; the competitive juices are starting to flow.

"What if you pulled out a win no one saw coming? It'd feel so good to see the looks on everybody's faces, wouldn't it?"

His eyes narrow. I'm ready to make my final move.

"You could save the garden, and it would make you look like a rock star to all the colleges, and you could go wherever you wanted. Your future would be on lock."

A hand shoves in front of Truman's face. The hand holds a phone belonging to Riley, who has returned and now stands next to us with cold determination in her eyes.

"What is your aunt's name again?" she asks Truman.

"We're fine here," I tell her. "We don't need your help."

"I'd beg to differ. You two have been going back and forth on this for twenty minutes, and it looks to me like you've accomplished exactly nothing."

Truman looks sheepish, and I have to cede the point. We do have a habit of going in circles. He takes her phone while she sits back down, leaning in to point at the screen. "I did a search for Margaret Blessing and got seven results."

I abandon my coffee to go look over Truman's shoulder.

"This one looks like a twelve-year-old cheerleader from Kansas. Pretty sure that's not her."

"Is she a mom from Maryland with a cooking blog?" Riley asks. "Does she do Roller Derby?"

"No and no," says Truman. Competition and intrigue have

teamed up to reel him in. He whips out his phone and does his own search. "Her name could also be Olmstead. She's divorced, but she might not have gone back to her maiden name."

"Olmstead, Olmstead . . . ," Riley says. "Here's a Henry Olmstead with a mention of a Margaret in the summary."

Truman sits up, excited. "That's Hank. That's my cousin."

I put *Henry Olmstead* into my own phone and it serves up results immediately, like hitting the jackpot on one of those machines where fruit and dollar signs roll into one matching line.

"Yes! Here's a phone number. Can you call him?"

"Wait a minute," Truman says. "Let's think strategically. We don't want to tip anybody off until we know exactly what we're doing."

"It looks like they both live in Chesterfield," says Riley.

I thumb Chesterfield into my phone's GPS.

"That's sort of up near Lake Champion. So about four hours away." I pull off my glasses and rub my eyes. "But I guarantee my parents are going to say no. They're super liberal until I want to do something that might actually require them to *be* super liberal."

Truman, on the other hand, picks up the granola bar he's been neglecting and takes a big bite.

"Guess who *is* going to Lake Champion next weekend," he says.

"Oh no, seriously?" Riley stares at him in horror. "Truman, no."

"Wait. What?" I lean in. "What's in Lake Champion?"

"State debate championship at Baldwin. The bus leaves Friday morning."

Riley slumps furiously in her seat. But as Truman's words sink in, they pump me back up. I put my glasses on again and grin.

"So, is it too late to join the team?"

CHAPTER TWENTY-ONE

"You're joining debate a week before the state championship? Skyler, that is the most far-fetched thing I've ever heard."

Dad brings glasses of iced tea to the kitchen table, where Mom and I are assembling salami sandwiches. I got home super late, or, to be technically accurate, super early in the morning, and then slept for six hours. Now it's lunchtime.

"It's nice that you're showing interest in a new activity, and debate is a great thing to put on your college applications, but do you know anything about it?" Mom asks.

"And don't you have to qualify for state?" says Dad. "I can't imagine they'd just let you slide in and compete."

"I'm thinking I'll have a supporting role this time." Truman already told me I couldn't actually debate, and I wouldn't want to; no way would I be able to do all the prep work it would take to argue about property rights with people who've been researching it all year long. "I'll be the debate version of a ball girl. I'll bring them water or carry their little laptop table things. I can make sure everybody has enough coffee."

Mom gives me a look. "What's really behind this?"

I make myself very busy, making sure my sandwich has just the right amount of mustard.

"Okay, so Truman's aunt lives in Chesterfield, which is near Lake Champion, and we were going to make a side trip to see her and try to get her to buy the Blessing garden. Before you shoot that down, let me tell you why! Harper loves that garden, and the fact that they're tearing it down is really bothering her, and there's a really good chance we could save it and not only make her happier but do something that would be good for this entire town."

Mom and Dad look at each other. I can tell the community crusader part of them is impressed. I lay down meticulous layers of salami, hoping their overprotective-parent side doesn't win out.

"How are you going to get to Chesterfield from Lake Champion?" Mom asks.

"Public transportation?"

"You've never taken public transportation in your life," Dad says.

"Except for that time in London," Mom reminds him.

"There's also Uber!"

"No," says Dad. "I do not feel comfortable with you taking Ubers in a strange area. Realistically, to do what you're talking about, you would need a car."

"Actually, that's just what I was going to suggest. . . ." Truman also told me the only bus the team could get was one of the short ones, and with so many of them qualifying, it was already going to be crowded. I lay down some lettuce, hoping . . . hoping . . .

"So you want to drive to Lake Champion on your own?" Dad says.

"I'd be following the debate team. And a bunch of parents are driving up there too. I wouldn't be on my own, really."

"Where are you planning to stay?" asks Mom. "I'm sure they've already made arrangements for the actual debaters."

"They'll be at a dorm. I can see if they have an extra room?"

"Or we can choose the obvious solution," says Dad. "You can stay with Piper."

"Dad, no." I was afraid they'd bring this up. "I don't need to be babysat by my sister."

"I don't understand why you wouldn't be jumping at the chance," says Mom. "You girls get to see each other so rarely these days."

She looks sad about my lack of enthusiasm. Maybe *she* would be excited to visit her sister at college, but she doesn't know how tense things have been lately between me and Piper.

"Piper is never going to agree to it. I'm sure she'll be too busy."

"Skyler . . ." Dad has that tone he always takes when he thinks I'm being unreasonable. "I can appreciate what you're trying to do, but you have to see how half-baked this whole thing sounds. We haven't even discussed the fact that you'd miss school."

"Just one day."

"How is your trigonometry grade?"

"I'm doing fine in trig."

"Really?"

"Fine. I get it." I push away from the table. "You don't trust me. I was going to figure out all the details this week, but it sounds like you're just going to say no anyway. So if you'll excuse me, I'll be over here abandoning everything that means anything to me and my friends. But hey, at least I'll be safe."

I storm to my room and shut the door; then I sit on my bed, feeling trapped. While I was fighting with my parents, Jordan tried to video chat. I hurry to call her back. I'm sort of desperate to talk after all the hurtful things we said last night.

After dropping the connection six times, my phone refuses to budge from my weather app, which conveniently informs me that the weather in Lake Champion is a beautiful seventy degrees.

There's a knock on my door as I'm tossing my phone to the foot of the bed. Mom comes in to sit next to me, followed by Dad.

"Your father and I have decided to let you explore the options for going to Lake Champion at school tomorrow," she tells me. "But you need to tell us what you're going to be doing there besides just talking with Truman's aunt."

"I'll cover it for the yearbook. I need a final project for my news-writing class anyway. I'm sure Ms. Stephenson will approve it."

"And then you'll stay with Piper," says Dad.

"I called, and she's willing to have you," says Mom.

"Why can't I just stay with everybody else? I'm going to look like a baby staying with my sister."

"Skyler . . ." Dad massages his temples. "Don't push it, okay? I'm offering this against my better judgement. But your mom wants to at least give it a chance."

He smiles the kind of smile that says he hopes our argument is over.

"We're giving you our best offer," Mom says just as a text comes through from Jordan. No apology, just two sentences:

She's still not talking

Otherwise they'd let her go home

We all look at my screen; then they look at me, waiting for an answer.

"Fine," I say. "I'll crash at Piper's."

Friday morning, ten a.m., I pull into the school parking lot in my dad's car, which he insisted I take instead of mine. He put on new tires. He had the oil changed and the interior detailed. For all I know, he installed a webcam to keep an eye on me. I wave at the dashboard as I drive, just in case he's watching.

I'm still amazed at how well everything came together: Mrs. Stephenson was thrilled about my idea to cover the state championship for both the yearbook and my newswriting project. Mr. Milliken, the faculty debate coach, was thrilled for the publicity. And because the only time Truman and I can make it to his aunt's without messing up his debate schedule is early Saturday morning, he and I decided that he'd stay Friday night at Piper's too. Truman's roommate for the trip, Oscar McLearen, agreed to cover for Truman, pulled in by the lure of having an entire room to himself and maybe also having Tessa Martinez share it with him. And since the bus was full, everyone agreed I could drive as long as I followed close behind.

I park and watch people clamber onto the bus with their backpacks, laptop cases, and garment bags. The two guys who accosted me outside of English class get dropped off with Riley, who carries a bagel box from Blue Sky. My stomach growls. I'm trying to spot Truman in all the activity when a knock on my windshield almost makes me spill my made-at-home coffee.

I roll down the window. "Geez, Truman. What?"

"Mr. Milliken said he'd feel more comfortable if you weren't driving alone. Nobody else volunteered to ride along with you, so here I am."

"Too much honesty," I say. But I know I can't really be upset. I'm in Truman's world now. Still, I'm happier when everybody is on the bus, not milling around, peering through my windshield like *Why in the hell is she here?*

Truman loads up my car, then gets into my passenger side. Mr. Milliken comes over, and we agree that if we get separated, we'll meet up when the bus stops for lunch. Finally, the bus starts moving. I follow it away from school, through downtown, over the bridge that overlooks the Blessing mansion. And then we're on the highway, and I realize that I have no idea what Truman and I are going to talk about for four hours straight.

Assuming we talk at all. Truman seems more than happy to stare out the window, letting me choose the music and control the AC. I speed up to see if I can get him to say something. I slow to a crawl, making the cars behind me honk. Finally, I bring up the one topic that's pretty much guaranteed to get a response.

"Do you have to pee?"

"No," he says. "Do you?"

"Not really, but if you did I could pull over. I saw a sign for a rest stop up ahead."

"I don't think that was for a rest stop. I think it was a national park."

"I read it. It definitely said rest stop."

"I read it too. I think it said restaurant. Many parks have those in their visitor centers."

"I know what I saw."

"But is what you saw correct? When was the last time you had your eyeglasses prescription checked?"

"My glasses are fine. And even if it did say restaurant, those have bathrooms. We could get food *and* go pee."

"Well, not now, because you just passed it."

I look in my rearview mirror to see the exit slipping away.

"Fine. You tell me when you want to stop. I won't worry about it anymore."

I turn up my music to drown out anything he might say in response. Then I drive on, ignoring my own need to pee, which starts out faint then gets more intense with every mile. I will *not* pull over until Truman begs, which I pray he'll do soon. He had a ton of coffee too, so he'll have to go at some point.

But he just sits there, organizing the tabs in his ever-present black notebook. Finally, I can't stand it any longer. I pull off at the next exit.

"You're welcome," I shout after him as he moves quickly to the restroom.

I barely make it to the women's. After sweet relief, I buy myself a soda and some gum. When I return to the parking lot, Truman is leaning against the car. We get back in, get back on the road, and it's more long stretches of nothingness until I can't handle it anymore.

"I knew you had to pee."

"Most people would after two hours in a car," he answers.

"But you weren't going to tell me, were you?"

"I knew you'd pull over when you had to go bad enough."

His face is smug as he texts his teammates on the bus up ahead, and I realize I've been riding with classic Truman all along.

"I'm starting to remember why I dislike you so much," I tell him.

"And I'm starting to remember why I enjoy arguing with you so much."

"Well, I'm glad I can entertain you," I say, "but I'm done arguing now."

After a while, Truman gets another text. "They're stopping for lunch," he tells me. "There's a country buffet up here at Exit 32."

My stomach rumbles and my butt has gone numb.

"Awesome," I say. "I could use a change of scenery."

CHAPTER TWENTY-TWO

Except it turns out that being at a buffet in the middle of no-where with a group of hostile debaters is even more painful than being in a car alone with Truman Alexander.

We are the youngest people at the restaurant, which appears to be the local spot for sitting and visiting while having coffee and pie. Since Truman and I have arrived late thanks to our bathroom break, everyone's already seated. Riley immediately leads him away to a packed table.

I find a booth in the back corner and put down my bag, then head to the buffet. I might be on my own, but at least the food looks good. I load up on fried chicken with gravy and sides. When I return to my seat, Truman is there, his notebook on the table next to a second water glass.

"Don't tell me. You asked if you could invite me to your table and everybody said no."

"Since you requested that I not tell you, I won't."

"Won't your girlfriend get mad if you're spending so much time with me?"

"Riley isn't my girlfriend." He nods at the notebook. "Will you watch that for me while I go get lunch?"

While he's gone, I text my parents that I'm okay, sending a photo of my plate as proof. My phone makes a weird sound, then belches out a notification from the reunion website.

Alton HS Reunion Message Board—New Posts (17)

This is something new: a message board.

I'll be avoiding it. The last thing I need is a bunch of golf posts from Ryan Oard.

Truman returns to the table. I put my phone facedown on the seat next to me. "Is that all you want?" I ask. On his plate is a spoonful of cottage cheese, one sad-looking baked pork chop, and a dinner roll. "Aren't you hungry?"

"I'm famished." He pulls his knife out of his napkin and starts cutting his pork chop into little pieces.

"So why didn't you get more? Or more to the point, why didn't you get something more exciting? We're at a buffet. You can have anything you want."

"This is what I want."

"Are you a toddler?"

"No. I'm perfectly happy with my selections."

He nibbles a small bite, and it's clear he's not trying to engage in an argument this time. Truman, apparently, is fine with safe, bland, and boring.

It's unexpectedly adorable. It's also completely unacceptable.

"Why are you so fixated on what I'm eating?" he asks.

"It's what you're not eating that disturbs me. Try this." I hand over one of my drumsticks, which Truman regards with suspicion. He uses his knife and fork to cut out a miniscule piece.

"Ugh! Truman! You have to enjoy it. Like this!" I shove my own drumstick into my face and gnaw off a chunk.

He picks off a bigger piece with his fingers, puts it in his mouth. "It's very good," he admits.

He reaches his fork across the table and snags some of my grits. I watch as he tastes them, and the way his features relax with pleasure fills me with something more than vindication—it turns out I sort of like seeing Truman happy. I head back to the buffet to get him some chicken of his own.

Once we've stopped shoveling food into our faces, he opens his notebook and says, "So I've worked out the timing for tomorrow. If we leave your sister's by six a.m., we'll be at Margaret's by seven. We get back on the highway by eight, and we're back at the dorm by nine, in time for the team meeting before first round. It's tight, but it should work if we're efficient and stick to the schedule."

"Piper is thrilled we're coming, apparently. I'm sure you two will have a ton in common."

Truman furrows his brow, like he does in class when he's thinking up an angle to argue.

"What?"

"I'm just trying to figure out how we get from a sister at Duke and then law school to you going to State," he says.

"There's nothing wrong with State."

"There's nothing great about it either. We're talking about the rest of your life here."

"No one asked for your opinion."

"I'm just being honest."

"And I'm enjoying lunch. Let's not ruin it."

"Well, then think about it like this. State is baked pork chop and cottage cheese. You've got a whole buffet of other choices. Why not try something more exciting?"

"Cute metaphor, but it's not the same."

"I don't understand why not. You could go anywhere you want."

"No, I really can't."

"If it's a financial issue, then you could look into aid. Or scholarships. It can be a lot of work to find them sometimes, but if you're motivated, you'd be surprised what's out there. I've already identified three that I'm going to apply for, and I'm tailoring my résumé to hit the high points I know those particular ones are focused on."

"Oh my God, would you shut up?" It's like Piper invaded Truman's brain to lecture me. "If I don't get my trig grade up, State may not even be an option."

"That can't be true. Just get a tutor and—"

"Listen to me, Truman, I don't just suck at trig, I'm failing it. Even with a tutor. And don't try to reassure me that it's not a big deal, because I have seen my future. Every crappy grade I get in that class leads me deeper into adult failure."

He looks surprised. "You can see that kind of thing?"

"Yes! I told you it wasn't just pictures of you and me on that website. It keeps changing and adding things, and in some cases, subtracting things, and I've seen more than I ever wanted to see about myself and all sorts of other people. Congratulations, you're on track for an amazing life, while I'm probably going to end up the lonely town cat lady, and there doesn't seem to be anything I can do to change that."

I immediately regret this sudden burst of honesty. Now I've all but invited him to feel superior. I get up and go to the dessert bar, where I help myself to a slice of chocolate silk pie. If I have to listen to more Truman advice, maybe chocolate will make it more bearable.

When I get back, Truman has put something next to my water glass. It's the sculpture he was working on at the bowling alley—the one that looks like a man, with the childlike eyes and the glazed swoop of a body. He reaches out, turns his hand over, and there's another sculpture hiding there. He sets this one down too. It's only half-finished, but it looks like a little boy with a face that's eerily old and, again, those huge expressive eyes.

"You might not believe this," he says, "but listening to you just brought back a lot of awfully familiar memories. And when I say awful, I mean it."

I pick up the little man, rolling him between my fingers. "I know your parents are hard on you. It's not the same thing. My parents are supportive. It's me who's the problem."

"It's not just that they were unsupportive, it's that I couldn't focus on anything for more than a few minutes at a time. My brain was like a hamster wheel of thoughts and worries that would loop and loop until I felt like I was stuck in some kind of nightmare. I couldn't sit still to save my life."

"They have medication for that kind of thing."

"Once we found the right ones, it helped me get off the wheel. But up until then, my dad was pretty frank about not seeing any future where I wouldn't be a total disappointment."

"That *is* awful. What did you do?"

He glances at the notebook with its tabs fanned in a well-ordered rainbow. "I got focused. And then . . ." He picks up the half-finished little boy. "This gave me someplace to put the extra energy—something to do because I wanted to do it, not because I had to."

218

The man in my hand looks as if he's trying to say something inexpressibly important. I run my finger over his face, feeling the fine bumps of his features.

"I just can't believe how talented you are, Truman. These are incredible."

He nods at my hand. "You can have it."

"Really?" The tiny face tilts up as if to say, *Yes, really. Put me in your pocket and take me anywhere you need help feeling confident and strong.*

"I'll call him Miles. Get it? Because he's traveling all these miles with us? He'll be our trip mascot."

Truman grins, then says, "But seriously, Skyler, don't be so down on yourself. You're incredibly smart. I really think you'd be surprised at where you could go."

This whole conversation is so un–Truman Alexander–ish, or at least so unlike the Truman Alexander I thought I knew. I could sit with this Truman for hours, eating pie and talking about the things that stress us out about the worlds we live in. But there's no more time. Everybody else is getting up to leave.

Oscar comes over and looks at me with disdain.

"You guys ready?" he asks.

"Never readier!" I say, extra enthusiastic. Truman looks at me funny. "What? I'm just making a point." Instead of being disdainful, Oscar should be thanking me for taking his roommate tonight and making it possible for him to hook up with Tessa.

"Okay . . . ," says Truman while Oscar walks off.

"I'm here to learn the finer points of debate, Truman. Maybe some of these guys could learn the finer points of having fun."

"You clearly have never been to a debate party," Truman says.

"So invite me sometime."

"You have to earn your way in."

"If that means actually joining the team, then I'm still in the nope column. But nice try!"

I put money on the table. Truman goes to talk with the rest of his teammates, and I head back out to the car. We're starting the final leg to Lake Champion. Truman and I are going to talk his aunt into buying the garden. It's all coming together, and that, it turns out, is super exhilarating.

I take Miles out of the pocket of my shorts, put him on the little ledge next to my steering wheel, and *boop* his tiny nose for luck.

It's showtime.

CHAPTER TWENTY-THREE

The closer we get to Lake Champion, the less exhilarated I feel. I'm not ready to see my sister. I don't want one of her inspirational speeches. And I don't know if I can pretend to be enthralled by her many new accomplishments. I love Piper, and I'm proud she's doing so amazing. But if I had a dollar for every time I've felt less-than-amazing in comparison, I could buy the Blessing garden myself.

Truman has his laptop out, legal pads spread all over the dash, and he's helicoptering that black Sharpie around his fingers, only stopping to write down notes. When he's not taking notes, he's rehearsing his points to the air. I don't interrupt—I'm not up for conversation anyway. He and I are both in our own worlds, each nursing our own anxieties.

We follow the afternoon traffic into the city, then follow the road signs to Baldwin. The tournament is being held at the university's fine arts center, with competitors staying at the dorm on the other side of a grassy quad. The streets around the campus are clogged with buses, and everywhere you look are groups of people carrying briefcases and backpacks, everybody sizing everybody else up. It's like a show choir competition, only our show choir has never advanced to a meet this big. I take some photos with the camera Ms. Stephenson loaned me. I do a few interviews. I get a rundown from Mr. Milliken on how everything works. Then I have a lot of time to kill while the team gets registered and checked into the dorm.

I find a place near the auditorium and sit on a bench with my phone. When I wake it up, a handful of texts from earlier in the day pop up. One of them is from Harper.

> Where are you?

Her mom told me she'd be returning to school, but I haven't seen her all week. Monday I went to her house and promptly left when I saw Jordan's car in the drive. Tuesday her mom said she was at therapy. Wednesday she was too tired to hang out, and then I had to get ready for this trip, so this is the first I'm hearing from her directly since prom.

My phone burps out another old text.

> Jordan says you're with Truman? Debating?!?

There are two missed video calls, as well. When I call back, Harper's face is fuzzy and the sound is scratchy, but at least we're finally connected.

"Hey, Skyler!" she says. "I missed you today!"

It's the weirdest thing. I've been trying to see her all week, and now that we're finally speaking, I'm angry.

"So I see you're talking again," I say.

"Yes . . ." She looks embarrassed. "I'm sorry about prom. The new medication I'm on gives me these wicked mood swings."

"How are you feeling now?"

"Better."

"Good."

"Hey, are you fighting with Jordan? She's mad at you but she won't tell me why."

"It's nothing." I pinch the bridge of my nose, trying to ward off the headache starting behind my eyes. "Don't worry about it."

"If it's because of me, you can say so. You don't have to protect me. I'm not a baby."

Was the fight about Harper, though? Harper was definitely the spark, but by the time I left Jordan in the hospital driveway, it felt like we'd gone someplace far deeper. One thing I do know: Harper doesn't want anything to do with the reunion site. Harper *shouldn't* know about what it's shown me lately. And since all that is tied up with everything else, I don't think it's something I should talk about at all.

"It's just the usual stuff," I say. "You remember how Jordan and I used to go at it."

"It was never like this, though." She frowns. "You both treat me like I'm going to jump off a cliff if someone tells me something difficult."

"Well, to be fair, Harper, you did attack a bulldozer."

"Yep. You know what? I humiliated myself in front of everybody, and now I'm never going to be allowed to forget it."

"But you went two whole days without talking."

"Look," she says. "I get that people are worried. If you're worried, think about how I feel. My emotions are all over the place, and the things that are supposed to be helping have side effects, and it's hard. But you treating me like some fragile flower isn't going to fix what I have to do. I love you, Sky, but it's just not that easy."

Speaking of things Harper has to do, a question pops into my head.

"How's your homework? You know, your action plan?"

She says, "Fine." But the irritation in her voice makes me want to keep pressing.

"I mean, you always tell me about it, and you haven't lately, so . . ."

"I'm doing it now."

"But you weren't?"

"I don't know." She pushes her hair out of her face. "Sometimes I don't do things even when I know they're good for me. I would think you of all people would understand that."

One thing that hasn't changed about Harper is her ability to cut to the bone. It's almost as if the universe is staring right at me when a text comes in from Dad.

> Just got a call from Mr. Bannister informing me that you are failing trigonometry. I thought you said you were doing fine in there?!

"Harper, I have to go. I'll tell you what I'm doing here when I get back, okay?"

"Fine," she says. "Have fun with Truman."

I try to text Dad back, but it won't go through. I consider texting Jordan, but I don't feel like listening to any more of her *realness*. I get to my feet and shake out my arms, my legs, my butt. I have to clear my head.

I make my way through the crowded lobby, and once I'm outside, I want to walk. Striding down tree-lined sidewalks, I watch the college kids studying on the lawn and hanging around outside the dorms. This is a gorgeous campus—much nicer than State, and a lot harder to get into as well. A guy runs in front of me, chasing a Frisbee. He catches it, then falls down on a blanket where two girls have been reading under a tree. This is the kind of thing I've always pictured when I've imagined what college would be like. If the reunion site is right, and if I can't figure out how to do better in math, then that vision probably won't include me.

I head back to the fine arts building, where I find Truman on a bench in the quad, bent over his black notebook, pen spinning around and around on his fingers.

I take a photo with Ms. Stephenson's camera, then sit next to him.

"This much focus and dedication should be captured for posterity. Do you want to be in the yearbook?"

He puts his pen down. "Why not? Maybe it will help my nerves."

I get out my reporter's pad and a pen. With my phone so unreliable, I'm doing things the old-fashioned way.

"So why debate?" I ask. "What's the appeal?"

"Debate is a time-honored exercise in eloquence, sportsmanship, and discourse, allowing participants to hone and perfect both their research and public speaking skills, enabling them to persuasively prevail in any setting where an exchange of ideas is warranted."

My hand cramps trying to keep up.

"I need some ranch dressing and croutons to go with that word salad, Truman. You lost me at *eloquence*. Try normal people language. Why do you love debate?"

"Because I'm good at it."

"But your sculptures are better. You should be making those all the time."

225

"Art isn't exactly a prestigious career."

"So prestige is what really matters to you. Nice."

"You're asking me why debate. I should be asking you why *not* debate? You were amazing at the city council hearing."

"Eh . . ." I stretch out my legs, peering across the quad to see that the girls with the blanket have gone inside. "I don't think you want to use that as proof of my mad skills. Isn't debate about convincing people? If I'd done a better job of that, I wouldn't be here right now."

"I don't think that's really what's bothering you, though. I think you're resisting simply because it was my suggestion." He flips over a new page in his notebook and starts to write. "Resolved: that Skyler has a bad attitude about debate because she has a bad attitude about me. Do you want to argue neg or aff?"

"Negative, obviously. I don't have a bad attitude about you. I have a perfectly justifiable dislike based on years of experience. I'm sorry if debate is a casualty of that."

Truman jots this down, punctuating the last sentence with a big, bold period.

"Make three key points about why you dislike me and back them up with evidence."

"Oh, this will be easy. Number one: You're irritating."

"Evidence?"

"You're sitting right there. You're irritating me. I don't have a mood-reading machine to prove it, so you'll just have to take my word on this."

If I did have a machine to quantify my mood, *irritated* wouldn't be the readout. My skin tingles, but not in the creepy way it used to around Truman. Maybe it's the fact that we're four hours away from our regular lives, but I'm having a good time talking with him—maybe even more than a good time. I sort of want to kiss him right now.

"So your first point is that I'm irritating," he says. "What's your second point?"

Just as I prepare to launch into my second point, my phone pings.

"Do you want to check that?" he says.

"It's probably my dad harping on my trig grade again." I peek at the screen and see a notification about some new message board posts. "Wait, it's not my dad, it's the other current bane of my existence."

"The reunion site?"

"Sorry, I know it bugs you."

"Actually . . ." He peers at me from under a flop of hair that's fallen into his eyes. "You said you could see other peoples' futures. Can you see mine?"

"I mean, I can only see whatever people decide to post at any given time. And things are always changing."

"Could I see it?"

"I thought it freaked you out."

"I've been thinking maybe I should get over it. To be honest, I'm nervous about how this whole thing is going to go, sneaking out to see my aunt and then the tournament tomorrow. I guess I could use a little reassurance."

"Okay, well . . ." I give my phone a shake. "Let's see if I can even get the thing up. My phone is literally gasping its last breaths right now."

The reunion site doesn't look much different from the past several times I've checked it—same swanky party, same shiny new Alton. There's the album of reunion photos, and the "School Days" album, which consists of all the photos our future classmates are posting of our Present-Day selves. And then there's that new message board—the one that's been sending me notifications all day.

"So at one point, there were actual bios here," I tell Truman as he scrolls. "You were this amazing world traveler."

"What was my job?"

"I don't remember."

He looks at me, annoyed. "These are important details, Skyler."

"Well, if I'd known you were going to all of a sudden be interested, I would have taken notes."

Truman can't find himself on this new website, and I can't find myself either. I never thought I'd say this, but I miss the old site. It was so detailed and nicely put together. Future Jordan was creating the site when I first accessed it, now apparently she's not. And I can't find Harper, either. Maybe in this new future, none of us are friends anymore.

When Truman gets too frustrated, I take the phone and open up School Days.

"The good stuff appears to be in here now," I tell him. A ton of new photos have been posted—people messing around in the commons, cheerleaders at games, sports teams posing together. I scroll a bit, then, "And well, well. What do we have here?"

"What?" says Truman. "What is it?"

"Here you go. See?"

It's a group picture of the debate team with Truman front and center, a state championship banner behind them like the one that hangs in the lobby right now. Several of them hold trophies, including Truman, who holds the biggest one of all.

He breaks into a grin. "Wow. That's . . . I mean, not that I'm surprised, but still, wow. So it's all going to work out then." And now he's hooked. He taps and scrolls and taps and scrolls until he opens up the new message board. More tapping and scrolling, until . . . "Wait a minute. What's this?"

Senator Stevens Embezzlement Scandal—
Alton High School Connection?

He opens the thread, and I read over his shoulder.

Kiran Smith: Did you see this story about Sen. Stevens stealing massive amounts of $$$ from the charity his father set up to help disadvantaged kids go to summer camp? Looks like he used it to fund his campaign. And look who his campaign manager is. Didn't Truman Alexander go to school with us?

"Oh my God." I remember Truman rattling off his plans that day at my house, telling me about his goal to work for Stevens someday. The thread has fifteen responses already.

Darius Johnson: Truman was always soooo full of himself. Couldn't happen to a better guy.

Fia Reyes: Who didn't want to smack Truman every other day in class? Dude couldn't shut up to save his life. Enjoy prison, big mouth!

Anna Larkin: Come on, guys. He may not have had anything to do with this.

Ramesh Patel: Maybe not, but it still looks bad. Stevens has been slimy since the dawn of time. Surprised Alexander would want to be associated with him.

Truman looks green as he reads. I reach out to touch his arm. "Are you okay?"

He gives me back the phone. "Why wouldn't I be? Everything is going to happen just the way I've planned it."

"You aren't planning on taking part in criminal activity, are you?"

"This kind of thing happens all the time in politics. There are misunderstandings and gray areas, and often these kinds of scandals are manufactured by political rivals. Most likely, he'll be cleared of all charges. If I'm working for him, I'll see to it that he is."

"So you're okay with this?"

"A little scandal is to be expected at this level of achievement." Truman's voice now is firm. "I'm going to have to make some compromises, clearly."

Yeah, I think. *Compromises to your integrity.*

Truman's entire team is out on the quad now. Mr. Milliken shouts that it's time to get dinner. "Skyler," he says. "Are you joining us for food?"

I can't say no, even though I don't have an appetite anymore. I'm supposed to be reporting on all the weekend's activities, plus Truman and I aren't due to go to Piper's until much later. It's only five o'clock now. I tell Mr. Milliken I'm coming, and I tell Truman I understand when he tells me he has to spend some time with his teammates; then I sit by myself at the head of a long table in a pizza restaurant, watching him hold forth over at the other end. He's in full Team Captain Mode, doing his classic pompous Truman act. Inside the pocket of my jacket, I find little Miles—the sculpture he gave me earlier today.

I run my fingers over the smooth bumps of Miles's face. No one knows this other side of Truman, and who knows if they ever will? According to the reunion site, he'll go from victory tomorrow to whatever other achievements he's destined for, all the way to a level so high that he will wind up getting accused of national election campaign violations.

My phone shows that I, on the other hand, am still an Instagram housewife, apparently with a lot of time on my hands to post inspirational quotes. The latest is superimposed over a photo of a highway stretching off into a sunset. *Don't judge each day by the harvest you reap but by the seeds that you plant. —Robert Louis Stevenson*

"Oh, shut up," I tell Future Me. My phone answers by blinking off and refusing to power on again.

CHAPTER TWENTY-FOUR

At eight-thirty, I pick up Truman two blocks down from the dorm. He told everyone he was going to bed early, now here we are, driving to my sister's place.

When my parents and I visited Piper at Duke, everything was *rah-rah* perfect: she lived in an ivy-covered sorority house, the perfect college girl, just like she was the perfect cheerleader, student, and sister back at home. I've always pictured law school as a more grown-up version of that. Now she'll be in a chic apartment, trading sweatshirts and side braids for cute sweaters and a bun held in place by a pencil.

But the GPS takes me into a less-than-great part of town, and when my phone tells me we've arrived, I tell Truman to double-check it, certain there must be a mistake. The apartments in front of us are a dank strip of depressing.

"This is it," Truman confirms. I pull into a parking space and stop.

"Wait down there and I'll come get you," Piper says when I call her. "It's hard finding my apartment."

Two minutes later I see someone I barely recognize coming toward us. Her hair is piled into a straggled topknot. She wears faded yoga pants, a flannel shirt, and no makeup. She's at least ten pounds heavier than the last time I saw her.

She squeals when I step out of the car, throwing her arms around me. "Skyler! I can't believe you're here! Who is this?"

"This is Truman. He's . . ." I pause, completely unsure how to characterize what Truman is to me. "He's a friend."

Truman lets Piper hug him too, managing to look only slightly stiff while she talks a mile a minute about how she hopes we'll be comfortable at her place, how it's super small but she's thrilled to have us and can't believe I haven't visited earlier. We follow her around the corner of the building and into a musty hallway. She leads us to a door tucked behind the elevators, opening it to reveal that she wasn't lying about how small her place is. It's literally a kitchen counter with a sink, range, and fridge, and an open area where a table, sofa, and beanbag chair compete for space with a TV. There are two other doors—one that must lead to a bathroom, and another that leads either to a bedroom or a closet.

"I'm sorry it's not much to look at," she tells us. "I don't have a lot of time to decorate. Or clean." She pushes a carton of mostly eaten fried rice into a wastebasket, then apologizes that she doesn't have any drinks or snacks. "I also haven't had time to shop, and I feel terrible I can't hang out tonight. I'm completely overwhelmed with studying. I barely have time to shower."

"You're majoring in tax law, right?" Truman says. "I've heard that's especially challenging."

"Yes." She adjusts the scrunchy in her hair and says, "Believe me, I'm regretting it."

Truman goes back out to the car to get our backpacks, and Piper starts gathering up her study materials.

"Do you and Truman want the bed tonight?" she asks. "I can

sleep out here on the couch. It's no problem as long as you aren't too noisy. The walls are thin and the neighbors can hear everything."

"We're not together that way!" I say. "Besides, aren't you supposed to be making sure stuff like that doesn't happen?"

She laughs. "I don't care what you do. And I'm assuming Mom and Dad don't know he's here, right?"

"Maaaaybeee not . . ." This is a fine balance, making sure everybody knows what they need to know but not enough to compare notes.

"Relax," Piper says. "I wouldn't have time to chaperone anyway. I'm late for my study group."

"Truman can have the couch. I brought my sleeping bag. I'll sleep on the floor."

"Suit yourself," she says. "But he's cute, Sky. And I can tell he's smart. I like him."

"We're not . . ."

"Okay. Whatever." She grabs her car keys and heads for the door. "I'm just saying I've spent maybe three minutes with you guys and I can tell there's something there. You don't have to pretend like there isn't. It's not like you're going to marry him or anything."

When Piper leaves, there's nothing to do but watch one of three channels on her TV or study. We decide to study because of course that would be Truman's choice, and because I have another trig test coming up.

Truman notices when I get out my book.

"I can help if you want," he says. "I'm not trying to offend you. I'm honestly offering."

"You know me pretty well if you're worried I'd be offended."

"Are you?"

"No. It's just not easy to admit that there's something I suck this bad at."

"So what does the test cover?" He comes to sit beside me, bringing his debate notes along. I open my binder, he leans over, and that smell of soap and syrup hits me. The room tilts as I fight to stay focused.

"I don't think my notes are right. They don't make any sense."

He squints at my notebook, which brings him in even closer. Now my body buzzes as hard as my brain. It's crazy what happens when I'm next to Truman, like there are magnets under my skin, pulling me toward him. If I get close enough, I might just snap to him and stick. He shifts, tilting away, and I wonder if he's feeling the pull too.

"There's nothing wrong with your notes," he says. "They're just a really bad way to teach this concept."

He explains another method, which starts to make some sense. And then, as we work through the first few problems, something extraordinary happens: I see what the numbers mean. I see how one thing affects another. This isn't just a bunch of abstract rules to try and memorize, I'm starting to understand. Truman is fifty million times better at this than Lydia.

"Wait a minute," he says. "Why did you write it that way?"

"What way?" I peer at the paper. "That's the equation."

"You switched the numbers around."

"Oh." I take off my glasses to rub my eyes. "They . . . move sometimes. It's like they won't stay where they're supposed to."

He draws a grid and places the numbers from the equation I've been working inside.

"Information can get overwhelming, so you need a way to organize it. In debate you file it in a database—or a big box. Then you can call it up when you need it. Maybe that will help you too."

It's like putting animals in a pen. The numbers stay put so I can move them where they need to be. It's such a great feeling that I could kiss Truman. But I don't. I do more math. He turns his attention to his own stuff, and I work more problems, like a kid on training wheels whose dad has just given her a push.

But just like that kid, my balance only holds for so long. Pretty soon I'm pedaling uphill, going slower and slower.

"You've only done seven out of ten," Truman says. "You should keep going until you're sure you've got it. When's the test?"

"Monday."

"That's just three days from now."

I shove my book into my backpack and get out my phone. "I don't want to think about three days from now. I want to do something fun now. Is there a movie theater around here?" I start searching for show times.

"It's way too late for a movie," Truman tells me.

"How about bowling? I still have to pay you back for beating me last time."

The more I talk about going out, the more Truman shrinks into the couch. He fidgets, tapping his pen against his note cards.

"I need to work on this," he says.

He turns away and starts speaking under his breath to an audience in his own mind. I can see him imagining tomorrow's matchup and how he'll perform at it, tuning everything else out. As I watch, it hits me.

"You live in the future."

He looks up and frowns. "Sorry, what?"

It's clear to me now, the way Truman keeps himself occupied with big plans, every achievement getting him closer to some glorious someday but distancing him from whatever's happening in the present.

"That's why you're so obsessed with all these goals. It's why you're always thinking about two years from now, or ten. You're trying to escape."

"That's ridiculous. I'm not escaping anything." But he's let his guard down just enough for me to pluck the debate notes out of his hands.

"What are you trying to get away from, Truman?"

"Nothing." He lunges for the note cards. I put them behind my back.

"False." I take hold of his chin with my free hand, tilting it to bring his gaze level with mine. "Why can't you just live in the now?"

I study his face, the way he flushes over those high cheekbones. The way his normally full lips are set in a taut line. I see the hurt in his eyes as he says, "Because now has never been that great a place to be."

I let his notes drop to the floor and move my other hand to the place where his hair meets the nape of his neck. "Don't think about tomorrow or the next day or the day after that." I move closer, my body practically screaming for contact. I brush my lips against his, see his eyes flutter shut. "Focus on this."

His hands forget the notes. They come up to my waist, and as his fingers meet the skin on my back, it's impossible to resist the pull any longer. I wrap myself around him. He presses into me. This math makes sense: me plus Truman plus the miles between who we are at home and who we could be equals something hundreds of times bigger.

I kiss his jawline, working around to his ear.

"How is now now?" I whisper.

"Right now is pretty amazing."

Truman takes off my shirt. I take off his. Next shorts and bra, and now there's virtually nothing to stop from binding us in one moment, then another, with everything else stripped away but a picture in the back of my head of Truman and me together on a website.

If this is fate, then right now, in this moment, I'm fine with it.

Until it becomes clear that I'm in danger of creating a fate I absolutely am not fine with at all. I didn't come prepared. I'm almost positive Truman didn't either. And I'm not looking to add "pregnant at seventeen" back to my future.

I untangle, just enough to let us both cool off. "We should probably . . ."

He nods, breathing hard. "You're probably right."

Outside in the hallway, we hear the sound of jangling keys. Then those keys are in the lock. I scramble to grab a shirt, while Truman pulls a pillow over himself.

There's swearing as the keys fall to the hallway floor, then go back into the lock. A few seconds of wrestling with the dead bolt, then Piper shuffles in. She doesn't seem to care or even notice that Truman and I are on her couch, barely dressed. She looks completely wrung out.

"Hey, Sky," she says as she trudges to her bedroom door. "I need to get to bed. Do you need anything? Okay, then, good night."

Her door shuts and we're alone again, and it's weird. Something tells me not to move, to listen instead. Piper was right, the walls of the apartment *are* thin—so thin that we can hear her bed frame creak as she sits on it. We hear her shoes hit the floor as she removes them. We hear the covers rustle as she pulls them up, then another creak as she rolls over, then muffled sobs—barely there at first, but soon louder.

I pull on shorts to go with the T-shirt I scrambled into—Truman's T-shirt, it turns out—and pad to my sister's door. Gently, I push it open.

"Piper?"

It's a mess of clothes and books inside, sweetly stale smelling, with my sister a lump under a comforter on the bed. I pick my way over by the moonlight that seeps through the blinds.

"Ugh, Skyler." She sniffles when I sit on the edge of the bed. "I'm sorry. I know you need your sleep. I shouldn't be so noisy."

"We're fine. But what's wrong?"

"Ugh!" she says again, throwing her arm up over her head and glaring at the ceiling. "I'm just so freaking stressed. This stuff is super complicated, and no matter how much I study, nothing I do is good enough."

"That's not true. You're doing great."

"Maybe it looks like that from a distance, but I feel like a complete idiot most of the time. I've been sending you stuff about it. Didn't you get them?"

All the emails I've been forwarding to spam, all the messages I couldn't view . . . those were Piper trying to tell me she was struggling?

"I've had phone issues lately," I tell her. "I'm sorry if it looked like I was ignoring you."

239

"It's just, Mom and Dad think I'm burning it up out here, and the truth is I'll be lucky if I pass the semester and keep my scholarship."

"What's the matter? Is it just really hard?"

"It's everything. This damned major, this ridiculous course load I took on, living by myself . . . I'm really glad you're here, by the way. I'm sure you hated that Dad made you come."

"No, I wanted to see you."

This makes her smile, which makes me feel like a jerk. She sits up and wipes her face. "I'm sorry I was judgy at Christmas. I just wasn't prepared for how hard it can be. And I wanted you to do better when it's your turn. I just want you to be ready."

I let out a nervous laugh. "You're making the future look really attractive right now."

"That wasn't what I was going for either." She shrugs. "You have to live your life and make your own mistakes. Just maybe learn from mine and don't study tax law?"

"If it has anything to do with numbers I'll be staying far, far away."

She laughs, then looks at the clock by her bed. "But seriously, though, you need to get some sleep. Look what time it is!"

"Only as long as you're okay."

"I am. I promise."

She reaches out for a hug, and when I put my arms around her I can feel the tension in her body—the anxiety and the fear of failing. Whenever I've felt especially bitter about being in her shadow, when she'd lecture me or I'd simply get tired of feeling second-best, I'd imagine how great it would feel to show the world that the Amazing Piper Finch isn't as amazing as they think. But now that I've seen just how not-amazing her life can be, it doesn't feel great at all.

My sister and I are more alike than I ever knew.

I go back out to the living room to find Truman asleep on the couch in his boxers. I watch him for a few minutes, wondering what he'd do if I lay down next to him. There's no way to fit both of us on the couch without tangling together again, so I find the blankets Piper left, unfurl one, and cover him up. Then I lay out my sleeping bag on the floor and crawl inside.

CHAPTER TWENTY-FIVE

"Skyler."

Truman's voice is soft but pressing. I open my eyes to daylight and the sight of him kneeling on the floor next to me.

"We have to get on the road," he says.

The first thing I remember as I'm waking up is how good it felt to be in his arms. Even though I spent the night on the hard floor of an unfamiliar place, I actually slept well. No nightmares, just a peace that grows stronger as I look at Truman. I reach out to pull him into the sleeping bag with me.

But Truman is already up and moving to the kitchen to make the coffee Piper left out for us. His notes, which got scattered around the floor last night, are in his backpack, which sits by the apartment door. His blanket is folded neatly on the couch. And he's fully dressed in a suit and tie, which only draws attention to my outfit of underwear plus the T-shirt he had on last night.

"Hi," I say, reaching for my glasses.

"Good morning," he replies.

I get up and walk over and stand by the fridge, waiting to be acknowledged, though I have to admit I'm not sure exactly what kind of acknowledgment would be appropriate. Should he give me a good-morning kiss? Push me up against the counter and continue where we left off last night? Or maybe he could just smile. A smile would definitely be nice.

He pours a mug half-full of coffee, then opens the doors to the kitchen's two cabinets.

"I don't think your sister has cream or sugar," he says. "Can you do milk?"

"I like it black."

He fills the mug the rest of the way and puts it on the counter, like a waiter setting down my order. No brush of fingers over the porcelain. Not even a peck on the cheek. Just *plunk, here's your coffee* as he brushes past me to sit at the table.

He takes out his phone and consults his notebook.

"The local traffic report says the highways are congested. We need to leave as soon as possible."

Okay. In the time between when I went to comfort Piper and the sun came up, something changed. Maybe he's freaked out about how far things almost went last night. Maybe he's mad they didn't go as far as he thought they would.

Or maybe he's doing what Truman has done since the start of our enemies-with-benefits relationship, which is pull me in, then push me away. I've been here before, in that uneasy place after letting myself get close to him. It was supposed to be weird then because it caught us by surprise, and it was a foregone conclusion that we'd continue hating each other even after a bit of secret making out. But last night was different. Last night we were in the moment—lots and lots of really good moments—that felt like moving into a future I just might be okay with. Truman and

I aren't enemies anymore. Unless I've completely misread the past twenty-four hours, we are anything but. So why does it feel like we're going backward?

"I think I can get Piper to wash your shirt today," I offer in a lame attempt at acknowledging the big neon thing between us—the fact that I am wearing said shirt, and why is that, and what happens now?

"You can keep it," he answers.

Don't get offended, I tell myself. But I'm starting to feel ridiculous with my bare legs goose-pimpling in the chilly apartment.

"I'm going to take a shower," I say, then bolt from the room.

In Piper's tiny bathroom, I stand under the water, hating how disoriented I feel. I know I didn't imagine the connection between Truman and me last night. It was real, and today it's gone.

When I come out in clean clothes, the apartment door stands open. Truman's in the parking lot loading our backpacks into the car.

"We have to . . . ," he starts.

"I know. I'll be right there."

I creep to Piper's door and crack it open.

"Hey." Over on the bed, she drags her pillow away from her face and squints open an eye. "No, don't get up. I just wanted to tell you we're going. I'll be back tonight."

"Drive safely," she says, her voice gravelly. "See you later."

"Okay." I go to shut the door, then lean back in, just for a second. "I love you. And I know everything's going to be fine. Don't worry."

"Thanks, Skyler," she says. "I love you too."

Getting to Chesterfield takes way less time than expected, though the ride feels longer because I'm not speaking to Truman. Does he notice? Doubtful, since he's spent the entire ride prepping for today's tournament. We've made such good time that it's not even seven o'clock when we pull into town.

Chesterfield reminds me a bit of Alton, with its downtown that looks like someone built it based on what they thought a nice old downtown should look like, and the little local businesses that look like they're teetering on the brink of getting crushed by the big chains that are opening along the highway. We pass a diner that could be Big Sky's sad fraternal twin, and it's the only place around that looks like it has any activity.

There are small towns like this one everywhere. Even State is in a small town, although the university makes everything a little shinier and they have an Indian restaurant, plus a Starbucks. I love Alton, but as I'm looking at this town, which is so similar to my own, I realize that I want to see more. Do more. Be more.

"Turn here—this is the neighborhood," Truman says when the main street comes to an end. As we start down a street of smaller houses, his phone rings. Panic shoots through me. It's got to be Oscar, calling to tell us we've been caught. Or worse, Mr. Milliken telling us we are not only caught but on our way to getting expelled.

"Hello, Mom," says Truman.

I lean over the steering wheel and exhale relief.

"No, you didn't wake me. I'm just having breakfast with my teammates."

This annoys me—irrationally, I know, since Truman obviously can't tell her the truth. But he hasn't said a word to me beyond giving directions, and he doesn't even glance my way now.

Considering everything else between us this morning, I might as well be invisible.

He's silent for a long time, and I can hear his mom's voice faintly through his phone. I can just imagine the kind of ice-cold pep talk she's giving him.

"Yes," he tells her. "I'm ready. I'm feeling really confident."

And again I'm annoyed, but this time not so irrationally, because Truman was sort of a nervous wreck before the reunion site told him he'd win today. For the longest time, he was freaked out about the site. Now he's treating it like his own personal insurance policy. I want to smack him.

I do smack him once we're sitting in front of the little yellow house that is supposed to belong to his aunt. Because Truman is still blathering, this time to his dad, about how great it would be to win state, and about how good going to nationals as a junior is going to make him look to Johns Hopkins.

Truman puts his hand over his arm where I hit him and glares at me.

"Dad, I have to go," he says. "I need to lead a team meeting now."

I roll my eyes as he puts his phone away. "Are you ready?"

"Yes." He gets out of the car and starts up the walk while I scurry to keep pace. Every step brings a pang of anxiety—the same as before the city council meeting. *We haven't prepared enough. We haven't even decided what to say.* But there's no time to figure any of that out because Truman is ringing the doorbell.

We wait. And wait. Finally, the door opens and a woman's head peeks out. She has that red hair I remember from the reunion site, and it's slightly mussed from being in bed. She peers at us, confused.

"Good morning. Aunt Margaret? I'm sorry if we woke you up. It's Truman. Do you remember me?"

Recognition spreads across her face, mixed with disbelief.

"Truman? Really?"

"I know it's early, but I came to see if I could talk with you for just a little bit."

She looks past him to me, clearly struggling to understand.

"This is Skyler," Truman continues. "She brought me here."

I want to step in and introduce myself—properly and pointedly. But I have to make a good impression on this woman, who's looking at us like we just stepped out of another dimension. I tell my touchy side to settle down and give Aunt Margaret a little wave.

"You'll have to excuse me," she says. "I'm just surprised. In a million years I never would have expected to see little Truman here at my house. But you're not little anymore now, are you?"

"I'm seventeen," Truman tells her.

"Has that much time gone by? I remember you when you were a baby, toddling around the old house. You used to love the garden. Now look at you."

"The garden is why I'm here. Aunt Margaret, we have to get back on the road soon, and we have something to talk about that's urgent. Is there someplace we can sit down?"

"Oh! Absolutely! Come in."

She steps back, we walk through the door, and I can't help gasping. The house is filled from floor to ceiling with art, but not just art on display. The home itself is like one big artwork. The living room walls are different colors: one yellow, one turquoise, two a deep red, with the molding around the windows, ceilings and floors painted too, in intricate, colorful patterns. The furniture is mismatched in the best way—lots of retro lines mixed with funky prints, mixed with ornate woodwork and velvet cushions. At strategic places from the ceiling dangle disclike pieces of ceramic that create the impression of wind chimes. On shelves, on tables, and on the floor, sit pieces of pottery. They're not the same as Truman's sculptures, but there's something in the shape and essence of them that's similar.

The way Truman's eyes widen as he looks around, it's almost like he's come face to face with a ghost.

"If I'd known I'd be having guests I would have cleaned," his aunt says. She moves a stack of books off the couch. "But maybe some fresh coffee will make up for the mess?"

"Wow," I say while she's in the kitchen. "This is . . . I mean, it's . . ."

"Breathtaking," Truman says.

"Exactly. Did you know she was an artist?"

"Not like this."

We sit and admire our surroundings until Margaret comes back with steaming lattes.

"Your home is beautiful," I tell her.

"It's my sanctuary. My studio is in the back, but I like having everything all over so my clients can see and my students can find a little inspiration when they need it."

"This is what you do?"

"Yes, dear." She smiles at me, but I can tell it's Truman she really wants to talk with. "So tell me," she says to him. "What brings you to my corner of the world? I can't imagine you got so dressed up just to see me."

"I'm supposed to be in Lake Champion," Truman says. "For debate. I'm competing in the state championships."

"That's quite an accomplishment!"

"Yes. As the team captain, I've led a record number of qualifiers this year."

"Very impressive."

"Debate is my main focus, but I'm also a Merit Scholar and top-ranked in my class. Winning state this year would be perfect timing for my college applications. I'm EDing at Johns Hopkins." Truman seems to realize he's gone overboard with the bragging. He looks down and says, "Anyway, we made a side trip to see you."

"Then I suppose I should be honored. And I suppose I shouldn't be surprised you're so accomplished. I know that's what my sister wanted for you."

"Y-yes, well . . . ," Truman stammers.

"Truman's here for debate," I jump in. "But there's something we wanted to talk with you about."

She side-eyes me, and in that look, I see a flash of Truman's mother. It's a relief when Truman finds his voice again. He tells her about the plans to tear out the garden.

"What a tragedy," she says. "But I don't know what you expected. Even before Dad died, he knew people were picking over his bones. All that arguing and bitterness . . . Sometimes when I think about it, I absolutely cringe."

"It doesn't have to have a tragic ending," Truman says. "You could buy it."

"Why on earth would I do that?"

"So other people can enjoy it."

"Oh no. I'm not inserting myself into the middle of all that again. When I left I didn't look back. And I have no desire to own a garden—especially not when I live four hours away."

"We can get volunteers," I blurt out. "My friend Harper is in love with the place. She would probably live over there if she could. You wouldn't even have to come to Alton."

Truman's aunt looks at me, then back at him. "Do your parents know you're here?"

"No," he answers.

The barest hint of a smile flashes across her face.

"I imagine your mother would love to see the place razed to the ground. It's too bad everything is marred by so much negativity now."

"You could help fix it," Truman says. "Maybe if you save the garden, it will give everyone a chance to heal."

She studies him with piercing eyes. "Why are you really here, Truman?"

"Because it would be a shame if the garden got torn down."

"Lots of things are a shame."

"Because we have friends who really love it," I offer.

"Unfortunately, we lose a lot of things we love in life. It's what we take from those things that matters." She leans in to Truman. "I appreciate that you cared so much about this that you'd come see me. I understand what you're hoping for. But your grandfather did what he did for a reason."

"He left the garden to everybody," Truman says. "He wouldn't want it to be destroyed."

"He left *you* what's in here." She reaches over and points to his heart. "That can't be destroyed, unless you allow it to be."

Truman looks confused. But I know what she's talking about. I reach into the pocket of my skirt, feeling for Miles with his smooth, heavy little body. I take him out and hand him to her. Her face lights up when she sees the sculpture.

"Truman makes these. Isn't it incredible? He's working on one right now, and I've seen pictures of a bunch of other ones."

"I remember you helping Dad in his studio, Truman. I had no idea how much he'd taught you." Margaret holds Miles up to the sunlight that streams through the clouds outside her picture window. "This is beautiful. *This* is what would be a shame to lose."

"It's just a hobby." Truman snatches Miles away. He pushes the sculpture into his own pocket, and I can see his expression closing like those shutters on that window he guards so closely all the time.

A text comes through. He checks it. "It's Oscar. We need to go. They're asking where I am."

He stands, I stand, and I want to shout, *Wait a minute! We can't be done already. That can't be it.*

But that, apparently, *is* it. Truman is already at the door. He turns and says, "Thank you for your time, Aunt Margaret. I'm sorry we got you out of bed so early. And I'm sorry you don't plan to buy the garden. That's really disappointing, but I recognize it's your choice. I hope you have a happy life."

"I hope the same for you," she says. "And, Skyler, it was nice to meet you. Please tell your friend I'm sorry. Surely, she'll find something else to love."

Again I'm left with this feeling of disbelief—that our mission is done so soon, that we're actually failing—paired with a growing sense of sheer frustrated WTF-ness at the universe, at the reunion site, at whatever other cosmic BS made it possible for me to see the future in the first place.

If this is all there is, why was Margaret even on the site to begin with? If this isn't the thing I'm meant to fix, then what is even the point?

Truman has already made it halfway down the front walk. His nose tilts into the air. His eyes are arrogant slits. I scramble into the driver's seat of the car, glancing back to see his aunt on her front porch, watching us go.

Truman does not look back. He's rapidly thumbing texts to Oscar and to everybody else on his team, all of whom are now wondering where he is.

"This was a mistake," he says as I pull away from the curb. "I should never have let you talk me into coming here."

CHAPTER TWENTY-SIX

"Okay, wait a minute." I roll through a stop sign. It's still early, and nobody's out on the roads yet. "You were the one who thought up this whole bring-Skyler-to-the-debate-tournament scheme, so I don't know why you're blaming me now."

"Because you were the one who had the bright idea to try and find a member of my family who clearly had no interest in being found." He makes a disgusted sound. "Milliken wanted to do a team breakfast. Oscar said I had a stomach bug, now everybody's freaking out that I'll be too sick to compete. Meanwhile, here I am forty-five miles away."

"Maybe just tell them the truth. I was approved to stay with Piper. How much trouble can you get in if you just admit you were with me?"

"Honestly, I don't want to find out."

This knocks what's been bugging me all morning into focus. The feeling I've been getting from Truman is the same one I've had from Jordan all these months.

"So what's the real problem, Truman? Is there somehow something wrong with me?"

"What?" He twists around in his seat. "No! Why would you think that?"

"You've barely said two words to me since last night. You barely introduced me to your aunt. You're being awful now. What else am I supposed to conclude?"

He runs both hands through his hair. He's quiet for a moment.

"Fine. You're right. I might not be doing it consciously all the time, but the truth is that I do push you away."

"Right," I say, deflating even more. This is one argument that sucks to win. "Well, I've definitely learned the value of honesty lately, so thanks, I guess, for being honest with me."

"I'm not in *control* with you!" Truman blurts this out like it's a realization that can only right this very second be put into words. "I mean, look at me. I'm doing guerilla visits to an aunt I haven't seen in years, allowing myself to risk being late to the most important debate tournament of my career. I've skipped practices. I've snuck out of dorm rooms and lied to my parents. I don't do those kinds of things, ever. Except when I'm with you."

"You say that like it's a bad thing."

"Sometimes it is. You were right when you said I spend most of my time in the future. Because right or wrong, it's important to me. With you, all of it could change. And I'm not talking about some reunion sometime in the next ten or twenty years, I'm talking about next week. Next month. If I keep doing things that screw up my plans, then what good is planning in the first place?"

The sky rumbles, and a couple of raindrops plop onto my windshield. I look ahead to see a wall of clouds advancing over the houses up the street.

"If there's anything I've learned from that stupid website, it's that the future doesn't always turn out like you planned," I tell him.

254

"No matter how much planning you do. Other people do stuff that affects your future. Things happen that you never even thought to plan for. You can plan all you want, and it could all still turn out differently. So let it go, Truman. Live a little!"

"That is so easy to say when you don't have anything to lose."

"I could lose my best friend!" I pull onto the highway as a clap of thunder strikes. We're making good time, but it's a good thing we left when we did. "And speaking of people making choices, I know you were a lot closer to your grandfather than you want to admit."

He sits up and adjusts his crisp-pressed shirt. "That's in the past."

"Your art isn't, though. It could be your future too."

Truman looks out the window, his jaw twitching every few seconds. "Can we go any faster?"

I press the gas, checking my mirrors for patrol cars. "Don't worry. We'll make it in plenty of time. I'm feeling like the universe is on our side with this one."

The second I finish that sentence, the universe lets me know I'm wrong by unleashing a tsunami of rain that forces me to slow back down until I'm able to see out the windshield again. Everything's fine for a few minutes, until we spot emergency lights up ahead.

"There must be an accident," I say.

All Truman says is "Oh no."

While we're sitting on the highway, waiting, my phone starts blowing up too. Pissed-off texts from Riley, texts from my dad, still angry that I lied about my trig grade, concerned texts from Mom, wanting to know why I'm not answering . . . Each ping gets scratchier, until my phone makes a sound like a plane crash in an old movie—a long, descending whine that I almost expect to end with the sound of a far-off explosion.

After ten agonizing minutes, traffic starts again, but it's ridiculously slow.

"Don't freak out, Truman. It's going to be OK."

"Let me see your phone," he says.

"Why?"

"I want to make sure it's still showing us winning today."

I run my finger over the screen, trying to wake it up. I push the home button. I push the power and the home button together. I check to make sure the charger is plugged in. Nothing works.

"I think my phone died. For good this time."

He makes a sound that definitely sounds like freaking out.

"But what if it did still show you winning? Is that the kind of future you really want?"

"What kind of question is that?" Truman explodes. "Of course it is!"

"What if all your plans come true? Say you win today. And then you win nationals. And you win every scholarship you apply for, and you go to Johns Hopkins, and you keep winning all the way up to working for Senator Stevens. You saw what's going to happen. He's a criminal. Or if he isn't now, then he will be."

"You didn't like it when I judged your choices," Truman says. "Who are you to judge mine?"

"I'm willing to admit that some of your judging was right. I do want to go someplace better than State. I do need to put myself out there more. You were right about all that. And the fact that I'm willing to admit you were right should tell you how serious I am. You saw how people were talking about you on the reunion site. Is that really how you want to be remembered?"

Traffic is slowing again. There's another fender bender up ahead, and even though both cars are off on the side of the road, people are still crawling past. When Truman speaks again, his voice is cold and clipped.

"I appreciate your concern about my social standing more than ten years from now, Skyler. But right now the only future I want to think about is the one that I am dangerously close to missing."

We creep along, watching the minutes tick by, and I know I can't deny I've screwed up. I am potentially making Truman miss something that means everything to him, and for what? A community garden? Harper pretty much admitted she'd stopped doing her therapy homework for a while, and finding the right mix of medications for her sounds like a roller coaster. Drugs and action plans, plus any of the other little things that can happen on any given day . . . all that has an impact. So why did I think it was all up to me?

I've been searching for reasons to explain the reunion site, but maybe there's no grand plan. Maybe there's just something about crappy, glitchy phones that allows them to open up portals in time. Maybe it's nothing personal, and people like me around the world are trying to get directions on their GPS, only to find themselves staring at pictures of themselves as old people.

But one thing does poke at me, even as I'm realizing all this. When I think back to the first reunion site, I remember something I completely overlooked because I was so freaked out about seeing Truman and me together. I looked *happy* in those pictures. If I had asked Future Me back when all this started, she might have said that she wouldn't want me to change a thing.

By some miracle, this second traffic slowdown doesn't last long. We break free of the bottleneck and start gliding down

257

smooth highways. Before long, I'm pulling into Lake Champion. We're going to make it.

"Oscar says drop me off down the street," Truman instructs. "There's a back door he's going to meet me at. We'll pretend I came down on the elevators and we'll meet everybody at the buses."

As the dorm comes into view, he pulls together his things and glances at my lap.

"Is your phone still dead?"

I try again to wake it up. Nothing. Not even a croak or a beep or a burp.

"Yes," I tell him. "But maybe that's good. Maybe don't think about your future today. Maybe just enjoy that you're here. Maybe just enjoy right now."

CHAPTER TWENTY-SEVEN

STATE DEBATE TOURNAMENT—DAY 1 NOTES

Tons of people gathered in the auditorium of Baldwin U fine arts bldg. Alton feeling pumped. On the stage, a big bracket that gets filled in as the competition goes on. 9:45 a.m.—1st-round matchups posted, and people start splitting off. Everyone debating Alton looks scared. And everybody knows the top favorite to win it all—Truman Alexander. People stand aside to let him pass in the halls. 1st rounds take place in classrooms thruout the building. Impossible to see everything, but even early rounds have big audiences. Judges under strict orders to start at 10 a.m. sharp.

I look up from the back of the classroom where I've come to watch Riley debate a guy from Westwood Prep. Mr. Milliken suggested I start with her, which doesn't turn out to be as awkward as I'd thought it would be because she is in the zone and could not care less about me or anything else.

She stands at the front of the classroom in an actual suit and heels, looking like a total badass. "Is anybody not ready?" she asks.

The guy a few feet away from her looks like he might be ready to vomit.

She then proceeds to annihilate him.

I keep up my notes the best I can, shaking out my wrist to stave off cramping. I'm learning a lot and, actually, maybe, sort of enjoying it, but one thing is 100 percent clear: I have got to improve my handwriting.

DAY 1, ROUND 2 NOTES

These people talk fast! Truman doesn't seem so annoying when everybody else is doing it too. Tessa Martinez quote: "You're so well prepared, you get on a roll, and you just know when you're crushing someone. People don't look at debate as a sport, but it definitely feels like one." So far every Alton debater has won his/ her round.

DAY 1, ROUND 3 NOTES

"This should be legendary"—Quote from a girl in the bathroom before my first time watching Truman debate.

No, the girl did not know who I was, so no, her comment did not in any way refer to me, but still. With Truman's and my history, it felt appropriate. I waited a couple of rounds before sitting in on one of Truman's. And in order to witness his "legendary"-ness in action, I make sure to sit in the back—behind a large man with a large head, so I won't be easy to spot. It's impossible to truly hide, but with things ending on such a chilly note between us, I don't feel comfortable sitting right up in his face.

Turns out Truman barely glances in my direction. He sets up his laptop, gazes at the ceiling until his opponent and judge are ready, then lets loose his arguments like someone pressed play on a recording.

He commands the room, and it looks like he could do this in his sleep. But there's something sort of automatic about it. His opponent has the charisma of a soggy noodle, though, so it's not like Truman has anything to worry about. He wins easily.

Once the match is over, I feel like there's no longer any need to hide. "Good job," I tell him as I file out with the rest of the spectators.

"Thanks," he replies.

And that's it. He's packing up, and I'm pushed out the door with the crowd. I don't know exactly what I was expecting, but I'm not sure what I just saw rises to the level of "legendary."

That feeling is confirmed by the look on Mr. Milliken's face when I spot him out in the hall. He doesn't look like someone who feels secure about a championship. In fact, he looks just a little worried.

Overheard at lunch: Truman Alexander off his game.
Teammates say off the record that his heart isn't in it. 3 Alton
debaters lose their last rounds. Growing sense among the team
that the competition is tougher than originally thought.

QUARTERFINALS NOTES

Packed room. Truman vs. guy from Philips Country Day School
who is supposed to be some kind of debate god—second in fame
only to Truman "the legend." Truman arguing affirmative.
Alton teammates who aren't still debating sit together
in support.

Dad and I are big basketball fans. Every year when it's college tournament time, one of the most exciting—and excruciating—things is wondering which top seeds are going to perform as expected and which are going to choke. As Truman's quarterfinal debate gets ready to start, the atmosphere in the room feels like that. Nobody can put their finger on what exactly is up with Truman, but there's a feeling his position might not be as secure as everyone had assumed.

Truman and his opponent stand at opposite tables. If looks alone were the measure, then the other guy looks like no match—he's short and twitchy, with an actual receding hairline. Truman, meanwhile, appears calm, confident, and—heaven help me—extremely hot with his red tie and his floppy dark hair and his greener than green eyes. His opening argument could probably be considered a masterpiece of debate, if the reaction from his teammates is to be believed. Everybody relaxes a little. His opponent is good, but so far not threatening.

Truman starts his first rebuttal. Three sentences in, he stumbles over a word, then a sentence. It's not super noticeable. He recovers quickly. But that hanging-by-the-fingernails feeling is back. His eyes lose a bit of their steeliness. His teammates suck in their breath. His opponent does not stumble.

The next time Truman's up, he clears his throat. He starts talking.

Then he appears to lose his place.

"No," murmurs Tessa Martinez, next to me. "Nonononono..."

Truman looks down at his laptop. He scrolls. He clears his throat again. Ten excruciating seconds go by—I know, because for some reason I've started counting silently. Truman looks up.

He starts over. At the table across from him, his opponent stands straighter. Suddenly that receding hairline does look like a threat. A real, serious one.

On the other side of me, I hear Mr. Milliken whisper to one of the parent chaperones.

"This isn't Truman. What's wrong with him?"

Advancing to tomorrow's semifinals: Riley Brennan and Oscar McLearen. Not advancing: Truman Alexander. Reaction from team faculty sponsor Milliken: "Stunning upset"—Truman unavailable for quote.

No one knows how to feel when the competition day ends, and the names of the semifinalists are added to the bracket. They're proud of Riley and Oscar. And they're freaked out about Truman. After losing the quarterfinals, he packed up and hurried away. No one has seen him since.

I, on the other hand, can't unsee the look on Truman's face when he lost his place or his train of thought, or whatever caused him to pause, repeat himself, pause again, stammer, and then simply stare at his laptop screen for those few painful seconds. It was a look of disbelief and terror. Then his eyes flicked up to meet mine. I don't know what the expression on my face looked like. I don't even know what I was thinking, other than that I'd started counting seconds, and continued counting while our eyes locked. *Eight . . . nine . . . ten . . .* He looked away, started over, and the rest is, to coin a now-painful pun, legend.

Back at the dorm, Mr. Milliken orders Chinese food for a quiet night in so those who are advancing can rest and prepare.

"Skyler, do you want anything?" he asks just as I'm trying to sneak away from the death-ray glares people have been shooting my way. They know Truman was with me last night. They know he arrived this morning with just minutes to spare. They assume I've worked some sort of witchcraft to sabotage him today.

"Thanks," I say, "but I'm just going to go to my sister's."

"Are you sure? We have tons of food, and I don't want to be responsible for you passing out at the wheel from hunger."

He's been so nice that I don't feel like I can refuse. I take a plate and approach the food table. Riley's there, dressing up her lo mein with an alarming amount of hot mustard.

"Congratulations," I tell her. "You killed it today."

She grabs a pair of chopsticks, then turns to Sweatshirt Guy from Outside English Class—I know now that his name is Nawaf—and asks him for a napkin. They both pretend I'm not there. I put my plate back and turn to leave.

But something catches my eye out the window. Truman is sitting alone on the quad with his back against a tree in the sun.

I put a couple of egg rolls into a napkin and go outside.

"Um . . . hi?"

Truman has Miles in his hand, and he's just sort of looking at him. At the sound of my voice he raises his head. I can see the start of a sunburn across his nose.

"I didn't know if you'd be hungry," I say as I sit. I lay the napkin in his lap. He takes a bite of egg roll, then puts it down and sighs.

"I know I should be eating with the team. I'm just . . . I don't know, tired."

"Truman, I'm so sorry. Jordan told me I mess everything up, and maybe she's right. I shouldn't have kept you up so late."

"Skyler."

"I shouldn't have got you up so early and made you talk to your aunt."

"Skyler."

"I shouldn't have argued with you in the car. I shouldn't have even done this trip in the first place."

"It's not your fault," he says.

"But you were right. I talked you into everything."

He picks the skin off the second egg roll, nibbles it, then puts the whole thing in his mouth.

"Seeing my aunt was your idea," he agrees. "But bringing you along for the championship was mine. I guess there was a part of me that really wanted you here. Maybe everything that happened happened for a reason."

He takes the other, half-finished little man from his pocket and holds him next to Miles, studying both together.

"I've qualified for state every year of high school. This was supposed to be my year to win. But every time I got up there, I couldn't stop thinking about what you said yesterday. You asked me, 'Why debate?' And I realized, I don't really know."

"I do. Because it's cool. And these people on your team are cool too. They hate me, but they're crazy good, and they're passionate, and I can definitely see how this whole thing is a rush. I personally would advocate for less fast talking and more feels, but my perspective on debate has definitely changed."

Truman smiles, the first real smile I've seen from him all day. "Does that mean you're going to do it next year?"

"Are *you* doing it next year?"

"I said I needed to figure out why I'm doing it, not that I'm quitting."

"Would I get to argue with you?"

"Most definitely. There will be timers. And judges."

"Ah, so someone who's objective. I'm not sure I can resist the chance to officially win an argument every now and then."

"You'll be amazing at it, I'm sure."

We're sitting shoulder to shoulder, my head nearly resting in the crook of his neck. It's only an inch or two to bring my lips to his, but I wait. I don't want this to be another time when things just happen. I want this to be a moment we both choose.

Truman fills the gap. He kisses me softly, slowly, the kind of kiss that could go on forever.

"People are watching," I whisper.

"Good."

"What's going to happen now?"

He leans back and looks skyward. "Well, I have to support my teammates tomorrow. Then I guess I have to figure out something else to do this summer since I won't be going to nationals."

"I mean, what's going to happen to us?"

He takes my hand, slipping Miles inside my palm.

"I hope by now you know how much I like you, and maybe— more than maybe, actually—even love you. I just think I need some time."

This hurts, especially since I know, in spite of everything that drove me crazy about Truman or drove me away or drove me to do things I didn't understand, that I love him too. But I get it. I do.

Truman has to decide what he wants out of his future. Harper has to work hers out too. I don't have any answers, and I can't even look for them on the reunion site anymore because my phone truly is dead.

Besides, it goes both ways. I can't fix the future for my friends, and they can't fix my future for me. We can stand by one another. We can even help a little. But each one of us has to figure it out on our own.

CHAPTER TWENTY-EIGHT

SUNDAY MORNING SEMIFINALS/FINALS—NOTES

Riley Brennan advances to finals—Oscar loses his matchup, but still going on to Nationals. Final debate takes place on auditorium stage w/ packed audience—Alton sits together to cheer Riley on v. the Philips Country Day guy who beat Truman. Riley arguing negative. Match intense. Atmosphere electric. Both competitors look confident of a win. Judges take a long time deliberating. Final vote: 2/1 neg. Riley wins state tournament. Riley Quote: "I'm proud of how everyone on our team did, and I'm honored to be representing Alton this summer in Anaheim." Oscar Quote: "*&$% yes! Wooohooo!" Faculty sponsor Milliken: "What he said."

CHAPTER TWENTY-NINE

Truman does not ride back to Alton with me. He says he needs to celebrate with his teammates, and I can't argue with that, even though Oscar's sister Shelby, the sophomore Mr. Milliken pairs me up with instead, talks the entire four hours home, making me miss Truman's silent stretches even more.

The trip ends with the bridge over the river, and I can tell right away that something's different. I try to put my finger on what it is. To the left, you can usually just see the peaks of the Blessing mansion over a tangle of trees rising from behind a stone wall. As I steer onto the bridge, I realize that I can see too much of the mansion now. The towers are fully visible, as is the back of the house.

More of the house means less of what kept it hidden.

The debate bus continues over the bridge, but I veer onto the street that winds up to Truman's grandfather's place.

"Oh wow," says Shelby as the car bounces over the mud-caked road. "When did this happen?"

A very orderly tornado has flattened everything. The garden wall is gone, the stones sitting in a pile of rubble by the street. Overturned soil blankets the ground. The planks of the wooden shed have been stacked off to the side, a few lonely statues leaning against them. The mansion stands next to the wreckage, looking stunned and bare. The only color comes from yellow bulldozers that dot the scene like lions on their prey. I stop the car and sit, staring. They must have worked fast—all this was still here when we left Friday morning.

"Isn't that where you had prom?" asks Shelby. "I heard it was amazing."

"Yes," I answer. "It was. Can I use your phone?"

"Skyler?" Mom sounds close to frantic when she answers. "Skyler, where are you?"

"Back in town."

"Where? We came to the school to surprise you, and you aren't here. Mr. Milliken said you were no longer following the bus. I am furious with you! Why on earth didn't you call before now?"

"Because my phone croaked, and also I knew you'd be furious with me." I hear her stopped-up laugh and feel bad for making her worry. "I would be at school, but I saw the Blessing house when I came over the bridge."

"Oh, sweetheart, I know. They did it so fast it barely even made the news. You didn't talk Truman's aunt into buying it, did you?"

"No, which I guess is a good thing. There would have been nothing to buy."

There's a muffled moment where I can tell she's talking to Dad; then she comes back on.

"Your father says to tell you you're grounded. He's unhappy with your trigonometry grade."

"I know. Tell him I'm working on it, I promise."

"Just meet us at home. We can talk about all of this there. And we are getting you a new phone, I don't care how much it costs!"

"I'll be home as soon as I can," I tell her. "I have to drop Shelby off first."

As I turn the car around, I wonder if Truman saw the wreckage when the bus came over the bridge. I wonder if Harper has seen it too. I wonder if all this was happening when she and I were talking. And I wonder how they'll both feel now that the garden is gone. The rubble is like a period at the end of a long sentence: whatever future had all of us meeting here for our reunion, it's been wiped away.

What happens now is anyone's guess.

CHAPTER THIRTY

"Where's Jordan?"

Harper approaches our usual table in the cafeteria with her tray. I glance around, conveniently overlooking the far corner, where Jordan sits with Kailey and her other prom committee co-chairs. Jordan has been sitting with them instead of me ever since our fight, and Harper has no idea because this is the first time since then that all of us have been back at school together.

"Is Jordan not here? I hadn't noticed."

Harper gives me one of her looks that says she knows I'm full of crap. She puts her tray down, along with two gift bags that have been dangling from her arm. She goes over to Jordan, pulls her to her feet, and walks her over. She points to the empty chair next to mine and orders, "Sit."

Harper sits across from us. Jordan side-eyes me. I focus on my sandwich.

"I come bearing gifts," says Harper. She puts one of the bags down in front of Jordan, the other in front of me.

I peek inside to find a stack of Harper's vegan cookies.

"Jordan," she says, "I wanted to make sure you know how incredible your prom was. People cannot stop talking about it. You did the most amazing job of anybody who has ever put on a prom at this school, and you should know that you are going to go down as a prom goddess. I have no idea how you're going to top yourself next year."

Jordan's bag has cookies too. Her frostiness starts to melt as she takes a bite.

Harper turns to me.

"Skyler, I wanted to say thank you for worrying about me. I'm pretty sure I know what you were doing this weekend, and I appreciate it, and I'm sorry the garden was destroyed while you were gone."

I take out a cookie of my own. I break off a piece and feel it melt on my tongue.

"I'm the one who should be saying sorry," I tell her. "I can't believe they actually tore it out. What are you and the other volunteers going to do now?"

"Volunteer somewhere else? It's just a garden."

She's right. Of course, she is. And looking back now, I can see how all the things I told myself—about the garden, about the reunion site, and even about Harper—were more about me than they were about her. When I think about it, the entire trip this weekend was probably more about me.

Jordan is sitting with her arms crossed, waiting for me to admit she was right. And she was, in a way. But I needed that trip to work through things she has no idea about.

So actually, I was right too.

"I just . . . I don't know." I break a cookie in half, then break that half in half, searching for the right words. "I had this idea that if I saved the garden, it would somehow save you."

"I don't need saving," Harper says. "I just need my friends to be friends."

"I told her that!" Jordan crows. She turns to me. "I told you that, Sky."

"Well, to be fair, Jordan, I wasn't completely operating on a hunch. I had reasons for doing what I did."

"Are we talking about that reunion thing again?" Harper puts her hands over her ears. "If so then shut up, shut up, shut up! I have no desire to know anything about what's on it."

"You don't have to worry," I tell her. "Not even the tech squad geeks at the phone store could get my old phone to work again. And I couldn't get the site up on the new one if I wanted to."

Harper has been playing with my new phone while we talk, admiring its sleek, shiny amazingness. Mom bought it last night. She got the best, fastest phone available to ensure that it wouldn't break down like my old one did. It truly is a phone to envy, and I would be gloating if I weren't so tired.

"There's nothing on it yet," Harper says. "Why haven't you taken any pictures?"

I haven't loaded the phone with apps or taken any photos because I went to bed immediately after setting it up. I slept without dreaming or, judging from the position I laid down and woke up in, moving until my alarm went off at seven a.m.

"We'll give Skyler plenty to post when she's ungrounded," Jordan says. "I'm planning an epic last-day-of-school party, and I've got a plan to get your parents to let you go, Sky. Not to brag, but . . . okay I'm going to brag. It's brilliant."

She's off again, embarking on another of her party-planning crusades. And Harper is listening, encouraging her with that spark lighting up her eyes. The tripod is balanced, each of us playing her part. But we know each other a little better now—the strong parts and the weak parts. Maybe it will make us all stronger.

"I just want to know one thing, Sky." Jordan leans in and, holding one hand up to keep Harper from hearing, says, "So before your old phone died and you couldn't see the future anymore, how did my hair look?"

After lunch, I take my trig test. Mr. Bannister grades it as soon as I hand it in. He calls me into the hall and hands me the paper, facedown. My stomach clenches as I turn it over: 72 percent.

"I got a C?" Relief spreads through me, warm and sweet.

"Just barely," he says. "But I'll take it, all things considered."

"Does this mean I'm not failing anymore?"

"As of right now you are just barely not failing. That's why I called you out here." He takes the paper back so he can record the grade. "We don't have much longer to this school year, and any more Fs could wipe out today's progress. I understand you've been working with a tutor. Would you say that helped you do better today?"

I nod. "Also my dad grounded me for the rest of my life until I get my grade up, so I guess that's some extra motivation."

"Well," he chuckles. "I think it's probably better if the motivation comes from you. But whatever works . . ."

"Actually, I did want to ask you something."

"Shoot."

"Well, I'll be applying to college soon. And I want to try for some scholarships. I'm sure this year's adventure in almost failing math isn't going to help me any. So what should I do if I want to look better?"

"Nobody likes to be told summer school. But there's a college prep program I do that I think you should sign up for. If you can show you've mastered the material from this year, then the school lets you take that average score on your transcript, assuming it's higher."

Ideas are starting to popcorn inside my head.

"When it comes to something like this," he continues, "I always say it's best to set a goal, then develop a strategy for achieving it."

"You're right. I just haven't always done that, which is going to change."

"So then, Skyler," Mr. Bannister says. "What is your plan?"

CHAPTER THIRTY-ONE

M s. Laramie opens the discussion of *Wuthering Heights* with a question about love. Gabriela Reitz jumps in immediately to gush about how romantic the book was. "Catherine and Heathcliff's love lived beyond the grave," she says. "It was so strong it destroyed them."

From across the room, Truman gives a slow eye roll.

"Heathcliff did terrible things out of a desire to get back at her and anyone else he felt had wronged him," he says. "There's nothing romantic about it."

"Truman's right," I add. "They were both terrible people who ruined the lives of everyone around them. Cathy basically pouted herself to death."

Gabby makes a sour face. "She was pining away."

"She had a baby who needed a mother. She had a perfectly good husband. Pining away for a jerk like Heathcliff makes her a jerk too."

Truman's mouth quirks up in a half smile and I nod, giving him the mental equivalent of a fist bump from across the room. Ms. Laramie leaves Gabby to her dysfunctional fangirling and moves on to another topic. When the bell rings, I hurry over to catch Truman before he leaves.

"Can we talk?"

"Of course," he says.

We head outside, moving slowly against all the other people hurrying to get away from school. He pulls himself onto the ledge that borders the hill down to the parking lot. He helps me up, and we sit with our legs dangling.

"Have you heard anything from your aunt?" I ask. We haven't had a real conversation in over a week—somehow it feels much longer than that. "Did you tell her they tore out the garden?"

"My mom told her."

"They talked?"

"Yeah, she called. And the funny thing is, my mom didn't know what to do when she found out I'd gone to see Margaret because I think she actually enjoyed talking to her sister. I was expecting to get the smackdown of the century, but so far, nothing."

"Were they disappointed about debate?"

"Yes."

"Oh."

"But I'm focusing on other things, so they can't be too upset. Believe it or not, I'm looking into art camp up at Baldwin. It's just a week, but it looks like fun. And then my dad put me in an Advanced Physics course online. I need to boost my STEM portfolio."

"I'm going to ignore the fact that you just used the word *portfolio* and say I'm glad you're staying around, because I'm doing some summer school stuff too. Maybe you'd like to be my math tutor? I can't pay you, I'd just be really appreciative."

He smiles his half smile. I catch myself smiling too.

"I'd like that a lot," he says.

"No one has to know anything else—especially your parents. And there doesn't even have to be anything else. I'll settle for just passing calculus, or whatever the next circle of hell is in the math world."

"Skyler."

"What?"

He kisses me, short and heart-achingly sweet. It's a "for now" kiss. I put my head on his shoulder, not wanting *now* to end. But then Dad texts to make sure I'm heading straight home because as far as he's concerned, I will not be allowed freedom—or anything remotely resembling fun—until I not only improve my math grade, but am also tracking toward toppling Truman from his top-of-the-class ranking.

I tell Truman goodbye, then hop down from the wall to go meet Jordan. Starting down the hill, I spot Eli walking slow and sure across the quad, like the world is watching and he knows it. And there's Brynn strutting next to him. They're shouting to their friends, laughing with each other, holding hands to dart away from a sprinkler that just spurted to life on the trampled grass.

They're not perfect people, but they are a perfect couple.

So at least one of the schemes I hatched to try and influence the future had a happy ending: Eli and Brynn wound up with everything they wanted. As I turn back to see Truman in his plaid shirt and loafers, pushing that dark hair out of his eyes so he can watch me go, I realize that even though I have no idea what's going to happen, and even though it bothers me more than I thought it would, in a weird way, I sort of did too.

CHAPTER THIRTY-TWO

Jordan's last-day-of-school party is the best-kept nonsecret ever. Everybody knows it's happening, but nobody knows where. All anyone knows is that the invitation will go up on Jordan's Instagram the morning of.

Even I've been kept in the dark—not that Jordan's been silent. Not even close. For days she's been making promises about just how spectacular this party is going to be. And true to her other prediction, she managed to talk my mom and dad into letting me go.

"It's a charitable thing," she told me on our way in to school this morning. "They couldn't say no to a good cause."

I rolled down my window and stuck my head out, gulping air. My grounding includes having minimal access to my car, so I've been getting up close and personal with motion sickness thanks to Jordan's driving.

"You mean I don't know what's going on, but my parents do?" I pouted.

"Nope, they know as much as you. Just don't mess up your curfew. I promised you'd be home by ten."

"It's ridiculous I even have a curfew. I'm passing trig now, but they won't unground me until Bannister posts the final exam grade."

"He'll probably be there," Jordan said. "You can bug him for it, then text your mom and dad for parole."

"Even teachers are coming?"

"I told you, it's going to be epic."

And so, while people pass their yearbooks around, waiting for first bell to ring, they're also obsessively checking their phones to find out just what Jordan's cooked up. At eight-thirty a.m., the post appears.

Happy summer and welcome to a new AHS tradition!
3 p.m. City Park, pavilion #11. Bring $ . . . You'll see
why! See you there!

The rest of the day, not a single thing gets done. At lunch, a couple of people drove to the park for a sneak peek and were met at the driveway to pavilion 11 by honest to God police officers. No one allowed in until three, they were told.

By the time last bell rings, the whole thing is still a mystery.

"Where's Harper?" I ask, back in Jordan's car for the drive over.

"Already there," Jordan replies. "Kimura let her out early."

"So Harper's in on this too? Why does she get to help and not me?"

"Because I was mad at you. And because you were grounded."

"Would you have included me if I wasn't?"

"Doubtful."

She pulls into the park, and we wind around to the picnic

pavilions. The first thing I notice is that the old house that's always been used as a maintenance shed has a new coat of paint and a cheerful red door. I sit forward when I see what's on the other side.

A tight-slatted wooden fence stretches from the side of the house, bending at the edge of the lot into a rectangle so big it's impossible to see around. A few trees peek over the fence, their branches draped in streamers and what look like twinkle lights. The sound of a DJ warming up comes from inside.

Harper stands in the gate. When she sees us she starts hopping up and down.

"I've been waiting to show you this!" she squeals. "You won't believe it."

She leads me forward as Jordan explains in my ear.

"You have to use your imagination, OK? It's going to take a while before it looks anything close to how it did, and we have a ton of money to raise. But you can sort of see the idea, can't you?"

Inside the gate is little more than an expanse of cleared land with a few trees here and there. Someone has built wooden paths throughout and a big wooden pad at the center. Leaning against the far side of the fence is a row of sculptures: cupids, gazing balls, and two twin angels, each clutching a heart in her hand.

Harper brings me to an easel next to the food table, which holds a giant map showing the layout of a garden next to an artist's rendering of a watercolored wonderland. Climbing roses, a koi pond, a gazebo . . . OLMSTEAD-BLESSING MEMORIAL GARDEN is emblazoned across the top.

"When did this happen?" I say. "*How* did it happen?"

Harper snags a pretzel from a tray piled high with snacks and says, "When we lost the hearing, I knew I couldn't just feel bad about it. I mean, I did feel bad, obviously. But the volunteers were all keeping in touch, and one of them asked the city if there was any place we could use to try and rebuild the garden."

"They basically donated this part of the park," Jordan chimes in. "And they found some money—just enough to paint the house and put up the fence."

"My dad did the tilling and the paths," says Harper. "We hauled over the sculptures last weekend."

Jordan points to the fence line. "They were even able to save some of the trees."

"That's the best part," Harper says. "A lot of the plants are from the old garden. They kept a seed library, and a bunch of things were getting overgrown. We can transplant them here and it will give them a chance to grow all over again."

People are starting to show up, pouring in through the gate, looking around, confused. Nick Kroger, who was enlisted by Jordan for his DJ skills, cranks up the music to make it feel more like a party, and the energy comes up a notch.

I, on the other hand, am completely floored.

"How were you doing all this and I didn't know about it?"

"We wanted to surprise you," Harper says.

"Then you got in trouble," Jordan adds, "which made it easier to get the finishing touches ready."

I scan the growing crowd, looking for an uptilted nose and wide green eyes.

"Where is Truman? Does he know about this?"

"He knows."

A hand on my arm, a voice that sends shivers down my back— I look over to see Truman beside me.

"Don't get mad, Sky," says Jordan. "Harper asked him to ask his aunt if she'd donate. She said yes!"

"It's not a lot," Truman tells me. "Just enough to put her name on it."

"Maybe your parents will give something too?" I ask him.

"That might be asking for too much."

"We'll get the money," says Harper. "Everest can donate."

I'm nodding along, caught up in her enthusiasm.

"Truman can use his mad persuasive skills. But I'll write the speeches so he doesn't put them to sleep."

"Speaking of which," says Jordan, "I should go tell everybody what all this is about. They look like they're starting to doubt my epicness."

She strides to the DJ stand, takes the microphone, and by the time she's done talking up the new garden, people are stuffing dollars into a flower pot that Harper passes around, and bidding on items at a silent auction table. Add the music back in, and the party is on as only a Jordan party can be.

It's perfect—a better solution than I could have ever dreamed of.

So why am I not happier?

I wade through the crowd and sneak out the gate, making my way around the fence to the back where there's nothing but gravel, bits of old trash, and a scrubby hill. I sit with my back to the wood, listening to everyone having a great time inside, and before I can even try to stop them, two surprise tears drip onto the fabric of my shorts. I take off my glasses and swipe at my cheeks, only to feel more coming.

"Skyler."

I put my glasses back on and run an arm across my snotty nose. "Truman. How is it that you always manage to find me when I'm a complete mess?"

"You don't look like a mess."

"Do you want to debate me on that?"

"Not really."

He sits, and it feels so good having him near that I want to start crying all over again. Because I'm grateful for everything my friends have done. Because the old garden is gone after all that effort to try and save it. Because Truman is here, and because I miss him.

"Hey," he says. "This is supposed to be a happy day. Why are you out here?"

"Have you ever had a hangover?" I ask. "I had one once, after a party at Kiran's. I spent the night at Jordan's and woke up with a massive headache, but that's not what I remember most about it. The thing I really remember is how wiped out I felt. I sort of feel like that now."

"It's been an eventful couple of months for sure." Truman places the yearbook he's been holding into my lap. We worked all day yesterday putting in the spring activities insert, fresh from the printer, and Truman's got it open to the page I put together about the state debate tournament. "You did a great job on this. Everybody on the team wants you for their best friend now."

"That's a change," I laugh through my tears. "I sort of figured I'd never get invited to one of those debate parties."

"You'd probably be the guest of honor if you wanted." He hands me a Sharpie. "Would you sign it for me?"

I look at the spread, feeling proud of the story and photos. Ms. Stephenson is submitting the version I did for newswriting class to a scholarship contest, and now I'm thinking I can see myself at journalism school somewhere.

One of the photos, though—the team shot with Oscar and Duncan and Riley holding their trophies—stands out for what it doesn't show.

"I still feel bad that you didn't get one of those," I tell him. "That whole side trip was an exercise in futility, as my dad would say."

"Maybe not. I didn't tell you this because I didn't want you blaming yourself any more than you already were, but the whole time we were competing I could hear your voice in my head. *Just be glad you're here. Just enjoy the experience. You don't have to win everything.*"

"Really?" I can feel the tears starting again.

"Yes," he says. "I've missed that voice."

His hand snakes across my leg, and when his fingers find mine a ripple shoots up my arm, all tingling and electric. What used to be millions of bugs is now thousands of delicious little bubbles washing over my skin.

"I've missed your voice too," I admit.

"Well, you're going to be sick of it again in a few weeks when it's all math all the time."

He's so close that it's nothing to bring my free hand up, capture that half smile and say, "Then maybe you should stop talking."

Kissing Truman with the sounds of the party at the new, second-chance garden behind us, I guess it's not surprising that the reunion site would find its way into my head. I've tried really hard not to think about it. But being with him unlocks something in my memory. Pictures start clicking into place.

All of us together in a gazebo surrounded by flowers.

Harper shaking hands with a redheaded woman—Truman's aunt Margaret.

I pull away.

"What?" Truman says. "Still too soon?"

"No, it's just . . ." I bite my lip, thinking it through. Maybe those photos weren't of the old garden. Maybe they were taken here, when everything has had time to grow and be loved to the point where it looks just as beautiful as the one that's no longer there. What if this is the future we were looking at all along?

"I'm going to tell you something," I say. "And if it freaks you out, then maybe we shouldn't be doing this, because I can't keep on wondering whether things are going to get weird again between us. *I* think it's weird, but I also think I should just accept that weird is the way things are sometimes."

"Okay . . ." He looks puzzled, and I plant another kiss on him—either to get him ready or to tell him goodbye. I pull everything I can out of the moment; then I tell him my theory. He listens. And I know he's picturing the same thing I am: the two of us with matching bands on our fingers.

"Does this mean we have to get married?" he asks. "Do you *want* to get married?"

"I have no idea, and I'm not supposed to because I'm in high school, right? I mean, as much as Jordan would probably love to plan my wedding, I'd rather just focus on my math grade."

Truman manages to look disappointed and relieved at the same time.

"What I mean is that I don't care about what happens later," I say. "All I know is I really, really like being with you now."

"I really like being with you too." Now he's the one kissing me, and it's not weird; it's the answer I need. Truman isn't anywhere else in time but right here with me, and I know that whatever the future might hold, for now we're going to be okay.

While we've been kissing, Jordan's been texting. I text back that

I have not disappeared, that I'm here, and no one should panic. I pull in a breath and stand, helping Truman to his feet. His hand stays in mine as we walk back around the fence.

Inside is a crowded crush of people talking, eating, and signing yearbooks. And more people are showing up too: parents, teachers—I even see a couple of city council people hanging out on the fringes. Over by the fence, I spot Mr. Bannister with Ms. Laramie. He catches my eye, gives a double thumbs-up, and I immediately text Mom and Dad.

> Passed trig exam. Can I stay out later?
> I've got a ride home—or you can come party too!

I thought you'd never ask.
Dad adds:
Proud of you. Leaving the office now.
"Looks like my parents are coming," I tell Truman.
"I'll be on my best behavior," he says.
"That's what I'm afraid of."

Harper spots Truman and me as we're checking out the snack table. Even though there's no real dance floor, she still manages to sweep us up into a threesome with Jordan joining in for a crazy quartet. I manage to get my arms around all of them. Laughing, we bounce to the music while Truman stands stiffly by. We dance around him until he has no choice but to join in. He starts bobbing and swaying with surprising abandon, throwing in what looks like a fencing move here and there.

"He's adorable," Jordan tells me as Truman does a booty shake in his cargos.

"Why did you hate him so much?" Harper asks.

All I can answer is "That was a long time ago."

Nick decides to take the mood down a notch. Jordan and Harper drift away, but Truman and I stay where we are. As we sway to the music under the late-afternoon sun, he brushes his lips against mine.

"So your old phone," he says. "Did you get rid of it?"

"Actually, I still have it. When they asked if I wanted to turn it in, I decided I didn't want it destroyed. But it's just a brick now. Truly. I don't even have any screenshots."

"Hmm . . ." He looks like I feel, like maybe it's best to not look back, but also like it would be nice to have some proof it all actually happened. Future Me and Future Truman *did* look good together. "I wonder where the reunion site is now," he says. "You really can't get it on your new phone?"

"No, and my future Instagram is gone too."

"So then what happened to us? Or maybe I should say what *happens*?"

I think about this. Who knows whether all the things I saw on that site will end up happening? And who knows why I was allowed to see it in the first place? I'll probably never have an explanation, but I sort of feel like I understand.

The events, the actions, and all the other parts of our lives that make up our futures are like puzzle pieces in a jar. Shake them up enough, and some of the pieces get bent to the point that they don't fit anymore. Truman and I have bumped against each other, connected, and broken apart so many times that our shapes have changed. I think that the universe, or whatever made it possible for me to see into the next eleven years, took a look at the picture of

Truman and me, threw up its hands and said, "Whatever, I give up. Surprise me."

I push my fingers through the dark hair at Truman's neck, pulling him just a little closer as a new song starts to play. I plant a kiss at the base of his ear, and whisper, "I think that's up to us to figure out."

ACKNOWLEDGMENTS

A lot of things happened in my life while I was writing this book, the biggest of which was the deaths of my parents. As it always has, writing helped me keep my equilibrium. And after a year of funerals and settling estates, I sent the manuscript to my agent, then took my family on a much-needed trip overseas. I came home to find that Wendy Loggia wanted to publish *Now & When,* if I would be willing to revise. Wendy and her wonderful assistant, Audrey Ingerson, saw "a rom-com struggling to break free" from the sadness and nostalgia that tinged nearly every page.

I'm so grateful to Wendy and Audrey for giving me the chance to rewrite this book and in the process to help write some fun and sunshine back into my life. Their notes and insights were the nudges I needed to find the real story. But more than that, I thank them for having faith in me. The same goes for my agent, Holly Root, who has remained a steadfast champion of my work. This little book is a great example of what can be accomplished when someone believes in you.

Draft after draft, I've had an amazing critique partner in Jules Hucke. You'll want to remember that name, because it's only a matter of time before Jules finds the right editor to believe in their books and bring them to the world.

I am beyond fortunate to have the love and support of my best friend and husband. He and my two daughters are the reason I do what I do. Adam, Bea, Margaret, I love you more than I could ever tell. A shout-out too for my "coworkers" Foster, Ruby, Muffin, Monica, and Fluffmaster. You can often see their "support" (otherwise known as begging for walks and treats while I'm trying to work) on my Instagram story.

I want to say a special thank-you to Ray Shappell and Ewelina Dymek for such a fun and pretty cover. Thanks also to all my friends and fellow authors in the writing community.

And finally, to my mom, Gayle Graham Bennett, and my dad, Tom Bennett, how I wish you were here to read the book I started in the living room of our house on Harahey Ridge. I finished *Now & When* in a much darker place, but with support and love and hard work, it ended up better, stronger, and happier, which is just the way you would have wanted it. Thank you for being such wonderful parents. I love you, and I think of you every single day.

ABOUT THE AUTHOR

SARA BENNETT WEALER grew up in Manhattan, Kansas (the Little Apple), where she sang in show choir and wrote for the high school newspaper. She majored in voice performance at the University of Kansas before transferring to journalism school and becoming a reporter, covering everything from house fires to Hollywood premieres. She now works in marketing. Sara lives in Cincinnati with her husband, two daughters, and a growing menagerie of pets. When she's not writing, you can find her at the ballet or obsessively watching ballet on YouTube and Instagram.

sarabennettwealer.com